Mary H. Krout

Hawaii and a Evolution

The personal experiences of a correspondent in the Sandwich islands during the

crisis of 1893 and subsequently

Mary H. Krout

Hawaii and a Evolution
The personal experiences of a correspondent in the Sandwich islands during the crisis of 1893 and subsequently

ISBN/EAN: 9783337381745

Printed in Europe, USA, Canada, Australia, Japan

Cover: Foto ©Andreas Hilbeck / pixelio.de

More available books at **www.hansebooks.com**

HAWAII

AND A REVOLUTION

THE PERSONAL EXPERIENCES

OF A

CORRESPONDENT IN THE SANDWICH ISLANDS
DURING THE CRISIS OF 1893
AND SUBSEQUENTLY

BY

MARY H. KROUT

NEW YORK
DODD, MEAD AND COMPANY
1898

University Press:
JOHN WILSON AND SON, CAMBRIDGE, U.S.A.

To My Father

THIS BOOK IS DEDICATED IN AFFECTION

AND REVERENCE

PREFACE.

WITHIN the past five years the Hawaiian Islands have been a centre of what might almost be termed international interest. From a state of dissension and public distrust — the outgrowth of a semi-barbarous monarchy — it has advanced to a state of intelligent and wholly prosperous self-government.

In this change the native Hawaiian has been an object of much misplaced sympathy on the part of those who know nothing of Hawaiian affairs, or who are, at best, merely superficial and not wholly disinterested observers. With the prosperity that has followed the founding of the Republic — a prosperity in which the natives have been permitted to share — many new laws have been enacted which have conferred upon them increased privileges and a degree of liberty which they have never enjoyed

under any ruler of their own race. This is especially true in the disposition of what were known as
Crown lands, which were held by the chiefs and
could not be acquired by the common people. Now
they are enabled to buy tracts of land freehold;
and this alone must prove an incentive to greater
effort on their part to fit themselves for the dignity
and responsibility of the householder.

It should be explained, as I have endeavoured to
show in my Introduction, that the President of the
Hawaiian Republic (Mr. Dole), the Attorney-General
(Mr. Smith), the Chief Justice (Mr. Judd), and others,
who finally approved the abrogation of the monarchy, were all Hawaiian born. Their mothers and
fathers had gone out to the Islands in the early days,
and had worked strenuously to civilise the people
and give the country the government of a civilised
nation. It was their country, therefore, as much as
it was that of any descendant of the Kamehamehas,
and they loved and served it as loyally as any native
Hawaiian could have done. All that it possesses
to-day of worth, as I have stated repeatedly in this
work, is due to their labour and to no other influence.
They had faith in the ultimate triumph of enlightenment and justice, and strenuously advocated the pres-

ervation of the autonomy of Hawaii, even through the long and turbulent reign of Kalakaua. When Queen Liliuokalani came to the throne, more perverse than her brother, more determined to restore native rule in its most aggravated form, her subjects lost hope, and realised that there were but two alternatives, — the relapse of the country into the state from which it had so painfully emerged, or the administration of the government by the Anglo-Saxon, aided by the natives of the better class. This has been brought to pass.

When I visited the Islands first, in 1893, I went prejudiced in favour of the natives, deeply sympathising with them because they had been dispossessed of their lawful possessions. A careful and conscientious study of the situation on the spot led me to change my views absolutely, and I perceived that whatever had been done had been done of necessity and with wisdom and forbearance.

In my account of the political changes that have occurred, I have had occasion to criticise Mr. Cleveland and his personal representative, Mr. Blount, with some severity, and in defence of my statements I will merely say that much that I have written I saw; the rest is a matter of public knowledge, and may

be found in a published report of the official inquiry
into the case by the United States Senate through
its committee of investigation. This is corroborated
by State papers recorded and on file in the Government building in Honolulu.

M. H. K.

LONDON, *January 9th*, 1898.

CONTENTS.

PAGES

INTRODUCTION 1–31
    The Old Kamehamehas. — The Crisis of 1887. — The Gibson
Cabinet dismissed. — Kalakaua's Debts. — The King's Extravagance. — Death of Kalakaua. — Queen Liliuokalani. — A Struggle for Supremacy. — Crisis of January, 1893. — The Queen and
her Cabinet. — The Provisional Government. — Mr. Willis' Mission. — A Republic established. — The Revolution of 1895. —
President McKinley's Proclamation. — An Uncertain Future.

CHAPTER I.

THE FIRST IMPULSE 33–41
    A Newspaper Manager. — A Rebuff. — Feminine Diplomacy.
— Success.

CHAPTER II.

DISAPPOINTMENTS 42–63
    A Farewell Dinner. — Disaster. — An Unlucky Family. —
Female War-Correspondents. — An Old Friend. — Shattered
Hopes. — The Expected Revolution. — Renewed Energy. —
Final Obstacles. — An Anxious Moment. — Departure.

CHAPTER III.

FROM CHICAGO TO HAWAII 64–77
    My Guardian Angel. — San Francisco. — The High-Binders.
— Voyage to Hawaii. — The Brighton of Honolulu. — First
Impressions. — A Living Fairyland.

CHAPTER IV.

A FIRST IMPRESSION 78–83
    The Royal Hotel. — The Native at Home. — Bitter Disap-
pointment.

CONTENTS.

CHAPTER V.

IN HONOLULU 84–100

    A Cosmopolitan Society. — The Labour System. — Japanese Immigrants. — The Hawaiian Jehu. — Houses and Habits. — Chinese Servants. — Hawaiian Women. — Society in Honolulu. — Schools.

CHAPTER VI.

THE HOME OF KAIULANI 101–108

    An Unusual Palace. — A Perilous Adventure. — Rapid Growth of Trees.

CHAPTER VII.

AN OSTRICH FARM 109–113

    Ostrich Incubators. — Division of Labour.

CHAPTER VIII.

A VISIT TO CAMP BOSTON 114–121

    Camp Routine. — Sailors' Occupations. — "Finnegan." — A Sailor's Handiwork.

CHAPTER IX.

KING KALAKAUA'S PALACE 122–137

    The Royal Picture Gallery. — Insignia. — The Royal Mantles. — Disused Crowns. — The Fourth of March. — A Scottish Wool-Grower. — Mr. Gay's Experiences. — Prospects of Hawaii.

CHAPTER X.

THE PRESIDENT'S COMMISSIONER 138–149

    President Cleveland's Action. — Great Expectations. — The United States Envoy in Sight. — Mr. James H. Blount. — His Credentials. — A Sad Disappointment.

CHAPTER XI.

THE LOWERING OF THE AMERICAN FLAG 150–164

    The Annexation Club. — Mr. Stevens, the United States Minister. — A Domestic Tragedy. — Day of Lamentation. — An Anxious Moment. — The Flag Lowered. — End of the American Protectorate.

CHAPTER XII.

VIOLATED CORONETS 165–171

    The Crowns are Stolen. — A Dog Fight. — General Holiday.

CHAPTER XIII.

PAGES

THE PRINCESS KAIULANI 172–177
Her Appeal. — The Princess in Washington. — Farewell
Manifesto.

CHAPTER XIV.

THE CHINESE POPULATION 178–186
Chinese Worshippers. — A Chinese School. — A Chinese Matron. — A Chinese Fire-Brigade.

CHAPTER XV.

THE QUEEN DOWAGER 187–194
The Queen's Apartment. — My Interview. — Native Dress.

CHAPTER XVI.

THE LEPER SETTLEMENT 195–202
First Signs of Leprosy. — Cheerfulness of the Lepers. —
Molokai.

CHAPTER XVII.

AN AUDIENCE WITH QUEEN LILIUOKALANI 203–208
Admiral Brown. — The Queen's Daily Life.

CHAPTER XVIII.

THE BLOUNT ADMINISTRATION 209–214
Mr. Willis. — Return to Honolulu.

CHAPTER XIX.

IN HILO 215–234
Mahukona. — A Rough Voyage. — A Titanic Highway. — A
Catastrophe. — Mrs. Bishop's Narrative. — Life in Hilo. — A
Female Pastor. — Native Cookery. — Blight and Parasites.

CHAPTER XX.

A LITTLE JOURNEY TO KILEAUEA 235–249
Chinese and Japanese. — Half-way House. — In the Crater. —
A Guest Book. — A Molten Sea. — A Narrow Escape. — Pelé.

CHAPTER XXI.

SOCIAL LIFE 250–263
Mark Twain's Experiences. — Effects of Education. — Hawaiian
Breakfast. — Manners and Customs. — Swimming Parties. —
Foreign Ships and Sailors. — On Board the *Boston*.

CONTENTS.

CHAPTER XXII.

AN INTERLUDE 264–294
    A Trip to New Zealand. — Samoa. — The Hurricane of 1889. — A Rebellion. — King Malietoa. — Kava. — New Zealand. — R. L. Stevenson. — Sydney. — Memorial Day. — The Republic Proclaimed. — The President's Address. — The Queen Agitator. — The Constitution. — The Courts.

CHAPTER XXIII.

ANCIENT CUSTOMS 295–302
    Music and Dancing. — Poetry and Religion. — Superstitions, Arts, etc.

CHAPTER XXIV.

PRODUCTS 303–311
    Flowers. — Wild Pigs. — Mosquitos. — Birds.

CHAPTER XXV.

THE PASSING OF THE NATIVE 312–321
    Natural Affection. — Native Houses. — Effects of Civilisation. — Childish Legislation. — Conclusion.

INDEX 323

ILLUSTRATIONS.

	PAGE
NATIVE WOMEN SELLING LEIS	*Frontispiece*
FORT STREET, HONOLULU	89
NUNANU AVENUE, HONOLULU	94
MARINES, CAMP BOSTON	114

Old Bishop Residence, former home of Liliuokalani.

THE EX-QUEEN LILIUOKALANÍ	203
PRESIDENT DOLE	287
HEDGE OF NIGHT-BLOOMING CEREUS, FIVE HUNDRED FEET IN LENGTH, AT OAHU COLLEGE	306

At the time it was photographed there were in bloom three thousand perfect flowers.

GRASS HOUSE AT WAINAHU PLANTATION	317

INTRODUCTION.

THROUGHOUT the year 1892 rumours of discontent and unrest in Honolulu were rife in the United States. King Kalakaua, who succeeded Lunalilo, was not descended from the hereditary ruling line, but was elected by the Legislature in February, 1874. His reign was turbulent and corrupt, the political abuses becoming so unbearable in 1887 that the demand for reform finally culminated in revolution. Others of less significance had preceded this, originating in the intrigues of corrupt adventurers who surrounded the King, taking advantage of his weakness and his financial embarrassments, and plunging the country into difficult and dangerous political complications. While without a single exception these men brought about their own undoing from time to time, the direct effect of their downfall was not so important and decisive as the resistance which was made against their encroachments in 1887.

The old ruling line, "the old Kamehamehas," as they are called by the Hawaiians, while frequently

possessing grave faults of character, had the wisdom
to choose as their advisers the ablest and most
public-spirited of the European and American residents in the Islands. From these were chosen the
chief members of their Ministry and the Justices of
the Supreme Court, but one native having served in
the latter capacity from the adoption of the first
constitution in 1840.

King Kalakaua became imbued with jealousy of
the growing wealth and influence of the white men
in the Islands, and gradually alienated all who
might have counselled him wisely and unselfishly.
He chose for his associates instead, so far as he was
able, those who flattered his vanity and intensified
his race prejudices, they securing from him in return
large sums of money and immense tracts of the best
Crown lands. He showed more and more a disposition to encroach upon the rights and privileges
which the whites had enjoyed under his abler prede-
cessors, and which it is only just to state they had
never abused. Whatever estates they acquired had
been purchased at equitable rates, and in several
instances where they had been gifts they had been
returned to the people and set apart for educational
purposes. This, in brief, was the situation in 1887.

In this year a secret league was formed which was
prepared to resist further demoralisation, and to
demand speedy and radical reforms. Arms were
secured, and in the guise of militia some five hun-

dred men were equipped and drilled, ready to act when the proper time arrived. Memorials had been sent to their respective governments by the American, English, and German residents, setting forth the existing state of affairs and asking for interference. In the interim the Rifles, as the military organisation was called, had planned a sudden attack upon the Palace; but it was abandoned, and more peaceable means of securing justice agreed upon. A public mass meeting was held, at which the grievances of the people were set forth, and at which specific demands for their relief were made of the King.

In his report to the Hon. J. H. Blount, who was sent out to the Islands by President Cleveland in 1893, Professor W. D. Alexander says of this crisis: "On the afternoon of the 30th of June, 1887, all business in Honolulu was suspended, and an immense meeting was held in the Armoury, on Beretania Street, composed of all classes, creeds, and nationalities, but united in sentiment as never before or since. The meeting was guarded by a battalion of Rifles, fully armed. A set of resolutions were passed, unanimously declaring that the Government had 'ceased through incompetence and corruption to perform the functions and afford the protection to personal and property rights for which all governments exist,' and demanding of the King the dismissal of his Cabinet, the restitution of the $71,000 received as a bribe from Aki (a Chinaman negotiating the unrestricted sale of opium in the Islands), the dismissal of one Junius Kaae from the Land Office, and a pledge that the King would no longer interfere in politics."

The Cabinet was one of the most corrupt that had ever existed in the Islands. It was composed of W. M. Gibson (a Mormon emigrant sent out from Utah as a missionary), Minister of Foreign Affairs; L. Aholo, Minister of Interior; P. P. Kanoa, Minister of Finance; Antone Rosa, Attorney-General, the last three natives. They were implicated in Customs Revenue frauds, the illegal sale of Crown lands, and other misdemeanours.

Kaae, it should also be explained, was one of the most dissolute of many conscienceless hangers-on at the Palace, and acted as intermediary between the luckless Aki and the King, receiving his share of the large sum that was demanded for the opium licence above mentioned. The result of this movement on the part of the people was that a committee was "sent to wait upon the King with these demands," as Professor Alexander's report goes on to state. "Kalakaua's troops had mostly deserted him, and the native populace seemed quite indifferent to his fate." The King, thus abandoned by his guard and his people, called together the representatives of the United States, Great Britain, France, and Portugal, all of whom were largely represented by citizens or subjects in the population, and offered to relinquish the Crown if they would agree among themselves as to some form of protectorate. This was naturally declined, as it was hardly probable that their respective governments would have consented to any such compact; and as they were certainly not personally or officially empowered to accept so grave a responsibility, nothing came of the proposition. There was no cable communication between the Islands and the United States, and many weeks must have elapsed before the action of either of the Powers mentioned could have been ascertained. The people had borne the gradual abasement of the Government as long as they were able to endure it, and they were in no frame of mind to tolerate either delay or evasion on the part of the King and his creatures. He was helped to a speedy decision also by those to whom he had sought to relegate his authority, and who very wisely advised him to accede to the demands of the committee, and that without delay.

The obnoxious Cabinet was therefore dismissed, Gibson the Mormon being ordered to return to San Francisco, narrowly escaping violence at the hands of the people, who very rightly regarded him as responsible for much of the trouble and loss which the Government had sustained; and the others speedily sank into obscurity.

The new Cabinet consisted of Godfrey Brown, an

Englishman, Minister of Foreign Affairs; L. A. Thurston, born in the Islands of American parents; W. L. Green, an Englishman; and C. W. Ashford, a Canadian, Attorney-General. This Ministry was sworn in July 1st, 1887, and was throughout one of the strongest and ablest that had ever been chosen.

The amendments of the Constitution which were then secured were of the utmost importance, both in the essentials of guaranteeing the people the possession of their rights and in bringing about conditions of material prosperity and unprecedented progress.

The suffrage was granted to the whites, which had been stubbornly withheld; and the Ministry, which had been hitherto entirely subservient to the King, was held responsible to the Legislature only, and this body was to be elected by the people. The white residents, who had no voice in public affairs, had been paying some 87 per cent of the public revenues —a political status not unlike that of the Uitlanders in the Transvaal.

The elections which occurred the following September were fair and honest, and there was a period of three years when what was called "the Reform Party," the party chiefly instrumental in carrying the revolution to a successful issue, gave the country the purest, best, and most efficient government it had ever known. In the meantime the King and his adherents carried on a continual struggle to regain their lost power and prestige; and the Palace then, as it was afterwards, became the theatre of successive conferences and conspiracies. The claim of Aki remained unpaid, and the King was urged by the new Cabinet to settle it before the Legislature should assemble. This he agreed to do, and the revenues of the Crown lands were to be set aside to satisfy the debt. A little closer investigation proved, however, that the King's liabilities of one kind and another amounted to more than $250,000. He was finally induced to make an assignment for the benefit of his creditors, Aki among them, three trustees being named. They refused to restore the money that had been paid for the opium licence, and the Chinese merchant brought a suit in the Supreme Court. Here it was decided, in conformity with the Constitution, which adhered to the old mediæval tradition, that the King could "do no wrong." This interpretation meant that Kalakaua "could not be sued or held to account in any court of the kingdom," but the revenue in the hands of the trustees was held liable to Aki's claim.

It should be explained that his irresponsibility in financial affairs, quite apart from the moral corruption of his Court, had been one of the chief causes of public discontent. It was almost impossible to get funds from the Legislature, which he absolutely controlled before the enfranchisement of the whites, for necessary expenses and improvements. The Islands were almost without roads, there were few proper wharves where vessels could receive and discharge their cargo, and as the dredging of the harbour had been utterly neglected, the great vessels plying between San Francisco and China were not able to dock. These improvements have since been made under the new Republic.

In 1881 the King, accompanied by the late Colonel C. H. Judd as chamberlain, and by Mr. W. N. Armstrong as Commissioner of Immigration, made a tour round the world. During this tour the King became inspired with an ambition to unite Polynesia in an autocracy, inspired by the example of the King of Siam, whose court and kingdom he found to be vastly to his liking. He displayed the unreasoning greed of a child in his envy of the rich insignia, the formality and ceremony, and above all the costly armaments of European monarchs. In Austria it was a field battery that tempted him, a caprice that cost the Government $21,000, the guns being of little use in the Islands, which are crossed by mountain ridges that in many places can be traversed only by steep and tortuous bridle paths.

King Kalakaua's return, October 29th, 1881, was made an occasion of great public rejoicing, the cost of which was also defrayed by the people. At the time of his election to the throne there had been no special ceremony beyond taking the oath of office as prescribed by the Hawaiian law. After his return from his long journey, and nine years after his inauguration, he decided to be formally crowned, the ceremony taking place in a pavilion erected in the grounds of the Palace, nearly all the European Powers being represented. The coronets, one for himself, and one for the Queen, Kapiolani, were purchased in England at the cost of $10,000 — not an exorbitant price certainly, but forming an item in a bill of expense which had already reached an enormous total. The King, as has been said, was not of the ancient and honoured lineage of the Kamehamehas, and had no sympathy from Hawaiians of high rank like Queen Emma, Ruth Keelikolani, and Mrs. Bernice Pauahi Bishop. The latter was a direct heir to the throne, but declined the difficult office, preferring the retirement of private life. She left the bulk of her great fortune to endow schools for her people. All these "chiefesses" of high rank absented themselves from the foolish coronation, which, far from being impressive, had many of the characteristics of an *opéra bouffe* ceremonial.

The building of the Palace was another enormous extravagance, and so far as its cost is concerned remains a mystery to this day. The contract was not put out to tender in the customary manner, but the work was given for private reasons to architects and builders whom the King wished to favour. There were no requisitions upon the Treasury, and bills were paid by the King without any Ministerial intervention. In addition to all this folly, which kept the country impoverished, and discouraged capitalists from engaging in profitable enterprises which might have developed its rich resources, large sums were squandered in barbaric funerals whenever a chief or chiefess died. The natives came to the capital from the surrounding islands, and four weeks of feasting and lamentation frequently ensued before the corpse was finally consigned to the earth. These funerals, the expense of which was paid from the State Treasury, cost frequently from $50,000 to $60,000.

In 1890, having failed in negotiating a loan of $10,000,000 with which to equip a standing army (an attempt that had been made unsuccessfully before), the King was urged by the reactionary party to call a revolutionary convention, by which a new Constitution should be framed, withdrawing the franchise from what was termed "the foreign element." All that resulted from this movement was the enactment of certain amendments; and, as Professor Alexander states, the most important of these was one "lowering the property qualification of electors for nobles" — the latter constituting the highest legislative body.

The King, worn out with incessant political turmoil and by the irregular life he had led for many years, accompanied Admiral George Brown to San Francisco in his flagship the *Charleston*, in November, 1890. He was hospitably received and entertained; but his health continued to fail, and he died January 20th, 1891, in the Palace Hotel.

Admiral Brown was commissioned by the United States to take the body back to Honolulu, and the Queen requested him to assume entire charge of the funeral ceremonies, which he succeeded in curtailing to a fortnight. The body lay in state for two weeks, and was then placed in the royal vault. As a mark of her appreciation of his services the royal widow presented the American officer with the King's ring, and a native ceremonial, called "the hookupu," was held at the dock in his honour on the day that the *Charleston* sailed for San Francisco; it consisted in the presentation of gifts of fruit, fowls, pigs, calabashes, fine *tapa*, and many rare curios of native workmanship. The offerings were so numerous that the ship was almost fully provisioned for her voyage, and many of the presents had to be left behind.

Of the King, personally, Professor Alexander, who was an unsparing though just critic, has written: "In spite of his great faults as a ruler and as a man, he had been uniformly kind and courteous in private life, and there was sincere grief in Honolulu when the news of his death arrived." This estimate is corroborated by others; and there were few who were brought into close contact with him who were not impressed by his amiability and sweetness of manner. His most serious defect was, without doubt, lack of will; and this made him unable to resist temptation, and an easy prey to the hordes of adventurers and parasites that gathered about him and that had access to the Palace at all times.

In this concise outline of events the heritage of political turmoil and social unrest to which Queen Liliuokalani succeeded will be easily perceived. To comprehend fully the events that followed, however, it will be necessary to go back somewhat. The Hawaiian law of royal succession was peculiar. The King was empowered to name the heir-apparent, who was usually his son or adopted son. Failing this precaution on the part of the King, the Legislature was authorised to elect a successor. Lunalilo, who was the immediate predecessor of Kalakaua, was chosen in this manner, being the chief of the highest rank among the native Hawaiians. He died without heirs and without naming an heir-apparent.

The real choice of the people was the beautiful and accomplished Queen Emma, the widow of Kamehameha V., the adopted daughter of Dr. Rooke, an English physician. She had been carefully trained and educated for the high position she was destined to occupy. She was married June 19th, 1856, and a son was born two years later, whose untimely death in 1862 was considered a national calamity.

Queen Emma, however, was a staunch adherent of the English Church, and there was reason to believe that she would have at least advocated, if she could not have accomplished, the establishment of a state religion, which the people, except those personally interested in the matter, were prepared to resist.

Furthermore, it was known that she would oppose the reciprocity treaty with the United States which was enacted in 1876, and by which the temporary cession of Pearl Harbour as a coaling station for its men-of-war was effected.   In return for this concession, Hawaiian sugar, the principal export, was to be admitted into the United States free of duty. It was always believed that the election of King Kalakaua was compassed by bribery, and the announcement of the result was followed by a riot, in which the Court House was attacked by a mob, and several of Kalakaua's partisans in the Legislature were killed and others forced to flee for their lives.

Marines were landed from the U.S.S. *Tuscarora* and the *Portsmouth*, and from H. B. M. corvette *Tenedos*.   The latter encamped in the Queen's Gardens, guarding the Palace and barracks, and arresting a number of the rioters.   History, it will be seen, a decade later repeated itself, although in the case of Kalakaua it was never charged that he was placed upon the throne by the connivance of British and American men-of-war.   But for their assistance, however, he would not have ascended the throne.

King Kalakaua had no heir, and he accordingly named his sister Liliuokalani as heir-apparent.   She had an intense jealousy of the whites, and at the time of the adoption of the Constitution of 1887 was in England in attendance upon Queen Kapiolani, who had gone to London to be present at the Golden Jubilee of Queen Victoria.

When she learned what concessions had been made to the men whom she regarded as aliens and interlopers, her rage knew no bounds, and it is not too much to assume, judging from subsequent events, that she never for one moment relinquished the determination to wrest from them the privileges they had secured and to restore them to their former status. It was of no consequence that the State Treasury was almost entirely dependent upon the taxes of which they paid so large a part, and that the colleges, the public-school system, the laws, the entire judiciary — all that the country possessed that entitled it to a place among civilised people — were wholly due to their efforts and support. Her attitude was perfectly well known to a few, but public confidence was restored when she took the oath to maintain the Constitution as it stood, which she did on the day that the King's body arrived in Honolulu.

She gave, however, on that day, January 29th, 1891, an intimation of the spirit which she had concealed with true diplomatic reserve. Mr. S. M. Damon, Minister of Finance under the Republic, and Envoy from Hawaii to the Diamond Jubilee, in an interview remarked, "What was needed was a responsible Ministry." She discouraged any discussion of the matter, and answered curtly and significantly, "My Ministry *shall be responsible to me*" — a bold usurpation of authority that would not be tolerated in any constitutional monarchy in Europe.

The Queen's niece, the young Princess Kaiulani, then in England, was named as heir-apparent.

The first conflict came at once over a constitutional question, with the Queen and her supporters arrayed on one side and the Cabinet on the other. The latter claimed that the Legislature alone had authority to remove them from office, the Queen claiming that she had a right to choose her own Ministry. An appeal was made to the Supreme Court, and the question was decided in favour of the Queen. She thus scored the first victory; and being in some particulars an astute though short-sighted woman, did not fail to follow up the advantage she had temporarily gained. She not only had a Ministry of her own selection, but she made their nomination subject to conditions by which she hoped to control them.

As a further intimation of an approaching crisis, the Queen asked of this Cabinet the appointment of C. B. Wilson as Chief Marshal of the Islands — a measure that was expected to bear fruit later, when she might require the backing of an armed force.

It was the old story of the struggle for supremacy, the conflict of the people for their rights under the Constitution, and of the Queen for autocratic and unlawful prerogatives. There were the usual plots and counter-plots, vigilance on the part of the progressive element to keep pace with and circumvent the intrigues of the royal party, and attempts at resistance instigated by the Queen.

The Bill to legalise the sale of opium in the Islands, another to establish a national lottery, two schemes never relinquished by King Kalakaua during the latter years of his reign, were revived by the Queen and her party. And this, with the determination to abrogate the Constitution which she had sworn to support, to promulgate a new one in which the whites should be disfranchised, were the main issues of her brief rule. She went to the throne with the best wishes of her people, who hoped that the troubles which had distracted the country for twenty years were to cease. Had Liliuokalani been content with the authority of the sovereign of the British Empire she never would have been molested, and not only might have enjoyed a reign of peace and prosperity, but have been a true benefactor to her country and her people. It was a great opportunity, which, like most such opportunities neglected, will never return.

It is not necessary to review the steps which led to the crisis of January 14th, 1893, the final culmination of years of misrule, held in abeyance only when a responsible Ministry could be secured and kept in office. The people at last were forced to acknowledge that nothing more could be hoped for from

the monarchy. It brought them face to face with
the only possible alternative : the establishment of a
republic, with ultimate annexation to the United
States; or the abandonment of the country, its
relapse into barbarism, or its forcible cession to
Japan or to some European power.

The story of the Queen's last decisive act is briefly
told. From June 1892 until January 1893 a con-
test was waged between the Queen and the Legislature, the former claiming the right of personal choice
of Cabinet officers; the latter contending that the
Cabinet should represent a majority of the Legislature. Three of the Queen's Cabinets were voted out
in quick succession. The Queen then, apparently
submitting, appointed a Cabinet representing the
Legislature; but immediately entered into a conspiracy with persons seeking an opium licence law
and a lottery franchise, she agreeing to assist these
measures in return for their help in overthrowing
the Constitution and establishing a new one, disfranchising the whites and giving the Queen arbitrary powers. In pursuance of this agreement the
Cabinet was voted out, the opium and lottery bills
passed and signed by the Queen, a new Cabinet, supposed to be subservient to the Queen, appointed, and
the Legislature prorogued.

A deputation of the best and most intelligent
women in the Islands waited upon her before she
signed the Bill, and besought her not to take a step

2

that must be fatal to the morals and the real prosperity of the country; but their prayers were of no
avail.

On the morning of January 14th it became known
that the Queen had arranged to promulgate the
Constitution that day. She was admonished, but
refused to alter her purpose, and the Honolulu
Chamber of Commerce was informed of what was
about to happen. A message was also sent to the
late Captain G. C. Wiltse, in command of the U.S.S.
Boston, which was then in harbour, having returned
unexpectedly from Hilo, where the vessel had gone
for target practice. The Legislature was prorogued
at noon with unusual pomp and ceremony. The
anti-lottery members and the white residents were
absent. Those present, with forty members of a
royalist society called the *Hui Kalaiaina*, marched
to the Palace, one of the latter carrying a flat
package, suspended from his breast by ribbons.
This was a new Constitution. The procession proceeded to the Throne Room, the household troops
being drawn up in line from the west gate to the
entrance of the Palace, armed and wearing their
cartridge belts. Amongst the audience in the Throne
Room were some of the members of the Diplomatic
Corps, Chief Justice Judd, and the late Justice
Bickerton of the Supreme Court.

In the meantime the Queen was closeted in the
Blue Room of the Palace with her refractory Cabinet.

She was endeavouring to force them to sign the document which was to undo all that had been accomplished for the cause of justice and good government. They by this time had become thoroughly alarmed at the storm of public disapproval which they had roused. The Queen was in a measure justified when she upbraided them with "having led her to the brink of a precipice and then abandoning her to take the leap alone." She was told by her Minister of Foreign Affairs that her attempt to abrogate the Constitution was a revolutionary act, while the Attorney-General excused himself and his coadjutors on the plea that they had not read the document. The Queen is then said to have exclaimed, "How dare you say that when you have had it in your possession for a month!" She asked for their resignation, which they refused; and when she threatened to announce their refusal to the crowd of sympathisers which by this time had surrounded the Palace, three of them made their escape, one remaining in order to prevent the Queen from proclaiming the Constitution from the Palace steps without their sanction, and upon the plea that the Ministry and the Supreme Court refused to aid her in what she had undertaken.

The Attorney-General called a conference of four leading citizens, representing the Queen and the people respectively, and asked for instructions. The Ministers were urged not to resign, and in the midst of the discussion a message from the Queen arrived, commanding the Attorney-General to return to the Palace. The absconding Ministers received like orders. But all refused to obey, on the ground that their lives were in danger.

They were presently joined by the Minister of Foreign Affairs, who had remained behind.

The result was, after due consideration, that the Ministers were induced to concur in issuing a proclamation declaring the Queen in revolution and the throne vacant.

As on a former occasion, when aid was required at the time of the election of her brother King Kalakaua, the American Minister was notified of the Queen's conduct, and the assistance of United States troops was requested "to maintain order and support the Government."

It finally became necessary to organise a committee of public safety. A call was issued for a mass meeting, which was fixed for the evening of Monday, January 16th, and which was attended by a large audience, and was addressed by representatives of the American, English, and German residents, and the best of the native element.

The Queen's unlawful acts were unsparingly reviewed, and the outcome of the meeting was the appointment of a committee of thirteen, composed of representative men. A proclamation was issued, in which it was set forth that, five uprisings and con-

spiracies having occurred within five years and seven
months, it had become necessary to adopt radical
measures "for the preservation of the public credit,
already seriously damaged abroad, and to avert the
final ruin of a financial condition already over-
strained." It was pointed out that further forbearance would be useless; that an immediate guarantee
for the protection of life, liberty, and property was
imperative; otherwise, conditions already almost
intolerable would grow steadily worse.

A Provisional Government was organised, to consist of an executive committee of four members,
with Judge Sandford B. Dole, Associate Justice of
the Supreme Court, as its head. This was supplemented by a strong Advisory Council. The integrity,
patriotism, and statesmanship of Judge Dole were
beyond question; not even the Queen herself could
suspect the motives of a man who was, and still is,
one of the wisest and most devoted friends her
people have ever had. A committee of five men
was also chosen and dispatched to Washington to ask
for annexation to the United States. The proposition was favourably considered by President Harrison,
who was just retiring from office; but it was subsequently rejected by President Cleveland. Not only
was the treaty rejected, but, after a so-called inquiry
made by a commissioner, Mr. James H. Blount, who
was dispatched to the Islands in February, Mr.
Cleveland devised a Quixotic scheme of reparation,

which was to effect the Queen's restoration, with certain other compensations for what she claimed to have suffered through the interference of the United States authorities. The evidence of Mr. Blount, when it was finally submitted to Congress and carefully analysed, proved to be *ex-parte* testimony of the most pronounced type. Undue importance was given to statements made by persons, tools of the Queen, who proved to be wholly untrustworthy; while many who could have given, and were entitled to give, important evidence were shown very scant courtesy or set aside altogether.

Mr. Albert S. Willis, who succeeded Mr. Stevens as United States Minister, arrived in Honolulu on November 4th, 1893, with instructions to restore Liliuokalani, at the same time bringing letters of extreme cordiality and professed friendliness to the President of the Provisional Government. There is every reason to believe that these orders were to be carried out, peaceably if possible, by force if necessary, and in the latter case it would have meant landing American marines from the warships in the harbour to fire upon the American residents of Honolulu.

The tenor of the instructions given Mr. Willis was not learned until twelve days later, and in the meantime he had received the most cordial welcome, both from the citizens and from the heads of the Government. An incredible cablegram, which had been received *viâ* London, dated November 2nd, brought by a steamer from New Zealand, stated that the President "was drafting a message to Congress in favour of restoring the monarchy." This could not be believed, until all doubt was dispelled by the arrival of the U.S.S. revenue cutter *Corwin* from San Francisco a little later with decisive instructions.

In the interval Mr. Willis was negotiating with the Queen. One condition exacted by Mr. Cleveland was full amnesty for all who had taken part in the revolution. An unforeseen obstacle was encountered, which delayed decisive action on the part of Mr. Willis, and this was the prompt and stubborn refusal of the Queen to grant amnesty, and her savage demand that those chiefly instrumental in the organisation of the Provisional Government should be beheaded. Mr. Willis with great wisdom and discretion perceived that restoration was impossible without great resistance and probable bloodshed. He notified the Secretary of State, the late Walter Q. Gresham, and waited further orders. Business was entirely suspended, the Government building was strongly barricaded and fortified, and men and even women held themselves in readiness to defend the Provisional Government to the uttermost.

The course which Mr. Cleveland had pursued was extremely unpopular in the United States. By this time the flimsy pretext that the revolution had been compassed by the connivance of the United States Minister, Mr. Stevens, backed up by the marines from the U.S.S. *Boston*, was known to be false; and an attempt to restore a corrupt and incapable monarchy by the Chief Executive of a nation pledged to the support and maintenance of democracy raised such a storm of indignation that the project had to be abandoned. Even the best representatives of his own party condemned the President unsparingly; and the Press, even that faction which bitterly opposed annexation, grudgingly acknowledged that his efforts in the direction of arbitrator had been carried to an extreme.

The *status quo* having been finally restored, the Provisional Government began at once to prepare for the organisation of a republic. A constitutional convention was called, to be held in Honolulu. It met in the Government building on the morning of May 30th, all the members of the Diplomatic Corps except Mr. Willis being present, with the officers of the American and English ships. The test required of electors in voting for delegates to the convention was the oath of fealty to the Government — the usual test in all civilised governments. The deliberations of convention were conservative and moderate, and the Republic was finally proclaimed July 4th with great public rejoicings.

The Hon. S. B. Dole was chosen President, with an able and conservative Ministry. The Republic, thus established, proceeded at once upon the prosecution of necessary public works. Roads were built, a water front constructed at which ships might load and unload their cargoes, and, most important of all, the harbour was dredged, so that China steamers might dock, instead of discharging their cargo and passengers by lighters. Public lands were surveyed and placed upon the market, with special advantages given the native Hawaiians that would enable them to buy and own their homes at a low rate and on the easiest possible terms — a privilege they had never had when these lands were held by the Crown.

No restraint whatever was placed upon the Queen. She came and went at will, residing at her town house, Washington Villa. The attitude of Mr. Cleveland toward the sister Republic all this time was one of intense disfavour. He refused to recognise it as long as he could do so without absolute hostility, and finally carried his animosity to the extreme point of withdrawing the U. S. S. *Philadelphia* from the Honolulu harbour early in September, and in spite of the emphatic warnings of Admiral Walker, then in command of the Pacific Squadron.

Even the nominal support of Mr. Cleveland being thus entirely withdrawn, the ex-Queen secretly returned to her old methods. Plots were set on foot;

she sacrificed a great part of her private fortune in paying accomplices and in the purchase of arms and ammunition. A portion of these equipments was subsequently found carefully hidden in various places, and there were unearthed upon her own premises eleven pistols, thirteen Springfield rifles, twenty-one Manchester rifles, thirty-eight full belts of cartridges, one thousand loose cartridges, and twenty-one dynamite bombs.

Early in the year 1895 secret meetings of the natives were held in various quarters of Honolulu, and there were other evidences that rebellion was on foot. On the afternoon of Sunday, January 5th, the police were informed that natives were collecting in a house near Diamond Head, some miles beyond the city. A search warrant was issued, and as the officers approached the house they were fired upon by those inside. Four Hawaiian born foreigners — that is, men of American ancestry, but born in the Islands — who lived near by, hearing the firing, seized their guns, and went to the aid of the police. One of the number, Charles L. Carter, a young lawyer and a member of the commission which had been dispatched to Washington, fell mortally wounded, surviving only a few hours. It was immediately realised that this was the beginning of a serious uprising, and on the following day twelve hundred troops were under arms, and martial law was declared. Within two weeks the rebel leaders, who had been driven into the mountains, were captured, and the rebellion suppressed, but not until after a number of the natives had been killed.

The death of Charles Carter, and what has been termed "the anarchists' plan of attack, which, if carried out, must have resulted in the indiscriminate death of women and children," produced the greatest indignation. In addition to the arms and bombs found upon the ex-Queen's premises was the draft of a new Constitution, with commissions for the officials of her projected Government. She was arrested and confined in her old apartments in the Palace with proper attendants, and given the freedom of the gardens.

The trial of the conspirators was fixed for January 17th, 1895. It continued for thirty-six days. The ringleaders were sentenced to pay heavy fines and serve long terms of imprisonment. Liliuokalani was sentenced to five years' imprisonment, with $5,000 fine, shortly afterwards remitted. She was finally fully pardoned, having signed a formal letter of abdication on January 24th, 1895.

The two years following upon the suppression of this final attempt to overthrow the Republic were years of uninterrupted prosperity. The Government strengthened itself and its position materially, and won the entire confidence of the best element in the Islands, including many of the more intelligent and thrifty of the natives. In the meantime the desire for annexation to the United States has been paramount, and has never been relinquished for one moment. The Presidential Election of 1896 was anticipated with the greatest anxiety, and the safe return of Mr. McKinley in November was considered a blessing to Hawaii, as it was a matter of congratulation throughout the whole civilised world wherever unimpeached national credit and honour are of value. The views of the President-Elect were well known. The courage and determination of President Dole, his firm and dignified resistance to gross injustice; the proof of capacity for self-government which the Government had furnished in its strengthened credit, the steady increase of its revenues, and the careful expenditure of these revenues; the unanimity and clemency it had exercised towards cruel and relentless enemies, had intensified the sympathy of its friends in the United States, increased their number, and refuted the baseless charges of American opponents as to the delay of the older Republic in the matter of annexation. While it has involved cruel suspense and certain dangers to the weaker Government, it has been in the end the path of wisdom. In this very delay the theory that the United States has been prompted in its interference by an unlawful desire to seize the possessions of a weaker people, not able to defend itself against the aggressions of a stronger power, has been absolutely disproved. In the five years of careful investigation, in the protracted discussion, both *pro* and *con*, the whole question has been thoroughly "threshed out," to use the expressive English phrase.

The nineteenth-century policy of territorial expansion is, and has been, strongly opposed, and rightly; but as some one has said, there comes, finally, with every people a crisis growing out of its duty to weaker nations beyond its borders, in which traditions must be relinquished and its accepted policy reversed.   In its attitude towards Hawaii this crisis has arrived with the Government of the United States.   As Captain Mahan, the highest authority that can be quoted, has said, "The United States finds herself compelled to make a decision; whether we wish to or no, we must make the decision."

In the annual message of President McKinley to Congress, upon its assembly in December 1897, he reiterated the recommendations which accompanied an annexation treaty negotiated in June 1897, and which was transmitted to the Senate for confirmation.   In this treaty the cession of the Islands to the United States in 1851 of Kamehameha III. was recalled, such a course being recommended by the King at the time as the only means of putting an end to the familiar difficulties which even then threatened the destruction of the country; the reciprocity treaties of 1875 and 1884 were noted; the invitation of Germany and Great Britain to unite in a protectorate and the refusal of the United States on the ground that the relations of Hawaii with the United States were sufficient for its protection; and what was termed "the continuous policy of exclusion" from 1820 to 1893 of all foreign influence save that of the United States was also pointed out.   It was shown that the ultimate negotiation of an annexation treaty was inevitable, and under such circumstances "a consummation, not a change."   The organic and administrative details were to be left to the judgment of Congress, and the document closed with an expression of the belief that the duty of the United States would be performed with "the largest regard for the interests of this rich insular domain, and for the welfare of the inhabitants thereof."

This, in brief, is the history of the relations of the two countries within the past two decades. All that Hawaii possesses of civilisation, of religion, of law, and of education is of purely American origin.

Whatever may be the ultimate decision of Congress (which may or may not be known before this is printed), to those who are familiar with Hawaii, with the characteristics of the natives, decimated and corrupted as they have been by disease, by the vices which contact with civilisation has engendered, their improvidence and inability to govern, there are but three alternatives — the anarchy of chronic revolution, the abandonment of the Islands by Europeans and Americans, or their permanent absorption by some stronger and stable power.   Whether this is destined to be Japan, England, or the United States time and legislation will decide.

M. H. K.

LONDON, *December* 1897.

HAWAII AND A REVOLUTION.

CHAPTER I.

THE FIRST IMPULSE.

IN 1892, in the course of a conversation with a friend who had recently returned from the Hawaiian Islands, it was remarked that a revolution, with a demand for annexation to the United States, was impending. At the time of his visit there was apparent tranquillity; but those who were capable of forecasting the future, basing their prophecies upon past history, were of the opinion that the crisis might come at any moment. The people might go to bed at night, and in the morning wake to confront revolution and anarchy and find themselves without a government.

So far as it was destined to influence my personal movements within the four years that followed, the speech was a momentous one. It meant thousands of miles of travel by land and sea, hours and days

and weeks of arduous and responsible toil, conferences with personages in exalted places, interviews
with heads of governments, and, mingled with these
rapid changes of time and place, harrowing anxiety
and racking and protracted physical pain. It will be
impossible to write of it impersonally, so indulgence
must be craved for the recurrence of the personal
pronoun.

With the natural instinct of a " newspaper woman "
— which is the preferred American substitute for the
more polite English term " lady journalist " — I was immediately inspired with an ardent desire to be present
when the crisis came. This was not the gratification
of a nature disposed to bloodshed and violence, but
the realisation of the professional opportunity to be
the one special correspondent in the field. With this
was a more creditable desire to witness the actual
making of history, the evolution of a people from a
semi-barbarous monarchy to a state of intelligent and
rational self-government.

My friend took his leave, and forgot all about his
speech. For more than a year I brooded over it, and
never ceased to plan and devise ways and means of
carrying my plans into effect. To be there prior to
prospective revolution, and so able to give an accurate
résumé of the causes which led to it, or, better still,
at the time, became the only thing in life worth
living for. It might have seemed an altogether
hopeless ambition to a woman of very limited

means and of uncertain health, but it was never relinquished.

Finally, a gentleman of great wealth, of reputed public spirit and enterprise, assumed control of the paper upon whose staff I had been employed for some years, and in him I believed I had found a sympathising friend and a congenial spirit.

One afternoon early in September 1892 I plucked up courage and invaded his private office, resolving to make a confession of my astonishing project, feeling almost confident of his approval. It was a luxurious office, a contrast to the sooty den to which he had relegated me shortly after taking possession. He did not ask me to be seated — a courtesy which was never forgotten by his elders and his betters in the staff — and, without apology, he interrupted the interview from time to time to carry on a conversation over the telephone with the members of his household some miles away.

His incivility was in a measure pardonable; and although the accurate account of it is necessary to the completeness of this record, I do not bear him the slightest grudge on that account. It was apparently a most foolish proposition — especially to one who was not a profound student of history. There was not the slightest breath of rumour at that time which could indicate any disturbance of Hawaiian political affairs. A little mild disturbance, half riot, half insurrection — well, yes, that would be as natural as the succession of epidemics to which ordinary childhood is subject; but anything graver than this — it was absurd!

There dwells in the soul of every man living — and from this category not one is exempted — a fixed belief, confessed or unacknowledged, that political problems are wholly beyond the comprehension of the feminine intelligence. It is not in the least worth one's while to combat this inherent and inherited prejudice. All that the feminine intelligence can do is to show itself capable of grappling with political questions and situations, and it will then be rewarded with a special verdict that one exceptional success simply proves the rule of unalterable incapacity.

My chimerical scheme was hesitatingly unfolded. I was pretty well read in Hawaiian history by this time, and, in order to prove the correctness of my theories, dates, facts, and names were glibly rattled off — the latter subject to painfully acquired amendment afterwards, when the correct pronunciation was acquired.

It was a hot afternoon, as hot as only a September afternoon in Chicago can be, with a burning sirocco sweeping across the prairies from the west, bringing with it the stench of slaughter-houses and pork-packing establishments — a little addition which millionaire pork-packers are permitted to contribute to the public discomfort.

The new man was warm and tired; he was

nervously irritable; and, moreover, he was distraught with the pains and perplexities of an amateur editor who has a lot to suffer as he acquires his experience.

He looked at me coldly through his spectacles; upon his sharply cut features and the tightly compressed lips there was an expression of justifiable weariness. He looked at me, and then remarked, with an effort to be satirical:

"Do you think anybody is interested in Hawaiian politics?"

"But it is not a question of Hawaiian politics," I protested; "it is a matter of international politics." And as I write these words a woman's spiteful sense of triumph comes over me when I think how time obligingly verified that rash assertion.

The interview was not prolonged. It became evident that my speedy withdrawal was urgently desired, and the unspoken wish was respected.

As I closed the door, I said with fervent relief:

"Thank Heaven, you are only the publisher; you are not the editor, and there still remains the court of final appeal."

This rebuff was only an encouragement to new and more determined effort. All the data that could be obtained were collected, and with them some forty letters of introduction, twenty of these from a relative then in command of the Pacific squadron, Rear-Admiral Brown, who had been a warm friend of the Hawaiian sovereigns and their people. These included letters to the Queen's Chamberlain, for the monarchy, which, though even then cracking in places and peeling off in spots, was still intact; the chief lady-in-waiting, a most charming and cultured Hawaiian woman; the Chief Justice and Mrs. Judd, one of the historical families of Honolulu; with others to the American Minister, Mr. Stevens, the American Consul, and men of equal consequence and social position.

Successful newspaper work may have been accomplished once by a system of spying and eavesdropping and backstairs espionage; but all astute editors and correspondents know nowadays that, quite apart from personal qualities of endurance and perseverance, with a greater or less ability to write grammatically, it has become almost a question of credentials and introductions. Twenty facts of value are to be obtained at an official dinner-table, where one is picked up regularly or irregularly in the highways and byways, and the continuance and worth of future information worthy the name depends upon the manner in which official confidence is abused or respected. This will be considered heretical by those who advocate other and more enterprising methods; but it is one that has been tested, and has been found to serve extremely well. The collection of letters was a sort of treasure, counted over with something of miserly satisfaction, and read and re-read some scores of times. With

all their undeserved reputation for cowardice and
distrust of adventure, women after all have ten times
the daring and resolution of men; and if the gene-
rality of them only knew how safe are the high roads
and even the uninhabited places of the world, and
how purely imaginary are the dangers that seem
to threaten when one leaves the beaten track, there
would be a hundred explorers like Mrs. Bishop and
Miss Kingsley where there is one to-day.

I had learned wisdom.   Masculine prudence did
not look kindly upon my views.   Denial should not be
rashly and carelessly risked again.   Columbus had
appealed to kings and courtiers, only to be repulsed
with indifference and scorn.   It was the Castilian
Queen, alone, who listened, believed, and pledged her
jewels to enable him to sail away into Nowhere — as
all the world of that age confidently believed.

The Isabella of my expedition was my friend
Mrs. N——, the wife of the managing editor of my
newspaper, to whom I already owed encouragement,
appreciation, promotion, and kindnesses innumerable.
She was a woman of liberal education, a fine linguist,
she had lived much abroad, and her mind had
been liberalised by contact with the world.   As is
inevitable with such women, she had great influence
with her husband, who relied much upon her judgment, and respected her opinion, and always found
it profitable.

The matter was discussed with her over a *tête-à-tête*

supper at her house one dreary November night. The letters of introduction were produced, and all that it meant for the newspaper and its correspondent she fully and immediately realised. She did not ask chillingly, " Do you think people are interested in Hawaiian politics?" but she said, "I believe it is an admirable plan, and that it will be well worth while."

Thus far we were able to discuss and reach conclusions with the dignity and self-respect of rational human beings. We might contrive to rise superior to conditions of possible danger, inevitable discomfort, fatigue, and disappointment; but we could not sweep away by one bold stroke, with all our audacity, the inevitable limitations of sex. We both knew that, just, generous, and kind as her husband was, the chances were that if we approached him singly, consecutively, or even in pairs, he too might fail to perceive the practicableness of our designs.

We were forced to resort to schemes and conspiracies, to the exercise of so-called "tact," as usual when women must deal with men in matters a little out of the common, and attempt to demonstrate the performance of the impossible. We sat in silence for a moment, and then she remarked thoughtfully: "I will talk to Mr. N—— about it to-morrow, and then you can see him the next day." This, then, was the plan of attack when we parted, I setting out to my home across the city in the teeth of a driving storm, and we carried it out to the letter.

She did talk to him on Monday, and I saw him on Tuesday. As should always happen after such conferences between a liberal-minded husband and a persuasive, intelligent wife, I found him, not convinced, but mollified; hesitating, but open to conviction.

"I feel so certain that it means everything for me professionally, that I am willing to bear my own expense to Honolulu, and return, if you will let me go," I said.

He gazed meditatively out of the window, suppressed a yawn, and then said, "Well, I suppose you may as well go."

I walked out of his office without delay, fearing that he might reconsider his decision. My heart was swelling with pride and triumph — a frame of mind that, in the uncertainty of human affairs and the vanity of human ambition, I might have known could not endure.

CHAPTER II.

DISAPPOINTMENTS AND DELAYS.

THE staff correspondent of a newspaper is like a soldier — always under marching orders. The necessity of being in readiness induces one of two conditions: he, or she, has always at hand a stock of serviceable clothing; or the supply is reduced to a minimum, and this remnant so dilapidated that nothing can make it worse.

Thanks to very thorough domestic training in early girlhood, which included a mastery of the art of patching, darning, and mending, my belongings were ready to be packed on short notice. Only three gowns were required — the orthodox black silk for solemn ceremonials, a white satin to be worn when I should make my bow at court, and a flannel dressing-gown for the steamer.

Shopping has always been to me a purgatorial penance, and I have learned that its torments may be appreciably mitigated by deciding in the privacy of one's chamber just what is required, the colour and fabric, and what it ought to cost. These are requisites that any one with ordinary common sense ought to decide in a few minutes, and it will be found to save an immense deal of time and of nervous wear and tear. The purchases were made within an hour, and in the hands of the dressmaker without delay. Four days later the gowns were finished, quite splendid, well-fitting, and altogether satisfactory — an example of Chicago skill and dispatch. They were accompanied, when they were sent home, by a bill as long as the train of the court dress.

There was a farewell dinner — a festal occasion at which a dozen friends assisted — a delightful company of artists and journalists. Toasts were drunk, speeches were made, and the ices came in with a tiny American flag in each pink and yellow mould — a delicate reminder that this protecting ægis was soon to be left behind, and life, liberty, and the pursuit of happiness to be sought and found under quite a different arrangement of colours and symbols.

On Saturday, December 10th, the final arrangements were made. I went to the newspaper office for the last official instructions. There I was given my railway tickets, the ticket for my berth in the Pullman, a telegram reserving a state room on the *Australia* of the Oceanic steamship line, with another from my cousin, who was then at the Mare Island Navy Yard, and to whom I was asked to wire the exact time of my arrival in Oakland. A series of entertainments had been arranged during the brief stop I was to make in San Francisco to rest from the fatigue of the long overland journey.

Several invitations had come for Sunday; but wishing to spend the day with Mr. and Mrs. C——, of whose household I had been a member for two years, I declined them all. Friends called, and made their farewells during the afternoon; and at six o'clock I went to my room to change my gown, preparatory to paying the one visit I felt could not be neglected, upon the aged mother of a dear friend.

We left the house together, Mr. and Mrs. C—— and myself.   We took a horse-car, and at the corner of Thirty-First Street I left them to catch a cross-town car, which took me almost to the door of my friend's house.   Even in the rehabilitated state of the city since the fire there are many things neglected and left undone by the municipality of Chicago that would shock the conservative ideas of Europe. Its side-walks in the outlying streets are one of these evils, and one from which I was destined to suffer, probably for the remainder of my life.

At the corner where I stood waiting for the car, whose green light I saw approaching far off, the side-walk was elevated at least two feet above the level of the street.   There was not the slightest protection in the way of a railing or coping; so when the car halted, throwing a dense shadow across the gutter —

a black abyss — I stepped down into it without in the least realising its depth. I had planned for a slight descent of two or three inches; I made a plunge of two feet, with the momentum that can never be computed until one feels the sudden fetch-up that follows. I felt it in the next instant in every nerve, and in one burning agony that seemed to concentrate itself in the heel and ankle on the right foot. The shriek which I gave ought to have collected a mob; but it was Sunday evening, and the righteous persons passing by on their way to church were so occupied with pious meditations that they either did not hear or did not heed.

I managed to crawl up out of the slippery chasm where I lay in a limp heap, and sat down on the curb, wringing my hands, and crying, "Will no one help me! oh, will no one help me!"

This moving appeal did finally penetrate the ear-muffs of two stout men, and they picked me up and carried me into a drug store on the corner. For the first time in my life I fainted; and when I recovered consciousness, the druggist himself was holding a wineglass of brandy to my lips, and a motherly woman was kneeling down beside me unbuttoning my boot. When I came back to life, the first thought that flashed across my mind was, "I have lamed myself, and *now* I cannot go!"

It was Sunday; the time for my departure was Tuesday night! After more than a year's effort, and after surmounting almost hopeless obstacles, to fail now, — it was sickening!

Furthermore, I had had before two separate experiences in lameness — a displaced knee-pan, which healed, to be hurt once again two years later. I had spent altogether about four years upon crutches, and, expert as I had become, there was nothing attractive or pleasing in the prospect of being again reduced to artificial locomotion. In the event of being able to compass the revolution in the face of this last and greatest of all possible and unanticipated disabilities, I could not run, and in event of a collision I should be forced not only to stand and take it, but to stand on one foot at that.

In some mysterious way I managed to get into an Indiana Avenue street-car once more, and started home. A gentleman helped me off, gave me his arm, and, as I limped by his side in the darkness, he talked to me encouragingly, and told me that he had broken his leg only a few months before, that he had entirely recovered, and he felt certain that my hurt was only a slight sprain, from which I would not be greatly inconvenienced. It was kind, but not reassuring; and after a four years' uninterrupted daily exercise in the art of applying a flannel bandage, I am bound to say that the cheerful prophecy was not fulfilled. He assisted me up the front steps, rang the bell, and when the servant admitted me bade me good night. I was suffering too in-

tensely to notice his face as the door was opened.
I never knew who he was; but I have often thought
of our strange ramble in the darkness, and have
still a distinct recollection of his agreeable voice,
his gentleness, and all that he said in his effort to
comfort me.

The C——s had been in one particular a most
unlucky family. Almost constantly some one of its
members was laid up for repairs; bruises, contusions,
sprains, and dislocations were not only their own
common lot, but that of their relations unto the
third and fourth generation, and of the stranger
within their gates. A lady who had been visiting
them some time before had slipped and fallen, and
had broken her arm and collar-bone, and it was
weeks before she could be removed to her home. A
sister was at that time walking on crutches from a
sprain of eighteen months' duration. I was the last
addition to the standing list of casualties.

When the good people returned from their call
a little while after my own arrival, they found me
in the library with my foot stewing in a bucket of
scalding water; their son, faultlessly dressed, with a
rose in his buttonhole, keeping it up to a boiling
temperature with more water, which he added, at
short intervals, from the tea-kettle.

When they came in, guileless and innocent, and
saw the touching tableau, I looked up out of a cloud
of ascending steam like some sort of a baleful wraith,

and remarked concisely, "I 've sprained my ankle — *but I 'm going.*"

Mrs. C—— threw up her hands with a cry, and sank down on a sofa.

After a while I was carried upstairs and put to bed. The surgeon came, made an examination, and said that the nervous shock had been severe, no bones were broken, but that the full extent of the injury could not be ascertained until the swelling had subsided; for by this time the injured member resembled the typical Chicago female foot as it is represented by New York and St. Louis cartoonists.

The next morning there was no apparent improvement, and my feelings were lacerated beyond expression by the spectacles of a trunk packed and strapped, of rugs, bags, and boxes, all in readiness for immediate departure. The crowning blow was the arrival of a sheaf of roses, pink and fragrant, with a charming note wishing me *bon voyage* from a friend who had not learned that, instead of *bon voyage*, it was to be *non voyage* — to judge from appearances.

The hurt, the disappointment, the inevitable postponement, the downfall of roseate hopes and lofty ambitions, was endured with stoical composure; but I am not ashamed to confess that when I received a time-table with the hour marked in red ink when my train left Chicago and arrived in San

Francisco, sent with a note of congratulation and good
wishes from another friend, I burst into tears.   More
than this, I settled down to enjoy that ancient
sedative to overstrung feminine nerves, a good
cry, and felt immensely relieved.   A prospective
war correspondent in tears is not a spectacle to be
seen every day; but it must be edifying, not to say
improving, when it does come within the range of
ordinary vision.   It simply proves that, even though
the war correspondent be a woman, she does not
cease therefore to be feminine and human.   But I
was destined to have more trials; first of all,
visits of condolence from friends, fellow-journalists,
and other well-meaning but not always tactful
persons.

I have always managed to be somewhere near
what in Kansas would be called the "cyclone
centre."   The previous summer, while on a visit
to my family in Indiana, the horses attached to
the carriage which was taking me to the railway
station bolted and ran away.   I was talking, and
did not notice the speed at which we were going,
and the gentleman who was my fellow-passenger
remarked quietly, without changing his ordinary
tone, "The horses are running off, but do not
jump out."

I had always inveighed against the folly of people
losing their heads under such circumstances, leaping
out, and being injured for life or killed outright.   It

was a fine opportunity to carry my theories into practice. I sat still, encouraged without doubt by the composure of the other passenger.

After a mad race of a quarter of a mile or so, the horses turned into an alley, the pole of the carriage struck a telephone pole and broke off, the right fore wheel collided with a heavy curb, and the frenzied brutes, entangled in their broken harness, came to a standstill, snorting and trembling. When the crash came, the carriage careened like a sinking ship, then settled and came down on its four wheels intact. The other passenger opened the door; we alighted, both a little pale and pretty well shaken up. As familiar objects flashed past us in our flight, the events of my whole life did not pass before me, as they are commonly supposed to do in moments of deadly peril, nor did I make any solemn vow to repent of my sins and make fitting reparation in the future. I knew perfectly well, even in that somewhat incoherent frame of mind, that I should not really repent of my sins, and that I could not make reparation if I tried. My one thought was pre-eminently practical and sordid: "I shall be killed, and my accident insurance policy has lapsed!"

When I reached Chicago, I went without delay to the office, and took out another policy, a prudential measure that was destined to be rewarded. I did not get the policy under any sort of false pretences. I told the secretary that early in life I had formed the habit of breaking my bones, and up to that time the record stood one arm, and two knees, or rather one knee, twice; there was also a miscellaneous and unimportant list of semi-drownings, falls, and other hair-breadth escapes.

The secretary set the confession down to an attempt to be humorous, issued the policy, and I thought no more about it, except on such occasions as it became necessary for me to pay the too frequently recurring premium.

On Monday — to return to the main narrative after this divergence — the insurance company was notified, and that evening its surgeon called to see the extent of the accident, and to give them some idea as to what it was to cost them before they had done with it. When he came into the room, I saw a tall, handsome young man, with features of classical regularity, fair complexion, fair hair, and a pair of remarkable eyebrows, in that they were not only perfectly arched, but jet black. It was a singular combination, and one that I remembered to have seen but once before in my life. He came to the bedside, and sat down.

"What is your name?" I asked rather abruptly. It was familiarity that could be ventured without undue rashness in the case of a young examining surgeon of an accident insurance company, and I meanly took advantage of the opportunity.

"Dr. H——," he replied.

I looked at him again, and the identity of the familiar face was identified.

"Ernest H——?" I asked again.

"Yes," he replied.

Years before he had been a pupil of mine, and I recalled him standing by my side, a white-haired urchin, eagerly receiving instruction in common fractions. I remembered him as a manly, honest, industrious, persevering lad; but I had not thought of him for years. His career had been one which the freedom and opportunity of the great Republic makes possible to those who are disposed to take advantage of them.

His father had been a plasterer — a poor man. The lad was taken from school to help support the family. He became a potter, and went west — to Kansas, to Colorado, to California. In his ramblings he lodged in a house with a young medical student, and became interested in medicine from hearing his friend read his text-books. He began to study himself, saved his money, entered a Chicago medical college, took his degree, and had just received his appointment while waiting to build up a city practice. We of course talked over the old days, and the strange chance that had brought him to my bedside after years of wandering and the thousand changes and dangers that had come to both.

At the time he was under my instruction I was enjoying one of my recurrent lamenesses; and I reminded him of this, and of the entire recovery that followed.

He remembered me as his teacher — a dim and shadowy figure that had risen suddenly out of a dim and shadowy past; I was venerable, not to say archaic, in the estimate of his keen and merciless youth. The hideous foot was unrolled, displayed, examined. I waited desperately for his verdict. He looked at it critically, handled it gingerly and professionally.

" How long will it be before I can use it ? " I at last managed to inquire. " You know I recovered from that second dislocation without much trouble."

He continued to prod and peer in silence. Then he looked up, and said, with the cruelty of the scientific devotee who under certain circumstances ceases to be human: "Yes, but you were younger then. Now" (a pause), — "*now* your age is against you."

In my bruised and broken state revolt was useless. I bore it as I had borne all the untoward events, the deadly disappointment, the nerve-racking anguish of the preceding forty-eight hours, and I lay back on my pillow with a moan. In the weeks of tedious and painful convalescence that followed my one dread was that the revolution would come and I not be there to see. I had tormented the long-suffering managing editor to distraction, and wrested a promise, reluctantly and hesitatingly given — for he had had more time in which to think about it — that I should go as soon as I was able to travel. I opened the morning paper every day with precisely the same emotion of dread and relief.

The crutches which had served me so faithfully in the two preceding engagements were sent for, and in due time the injured limb was encased in a silicate cast from the knee to the toes. The latter were exposed, and could be covered only by a man's sock, which was all that would go over the cast. Over this, to prevent the sock from becoming soiled and ragged, was worn a man's No. 10 india-rubber overshoe. A leather shoe of that size, with the weight of the cast, would have been a burden to carry, and a slipper would have been difficult to keep on. The only possible compensation that this structure offered was that it made the other foot look fairy-like by comparison.

The latter part of January the surgeon gave me permission to visit a friend in the West Side. My health by this time was seriously affected, and it was thought that the change of scene would be beneficial. A fortnight passed delightfully, with no evil tidings from the prospective seat of war. On Saturday evening, February 4th, when Mr. P——, the husband of my friend, returned from his office, his wife met him in the hall, carefully closing the door behind her. All this time, during the entire fortnight, I had talked of nothing but Hawaii, boring them incredibly, no doubt, of where I should go, what the country would be like, the adventures I was destined to have, breaking another bone or two being anticipated as a matter of course. The conference in the hall was lengthy, and it was carried on in whispers; but as I was reading by the fire, I did not notice it — I recalled it the next morning. Through the evening there was an unnatural gaiety in Mrs. P——'s manner, and a marked absent-mindedness and nervousness in that of her husband.

She related an unusual number of amusing anecdotes, and he laughed mechanically, and started out of a brown study once or twice when I addressed him suddenly. With the prospect of the scene in which they were destined to participate, I have reason to believe that their dreams that night were troubled and their slumbers much disturbed. In the five weeks that had elapsed since the accident the injury had not improved in the least; I could not walk a step without crutches, even with the apparent prop of a silicate cast weighing twenty pounds.

I came hobbling into the drawing-room on Sunday morning before breakfast in smiling unconsciousness of the last vindictive slap that Fate had delivered. There had been a terrible sleet-storm, which had prevailed all day on Saturday and throughout the night. The city was a solid glare of ice. The storm had ceased at dawn, the sun had come out, the sky was without a cloud, and it had turned bitterly cold. Sleighs were dashing up and down the avenue with a cheerful jingle of bells, their occupants swathed in furs from head to foot.

Without a word Mrs. P—— handed me the Sunday *Tribune.* I glanced at the staring headlines. There I saw it set forth in the biggest and blackest of letters, "*Revolution in the Sandwich Islands. The Queen Dethroned. The American Flag Hoisted.*"

It had come! All that I had dreaded had been brought to pass. Words were inadequate to express our feelings. As Miss Kingsley remarked of the East African natives, we simply sat down and had a "friendly howl" together. The tears streamed down my face, and we wept in unison. After the manner of his kind, the husband looked on helplessly, then discreetly retired to his bedroom. But it was only a burst of passing emotion; and, besides, there was no time to cry. When Mr. P—— joined us at breakfast half an hour later, he found us sad, but calm. After I had had a cup of coffee, I said:

"Order a carriage, and I will drive at once to Mr. N——'s house."

Half an hour later the carriage was at the door. The streets were like glass, and the horse had to walk at a snail's pace. A drive that ordinarily could have been made in less than an hour required two. When we reached the house at last, with deceit that

was in reality the last artifice of desperation, I left one
of my crutches in the carriage, risked the only neck
I had, which, once broken, could not be mended
with silicate, and dragged myself across the slippery
side-walk and up the slippery steps. That this
was accomplished without fatal results I can only
attribute to the fact that the frowning Providence
that had been glowering at me steadily for five
weeks, was temporarily distracted, probably by
some fresh savagery of a Chicago alderman, and
so I escaped.

The sunlight streamed cheerfully through the
drawing-room windows; it was warm, and there
were flowers everywhere about. It was the most reassuring prospect that I had had through a period
of protracted and heavy calamity.

Mrs. N—— was out of town—the champion, the
friend, that would have backed me up as valiantly
as of old had she been there. Mr. N—— was at
breakfast; but he came amiably into the drawing-
room, with his napkin in his hand, as soon as my
card was sent in. He divined my errand. He read
it emphasised in my determined air. It was of no
use to waste words; besides, I had talked of Hawaii
so much that I was myself by this time a little tired.
I went straight to the point:

"The Queen is dethroned, and *now*, Mr. N——,
I am going."

Mr. N—— did not look at the crutch which I

clutched, nor at the No. 10 overshoe; but he said, with mild and wholly unexpected acquiescence:

"Well, I suppose you will never be happy until you do. You 'd better telegraph to San Francisco and engage your passage on the steamer."

The entire interview may have occupied ten minutes. In another hour the wire was sent to the office of the company in San Francisco. I was to leave the following Tuesday, February 7th. And this is where the superior heroism of women is displayed. There was not a man of my acquaintance who did not think that it was the maddest folly to attempt such a journey, on such an errand, alone, on crutches, half-way across the continent and the Pacific. They said it would have been bad enough to go with a maid and a physician in time of peace; but unattended and practically helpless, to venture upon such an expedition, to find the country in nobody knew what state, was sheer idiocy.

The only two approving masculine voices which both, well for me, happened to be decisive ones were those of my good surgeon and my good editor-in-chief. The city editor, a tender-hearted Englishman, who had ruled me with a rod of iron, or tried to, in the old reporting days, was especially severe.

"If *I* had any authority in the matter, you should not stir a foot," he said.

I reminded him that, fortunately for me, he had no authority, and that it was true that there was but one foot that I *could* stir, but that I hoped to make sufficient use of that to compensate for being deprived of the usual complement.

I set out to the C——s on Monday afternoon. The only accident that happened *en route* was that the horses slipped and both fell down upon the track in front of a rapidly approaching cable-car.

Successive disasters had quite hardened me, and, beyond a feeling of pity for the poor brutes, I surveyed the accident with composure, and in the frame of mind of the heroine of a melodrama who has been abducted, robbed, arrested, imprisoned, survived the loss of friends, fortune, and family, and exclaims truthfully, "Nothing can hurt me now."

The poor horses struggled to their feet again — *they* could; the cable "slowed up," as the motorman would say; and no harm was done. I halted at the office a moment, and it was arranged that I should drive down the next morning and get my credentials, a fresh supply of railway tickets, and a second set of official instructions. Then I drove home, the luggage was ready, and as I said goodnight I remarked in fatuous confidence:

"Everything is done, M——; and when I come back from the office in the morning, we will have a long, quiet day together."

A long, quiet day! How my evil genius must have grinned at that vain speech! At ten o'clock I was ready to keep my appointment; but there was no editor visible, nor were there any evidences that he had arrived. I waited patiently until it struck eleven, twelve, then one, two, three, four! At four o'clock the door opened, and he came in, amiable and absent-minded. I had waited without luncheon, all day.

"The tickets, and the letters, Mr. N——," I began. "You were to be here at ten, and have them for me."

"Tickets — letters? Why, bless my soul, I sent them out to the house last night at seven o'clock!"

"They have never been received."

"Are you certain?"

I had a little habit of forgetfulness of my own, and was past grand-mistress in the art of losing things. I had lost my watch two months before, and had the entire office in a turmoil hunting for it. It was found among some clippings in a pigeon-hole of my desk. I was never believed on such a point as this afterwards; nobody charged me with wilful mendacity, but it was taken for granted that I supposed I knew, but in reality had forgotten.

I suffered for my sins on this occasion. There was no doubt but that the tickets and letters had been delivered, and it was hinted that I would probably find them on my writing-table or in a bureau drawer. The only alternative was to go home and look; there were yet six hours until the train left. Nothing had been seen or heard of any tickets or letters of any nature or description whatever.

It was the housemaid's afternoon out, and she had gone to visit friends on Blue Island Avenue, miles away across the city. She was usually prompt and reliable, and messages or letters or cards were at once brought to my room. It was barely possible, it was thought, that she may have forgotten to do her duty on this one momentous occasion; because, if she ever did forget, it would be at just that time and on that one particular evening.

We looked everywhere, the entire family joining in the fruitless search; not a vestige of a railway ticket or a credential was unearthed, and at length we desisted and held a solemn conclave. The last expedient was resorted to: the cook was dispatched to find the housemaid and bring her back, and M—— went into the kitchen to finish getting the dinner. Everybody was tired, anxious, depressed. I had on my travelling-dress, and had carefully secured the No. 10 overshoe, and then I toiled downstairs to wait in the drawing-room and apologise to the family for all the trouble and distress I had caused them. The cook had not returned; but just then there was a sharp whirr of the door-bell. A reporter had arrived and produced the lost documents. The explanation was simple, but incredible. A man had been sent to the district messenger office, and every little loitering wretch assigned to duty on the

South Side had been called up, catechised, and made to give an account of himself.   The guilty one was found.   He was forced to go with the reporter to the identical house at which the packet had been left.   It was next door, and the woman, who was my dressmaker, had forgotten to send it in to me!   Her servant had received it the evening before.

We held our breath, and wondered what possibly could happen next.   Very little dinner was eaten, and conversation languished.   The last hours passed rapidly by, as they always do; the carriage came, the good-byes were said, I hobbled down the steps, was helped into the vehicle, the door was slammed, and we rolled down the icy street.

"Do you realise what a journey you are undertaking?" said M——, as I put my crutches in the corner.   And I replied briefly, but undauntedly, "Yes."

At a quarter to ten I was comfortably established in my section of the Pullman car with all my belongings about me, innumerable farewell gifts from friends —fruits, flowers, books, and many creature comforts, after the kindly generous American custom.   Then, last of all, M—— said good-bye.   The negro porter made up my berth, and in fifteen minutes I was between the blankets, with a sort of vindictive and evil satisfaction that it was over and I still lived.

Presently the steam rushed into the air-brakes

with a hiss, the wheels revolved, and we moved slowly out of the great North-Western station. I sat up in my berth, drew back the blind, and looked out as the blue and green signal lights went by. I then said, as solemnly and as feelingly as if I were saying a prayer:

" I — am — really — off — at — last !"

CHAPTER III.

THE Japanese believe that huge, invisible spirits contend in the upper air for the mastery of human destiny, the one good and the other evil, and when misfortune is paramount the evil genii triumph, when fortune is propitious the good spirits have prevailed. As we rushed away through the night across the Illinois prairies, the demons that had thwarted me for weeks must have looked after the flying train, frowning and gnawing their nails in humiliating defeat.

They may even have hissed "Foiled," and so departed. At any rate, my troubles ended from that moment; at least they ended so far as the vexatious miscarriage of my plans were concerned, for the silicate cast, the crutches, and an ever-present ache were still with me. I had insisted that I would get on famously, that the porter would look after me, that friends would be raised up along the journey to aid me in dire extremity. I had put in my bag a package of postcards, upon which brief messages should be inscribed, giving a sort of bulletin during the three days' journey overland.

The next morning at nine o'clock I wrote:

"The guardian angel has appeared upon the scene. He is sitting in the seat opposite me, in a grey tweed suit and a travelling-cap. He is sixty, or thereabouts, with snow-white hair, blue eyes, and cheeks as rosy as a winter apple. He is humming 'Annie Laurie' to himself."

It was not a misleading intuition. He proved to be a retired Chicago banker of scientific tastes. It may be doubted by the unenlightened that there ever was such a person as a Chicago banker with scientific tastes; but here he was. He had graduated from Yale with honours years before. He had wanted then to devote himself to scientific study; but he had to earn money, and scientific study is not usually financially profitable. All his life he cherished the hope that he might one day realise his aspirations, and they were realised. He made his fortune, and retired — for Americans occasionally do retire when they make their fortune, though not often. He had given the years of his leisure to the study of astronomy, and had written much on the subject for scientific journals. He was making his fourth visit to Japan, and he said that it would vary the monotony of a journey that had lost all its novelty to look after me and render me any assistance that lay in his power. He talked much and most interestingly, escorted me to the dining-car and back again, and we shared the contents of our lunch-baskets as long as those contents lasted. The acquaintance was renewed upon my return home, and he and his charming wife are to-day among my warmest and most valued friends.

The negro porter, William, was the paragon of porters. The poor fellow had arrived in Chicago from the long journey eastward at seven o'clock, and had started back at half-past ten the same evening. He was worn out with fatigue, but his good nature and kindness were boundless; all that mortal porter could do he did, cheerfully, respectfully, and as if it were a pleasure. I began to think that henceforth I should make it a rule to travel with crutches.

The prairies of Iowa were white with snow. At Omaha the ground was bare; but a blizzard broke loose that rocked the heavy train until it was almost thrown from the rails. Here, too, when the wheels were tested, one was found with a broken flange — a timely discovery which saved us from being wrecked out on the plains, miles from assistance or a telegraph office.

In crossing Nevada the platforms were crowded with painted and blanketed Indians, who had been given the privilege of riding thus from station to station for the right of way across their reservations.

The last night we climbed the Sierra Nevada

Mountains, and as I woke and looked out of the window in the dim moonlight, I could see enormous snow-drifts, with paths like tunnels to the doors of the low houses along the railway. A little later there was a dense fog; and when morning came we were climbing down the western slope into the verdant Sacramento Valley. The floods were out, the river had burst its banks, and the lowlands were submerged for miles; but there were other miles of emerald fields, of blossoming almond orchards, of budding vineyards.

We had rushed down the mountain in the grey of the dawn, out of frosty winter into spring and sunshine. I had not realised that Oakland was the terminus of the railway line, and that San Francisco, which we saw miles away, must be reached by crossing the bay. The difficulty of a transfer by ferry was one, happily, which I had not bargained for, and consequently was spared the pain of worrying over it; but William was faithful to the end, and my scientific friend, after three days' unceasing and untiring ministration, said, "I will not desert thee."

Nor did he, until he saw me safely bestowed in my pleasant room at the Occidental Hotel, where I found a bright fire sparkling in the grate, a pyramid of fruit upon the table, which was presently supplemented by a great basket of dewy ferns and roses, sent up "with the compliments of Major Hooper," the proprietor. He was a retired army officer, a graduate of West Point, and had all the kindness and courtesy and gallantry of "an officer and a gentleman." Whoever fell into his hospitable hands was well cared for.

We were not to sail until Tuesday, and, arriving on Friday, I was supposed to be given time to rest; but the brief sojourn in the Californian metropolis was anything but that. There were calls, visits, sight-seeing, drives in the Park and out to the Seal Rocks, and last, but not least, a visit to China-town on Monday, the eve of the Chinese New Year, with a friend then on the staff of the San Francisco *Call*.

The shops and temples were gaily decorated, and the streets were thronged with people in holiday attire. All sorts of unappetising edibles were offered for sale — strange fruits and nuts, squid, dried ducks, and various sorts of salt fish. Firecrackers were popping right and left; and there was a babel of thin, high-pitched nasal Chinese voices, and mirthless, falsetto Chinese laughter. I hobbled about, intensely interested in the shifting panorama, for no one can drive through the steep, narrow thoroughfares. Suddenly two shots were fired. Instantly an officer hurried us into a police station near at hand. Shop windows were closed like magic, doors were fastened, and the streets were immediately deserted. It was like the retreat of animals into their burrows at some sudden alarm.

"What in the world is it?" I asked, as the door of the station opened and admitted a whimpering Mongolian, supported by two officers. I had supposed the firing to be connected in some way with the celebration of the New Year.

"High-Binders have broken loose again," said the policeman.

The High-Binders are a secret organisation, of a semi-political nature, banded together for their own purposes, which include the prompt assassination of their enemies. A hasty examination was made, and it was found that the man had been seriously wounded in the back. He was removed to the hospital, and we returned to the hotel.

That night, after I had gone to bed and had fallen asleep, quite worn out with the fatigue and excitement of the day, I was roused by a knock at the door. A reporter from one of the morning papers was in the drawing-room, and asked for an interview. I knew that failure to get the interview would mean a reprimand for the man, so a sort of professional sympathy forced me to get up and dress and go down and see him. It was a case where virtue had to be its own reward, for I found myself introduced to the San Francisco public, through his newspaper, afterwards as "the Mississippi Valley Campaigner and Correspondent to Hawaii." This extraordinary legend was accompanied by a picture which illustrated St. Paul's definition of faith — *re·*

versed ; for it was "the evidence of things seen, *not* hoped for."

The *Australia* sailed the next day at two o'clock —a convenient hour. My San Francisco friends had been unremitting in their attentions, and I left the hotel loaded with flowers and fruit; indeed, there was so much of the latter that quantities of it had to be left behind.   Among many gifts of books and little conveniences for my cabin was a comfortable steamer chair and a big, soft cushion.   On board I was passed over to the surgeon, Dr. S——, who was the embodiment of goodness and patience.   I had been given a cabin to myself, although the owner of the line besought me to give up the voyage and remain in San Francisco.   When I refused, orders were given that its difficulties should be made as easy as possible.   Dr. S—— had the upper berth removed, so that the lower one was converted into a lounge, into which one could climb easily and conveniently. Among the passengers were his two cousins, interesting and charming people.   He himself was deeply learned in his profession.   He had been educated in England, had lived much abroad, and was a fine talker.   We kept very much to ourselves, I through necessity, not being able to move about and having no desire to make acquaintances.   We made a little quartette at the surgeon's table, and were daily refreshed with the incomparable Kona coffee (the indigenous coffee of the Hawaiian Islands), with other little luxuries which he was able to procure for us.

The weather was enchanting; and we steamed down the Bay, through the Golden Gate, under cloudless skies, in floods of sunshine, past the grey craggy Faarallones peopled with seagulls, of which dominion the light-keeper is king. It was like a soft May day. The next morning I was roused by a knock at my door, and Dr. S—— said, "Look out of your air port, and you will see the *Monawai* passing." In these lonely seas one may sail for days without a glimpse of a mast or a funnel, so the passing of a ship is an event. It gradually grew warmer, and summer clothing was in demand the third day out.

Though the Pacific does not always deserve its name, the entire voyage was something never to be forgotten. The water was blue as sapphire, and peopled with living creatures: flocks of flying fish, like small white birds, leaped from the waves, ventured their short, swift flight, and sank back into their native element; occasionally the dim outline of a grey and ancient whale could be descried far off; the white gulls followed us half-way across, and the brown gulls met us in mid-ocean and escorted us the rest of the distance. As we approached the land, which was sighted early on the morning of February 22nd, the "bo'sun bird," as the sailors call the beautiful creature, circled round the ship, pure white, with two extraordinarily long white feathers in the tail, fluttering like pennons as it flew. As we neared the tropics heavy showers were frequent; they came on suddenly, the rain fell heavily for a few moments, and then the sun came out. Sometimes we could see half a dozen of these tropical showers descending from clouds at different points around the horizon; one could then realise the small area which such a rainfall covered. The rainbows were marvellous, spanning the sky with an opalescent arch apparently rising from and sinking into the sea. The phenomenon is so common in the Islands that the natives once called them the "Islands of Rainbows."

The first of the group to lift itself from the sea was Molokai, the prison-house of the lepers. From a distance it seemed to lie low against the water, like a giant tortoise; but it is in reality a mass of forbidding cliffs and almost inaccessible precipices. There are eight inhabited islands in the group, which have an area of six thousand seven hundred square miles; they are Hawaii, which is the largest, Maui, Kahoolawe, Lanai, Molokai, Oahu, Kauai, and Niihau.

Nothing could have exceeded the loveliness of the morning. There was not a ripple upon the bay; the wonderful colour of the water, the deepest blue, banded with pink, rose, violet, brown, and yellow, with streaks of palest green, was something that the

most fervid imagination could not have pictured.
The white surf was beating against the hidden reefs,
a fringe of tossing spray; to the right rose the
naked crag of Diamond Head, seamed and scarified
by primeval volcanic fires.   There were other
peaks, Tantalus and Round Top: there is always
a Round Top everywhere — such, in the matter of
fitting names, is the mental poverty of mankind.
These remote peaks were clothed with dense masses
of vegetation, the native forests which grow in these
higher altitudes; on the lower slopes, the merest
dots and specks, could be seen the white houses and
gardens of the industrious Portuguese; below these
there were stretches of fertile valley covered with·
velvet sward.   The city followed the curve of the
harbour from the docks to Waikaiki, a beautiful
suburb which Mrs. Isabella Bird Bishop has named
"The Brighton of Honolulu."   The name is hardly
a fitting one, since it is a succession of fine private
villas standing beside the sea in the midst of tropical
gardens, visited little by the public except select
companies of bathers and by those who drive out
along the well-kept road in the cool of the early
morning or evening.

The harbour showed a forest of masts; this should
have been anticipated, for it is not so very many
years ago since it was a most important port from
which whaling vessels set out upon their long voyages.
For some strange reasons on their first voyage the

Hawaiians made admirable whalers, the cold of the Arctic or Antarctic proving a keen tonic; the second year, however, they were of less value, probably because, their curiosity having been gratified, their interest waned and they had more time to brood over discomforts that did not disturb them at first. In those old days it is said that one could walk for a long distance by stepping from the deck of one whaling vessel to another, as they lay anchored closely side by side. Both Hilo, in Hawaii, and Honolulu were important ports in the whaling trade.

It was Washington's birthday, an American national holiday, and the three American men-of-war, the *Boston*, with the *Alliance* and the *Mohican*, were gaily dressed from bow to topmast. The great *Naniwa*, which had been dispatched to Honolulu, and was protecting the Japanese interests in the Islands, commanded by a cousin of the Mikado, and which afterwards took such an important part in the war with China, also displayed a mass of flags and pennons out of courtesy to the American ships. The four war vessels, with the English *Garnet*, were anchored side by side, constituting what was known as " Naval Row." As we steamed past them the sailors in their uniforms of dazzling duck crowded to the side and cheered us lustily.

The arrival of a steamer is always an event of importance to these island dwellers, cut off from closer contact with the world. We had taken a pilot on board outside the reef, and had learned from him that there had been no new developments in the political situation.   We passed the quarantine, and, being able to show a clean bill of health, were not detained.   All about us were boats filled with chattering Hawaiians, most of them barefooted, wearing blue cotton trousers, white cotton shirts, and straw hats. Around the latter invariably was a garland of yellow coreopsis or tuberoses, called *lei*, which was made by stringing the blossoms in a solid wreath on a bit of cacao fibre.   With the well-to-do the *lei* was a band of peacock feathers.   Many wore these garlands around the throat as well.

As we approached the landing-stage crowds of dusky brown urchins, wearing only a thin cloth about the loins, swam out and dived for coins — a custom that seems to prevail in all tropical islands.   The water was nearly as transparent as the atmosphere, and their lithe, slender bodies could be seen at a great depth, almost as much at home as their familiar friends the fish that darted about them.

There was a charming, picturesque multitude on the covered dock: ladies beautifully dressed in summer muslins, with white, pink, and blue parasols, and pretty lace-trimmed hats; gentlemen also in white, even to their canvas shoes.   They signalled gaily to friends on board, and were as gaily answered. The air was heavy with the fragrance of orange blossoms, tuberoses, and gardenias.   What a transformation scene! Less than a fortnight before I had left Chicago, a city stark and frozen, locked in ice, and here was a land of perpetual verdure and a fadeless summer.

With the Americans and Europeans were crowds of natives; the women wearing the *holoku*—a decidedly rational garment, vastly becoming, and invented for them by the wives of the missionaries. It consisted of a full, flowing skirt attached to a yoke, and the preference seemed to be for muslin, or stiff flowered silk. Each woman wore a garland of flowers, and they were talking volubly and laughing like children. At that crisis neither the white residents nor the natives had taken the revolution seriously. They had grown accustomed to little political upheavals like this, and they believed that this, like others that had preceded it, would blow over, and there would be an interval of peace — until the next time.

As events progressed, however, the public temper changed; there were in store for both days of anxiety, of carking care, of personal and national peril, and both the foreign residents and the natives were to be seriously affected by the phases through which they were destined to pass. They became subdued and apprehensive; both lost their cheerfulness and their sanguine faith in the future; suspicion became rife, feuds were engendered, and men who had been as brothers were divided and hopelessly alienated.

But, as I have said, this was a later phase of political development. There was among her adherents at that time some regret that Liliuokalani had been dethroned. Many of the natives were amiably indifferent, and the ex-Queen had not then wholly alienated the white population by the savagery that subsequently sought to satisfy itself with mediæval beheading and modern dynamite. But this was only the beginning.

The ordeal of the customs was simplified for me, through the thoughtfulness of Dr. S——, and, this formality complied with, we drove down to the hotel.

I had never seen anything that seemed to me half so wonderful as the beauty of that island capital and the wide, clean, sunny streets; the chimneyless houses standing in gardens crowded with palms, and mango trees, and feathery algarobas; the hedges of flaming hibiscus, and the long pendent garlands of rose-coloured bougainvillea. What a contrast it all was to my recent dwelling-place! It seemed a living fairyland, and I exclaimed, "I *know* that I shall never be as happy again in this life as I am at this moment!"

CHAPTER IV.

A FIRST IMPRESSION.

WE drove up the winding avenue into the grounds of the Royal Hawaiian Hotel. It was an inviting place, standing in an extensive and well-kept park. There was a central building, with wings on either side, and verandahs above and below. The back rooms were preferred because they commanded a view of the mountains, were much more retired, and were much cooler.

The house was quite full, and there was some trouble in finding a place for me. Miss Adeline Knapp, the clever correspondent of the San Francisco *Call*, had preceded me to Honolulu by some days. It was very difficult for me to get up and down stairs, although I could have managed it if forced to do so. My sister journalist, however, came generously to the rescue. She had the best and most desirable room in the house, one on the first floor, looking out upon the Punchbowl — an extinct crater at the back of the city — and shut off from the main verandahs by a private passage; it had also its own little secluded verandah, which could be converted into a cosy

and delightful open-air drawing-room. Besides all
this, it was screened with vines, shady, cool, with
the bath just across the passage outside. She at
once insisted upon vacating this desirable snuggery,
taking a far less comfortable apartment on the upper
floor, pretending that she was more than compen-
sated by the view. I was not deceived in the
least, and knew that I was profiting by her self-
sacrifice. She not only did this, but helped me to
get settled, unpacked my trunks, shook out my
crumpled gowns and hung them in the wardrobe, and
did not leave me until she had done all that she could
find to do.

The Royal Hawaiian Hotel was built early in the
reign of King Kalakaua and is still the chief hotel in
Honolulu. It was inconveniently arranged, but had
been furnished with a good water supply and the
electric light. The verandahs were broad and airy,
and liberally furnished with chairs and wicker
lounges. At one end was a *lanai* — an apartment
open on three sides, with curtains of matting which
could be lowered when it rained. It was connected
with the drawing-room, and was prettily furnished
with wicker chairs and tables, and hung with Japanese lanterns. But there was too profuse decoration,
and whenever I looked at the array of gimcracks it
seemed as if a vessel loaded with Japanese fans and
umbrellas and banners must have exploded there,
and its cargo attached itself in some mysterious way

to the walls and ceiling. I had once heard an authority on household decorative art solemnly expostulate against what he called "producing a spotty effect." Had he seen that collection of fans and banners he would have beheld the spotty effect in its most malignant and exaggerated form.

The drawing-room was cheerful and comfortable, but people seldom sat there, except when receiving calls, preferring the verandahs outside. One valuable and conspicuous work of art was a fine bust in marble of the late King Victor Emmanuel. I wondered much how it came to be there of all places in the world, and learned that it had been presented to King Kalakaua when he visited Italy during his tour around the world; he gave it to his Mormon Premier, the notorious Gibson, and he or his heirs presented it to the hotel. The dining-room was a big bare place with Chinese servants flitting silently about, and candour compels one to say that the cooking of itself would have been enough to incite revolution. That evening at dinner I thought the American who sat opposite me excessively rude when he called the Chinese boy and told him to take away the beef that had been set before him, adding sternly, "And bring me some more without any of that umbrella juice on it." In the course of time I learned to loathe the inky liquid myself, and almost everything else, except the delicate broiled mullet, the strawberries, and honey-sweet bananas.

The servants and officials about the house were about as heterogeneous a company as could have been mustered. The proprietor was English; the manager an Englishman, a graduate of Oxford; the day clerk was a Portuguese, married to a Japanese lady; the night clerk a Chinaman; the head steward was an Alsatian, married to a Parisian woman; the cook was a Greek; the barber a German; one of the bell boys came from the Canary Islands, and the others from the Azores. At the various tables were American and European tourists, and occasionally officers from the Japanese war-ship, with the diplomatic representatives of various countries.

After luncheon Miss Knapp took me for a drive out to Waikiki and Diamond Head. I had my first glimpse of the native at home as we passed a house crowded with idle, dirty women, squatting on the ground smoking. The furniture was scanty and dilapidated; the hut was dirty and disorderly in the extreme; there were numbers of cats; and the progress of civilisation was exemplified in a kerosene lamp and a small sewing machine worked by hand. By the roadside were groves of old cocoa palms bending their plumy heads toward the sea, young forests of graceful algarobas, and there were flowers, flowers everywhere. Clouds came drifting down the valleys along the mountain sides, soft as spun wool and as white. There is nothing so profoundly solemn in nature as this slow movement of

6

clouds; they are so wraith-like, so impalpable, passing, fading, dissolving. There was an historical fish-pond stocked with venerable gold-fish, that had gone on multiplying undisturbed, no matter what revolution might be on foot, and the water swarmed with them.

It was arranged that the cast with which my foot was still cumbered should be removed that afternoon. I must be indulged in this final mention of the hateful impediment, which will then disappear from this chronicle. On a former occasion, when a similar appliance had been taken off, after I had lugged it about for six weeks, I found myself able to walk, and I had looked forward eagerly to a similar recovery now. It was very warm, and the operation took something over an hour and a half. Dr. S—— with a huge knife cut away the solid mass, the perspiration streaming down his face. At last the remnant of the shell dropped off, and I felt as light and untrammelled as a newly hatched chicken.

I rose with trepidation and essayed a step, hoping and believing that I could walk as well as ever. Vain expectation! The useless foot, to quote the graphic description of a friend, "shut up like a razor." Except that the load which I had carried for five weeks was gone, I was no better off than I was before. It was the third bitterest disappointment I had ever had, and the good doctor, sympathising with me in it, patted me indulgently on the shoulder, and there was nothing to do but make the best of it, and arrange for the difficult work I should have to do as best I could.

In the evening many callers came. There was an open-air concert on the lawn by a substitute for the Queen's band, which refused to play after her overthrow, and the grounds and verandahs of the hotel were crowded with people. We had another drive in the moonlight. The air was steeped in the fragrance of jasmine and orange blossom, the streets brilliantly lighted, with shadowy gardens echoing with the notes of the guitar and mandolin, and with the soft pensive music of Hawaiian voices.

I went to bed at midnight, but I could not sleep. At two in the morning, when silence had fallen at last, I rose, wrapped myself in a rug, went out, and sat in my steamer chair in the verandah, watching the stars. How low they hung; how luminous, how large they were! The night wind stirred the boughs of the mango-trees; now and then a bird chirped in its sleep; far off I could hear the lowing of cows and the barking of dogs; footsteps came approaching out of the silence and then vanished. It was inexpressibly peaceful; it was beautiful beyond the power of words to describe; but there had been with it all that deep, indefinable melancholy which tinges our profoundest happiness.

CHAPTER V.

IN HONOLULU.

BEFORE arriving in Honolulu I frankly confess that my sympathies were wholly with the natives; I took the view — so easy to acquire from books and from other sentimentalists like myself — that the natives were being robbed of their birthright by the relentless whites, who, in their greed and with their superior cunning, had seized and held the balance of power.   It was a fixed hallucination which it took some time to clear away; and during the educating process the only judicious course to pursue was to listen, and observe much and say little.   At the end of a fortnight the question ceased to be one of sentiment; it became simply, stripped of all its verbiage and local colour — of which there was a great deal, and a variety of shades — one more ethnological illustration of that relentless law, the survival of the fittest.   The complication could be compared only to a temperance campaign in Indiana, where the feeling ranges through all varieties of belief — high licence, prohibition, and no licence; and

Indiana is named because there, as in the Hawaiian Islands, politics are the native element of the inhabitants. Never were there so many prejudices and suggestions projected upon which the unwary might tread. To think thrice before speaking once, was the mildest and most inadequate advice. One finally wondered if it were prudent to speak at all.

Society was a curious network. All Americans, most of the English and Germans, and some of the best of the natives and half-castes, favoured annexation to the United States — annexation pure and simple, as they put it. There were with these — an influential constituency — the adherents of the Queen, who believed that she had been cruelly wronged; the missionaries, who to a great extent control social affairs and constitute that dominating power supposed to be vested in the oldest families; last of all, there were prospective capitalists — Americans and English — who might have rendered substantial aid in developing the resources of the Islands. Besides these there were numbers of secret annexationists, waiting to find out which would be the popular and winning side, with some hundreds of Hawaiians bitterly opposed to the ex-Queen, and justly blaming her for the trouble she had brought upon the country. All, however, royalists and annexationists, were united in a desire for peace and for a stable form of government.

The times were exceptionally hard; money was

so scarce that it was difficult to borrow even small sums upon good security, while business had stagnated to such a degree that general bankruptcy seemed imminent. It has been realised by this time that the part taken by Mr. Stevens, the United States Minister, had not been an arbitrary assumption of power, but a measure of public safety. The Hawaiian Government had not been absolutely dissolved nor its authority set aside. When the American flag was hoisted over the Government buildings, the United States men-of-war saluted not only their own colours, but the Hawaiian flag as well, which continued to float from its flag-staff in the grounds. And when Captain Swinburne, in command of the marines which were landed, was questioned, his reply was:

"My orders are to protect the Legation, the Consulate, and the lives and property of American citizens, and to assist in preserving order. I do not know how to interpret that; I can do it in but one way. If the Queen calls upon me to preserve order I am going to do it."

This disposes entirely of the charge that the Revolution was premeditated and the Queen dethroned by the aid of United States troops. Japan at once dispatched the *Naniwa* to protect the interests of the thousands of Japanese labourers in the Islands, who are employed in the cane fields on the sugar plantations.

At the time of the Revolution the planters were dependent upon the contract labour system. The Japanese Government received a certain sum for every man permitted to leave the empire — a pretty substantial source of revenue when the number increased, as it did steadily. A strict account was kept of each labourer furnished. When the men arrived in Honolulu, they were selected by their employers and taken to the plantations on the other islands. Each man received $15 a month, a house, fuel, water, and free medical attendance. Women received $13 per month, and were employed chiefly in the mills as "feeders."

Opponents of the system condemned it without reservation, declaring it to be but little improvement upon negro slavery as it prevailed in the Southern States before the war. There was, in reality, a very great difference, with all the advantage in favour of the Japanese field-hand. He could return to his native country at the expiration of his three years' period of service; he could not be separated from his family; no species of force was permitted on the part of the planters, who, if they so much as laid a finger upon one obstreperous cane-stripper, could be fined for assault; and, in such instances, it was a rare thing for the verdict to be given for the defendant. With the warm climate, but little fire or clothing was required; the labourer had always his garden, and lived largely upon rice, which is very cheap; upon what he raised, and upon wild bananas, that could be had in the forests for the gathering. A careful system of book-keeping was carried on at the Japanese Consulate in Honolulu, where his savings were deposited, and an account was kept of the sum due him, which was paid him, with interest at the rate of four per cent., at the end of the three years. The Japanese was frugal and temperate, and it rarely happened that he returned to Japan empty-handed. Instead of regarding it as a sort of bondage, the Japanese labourer was glad to go to Hawaii, where he could live comfortably and cheaply, and his Government was willing to profit by his temporary absence.

The system being made one of the objections to annexation by many Americans — the employment of contract labour being prohibited by law in the United States — the unwillingness of the Hawaiian Republic to allow unlimited Japanese immigration led to a collision with Japan. There has been, how-ever, very grave reason for resisting Oriental en-croachments. Immigration increased subsequently at an alarming rate. The Hon. L. A. Thurston states that in 1896 and the early part of 1897 immi-grants arrived at the rate of two thousand a month, and that in 1896 the adult Japanese males outnum-bered those of any other nationality. He states further, that, at this rate, in one year "they would have numbered one-half the population," and in five years "would have outnumbered all the other inhab-

GOODS

itants put together, two to one."   "Considering the relative population of Hawaii and the United States," he continues, "it was as though a million Japanese a month were entering San Francisco;" and he very fittingly termed this, "not immigration, but invasion."

To put an end to this invasion the Government was finally forced to enact restrictive laws, which the Japanese Government considered a violation of its treaty rights. With this difficulty there has been dissatisfaction on the part of the planters, who have found no satisfactory substitute for the wiry, active, and energetic Jap.   Europeans or Americans have not been found in large numbers to work in the cane fields, and the Hawaiians will not; and the situation remains something of a quandary.

Honolulu is wonderfully clean, and the absence of poverty and squalor is striking.   There is no smoke or soot, and but little dust.   The streets are swept constantly.   There are no filthy alleys and unsightly premises, such as may be seen in American towns and cities; and the tiniest cottages, even in the Chinese and Portuguese quarters, are surrounded by neat fences and blooming gardens, wherein may be seen a myriad variety of flowers, vines trained against the walls, and figs ripening upon the trellises. In the business portion of the city the streets are narrow, and there is not much room for traffic when the tram is given its allotted space.   One sees in the shop windows tastefully arranged muslins, prints, calico, silks, and laces, like those displayed in American shop windows, and the prices are about the same. There are book, picture, and china shops, such as may be seen in any European capital; and if the proprietor happens not to have an article inquired for, it is promptly ordered.

There are five churches, not including the Japanese and Chinese missions, — the Union Church, which is professedly Congregational, but which is attended by people of all religious beliefs; St. Andrew's Cathedral and second congregational Church; Christian Chinese congregation; a Roman Catholic Church and Convent.

The street-cars are little patronised except by the natives. Every one drives either in his own carriage or in one of the numerous vehicles that may be hired at any street corner. These are neither cabs nor victorias, but what in America are called "double-seated carriages," drawn by one horse. The animals are generally in poor condition, hay and oats having to be imported from California. They are driven, however, at a rattling pace. The numerous and convenient carriage-stands are an evidence of the extensive tourist population. Rates are dearer than in London or Paris, and a great deal cheaper than in New York or Chicago — $1.50 cents an hour for one passenger, $2 per hour for two, and twenty-five cents to any point within a radius of one mile from the centre of the city.

Jehu in Honolulu is an eminently social creature. He does not answer questions gruffly, like his American *confrère*, or point out objects of interest with chilling reluctance. He feels a simple and sincere interest in your well-being, and takes for granted a corresponding politeness on your part. If he is driving two "fares," he freely joins in the conversation, gives you his views, and concedes your own, or gently but firmly disputes them. And he is a revolutionist first, last, and all the time.

The abolition of the monarchy was a stirring crisis in Hawaii, and no one realised this more keenly than the ubiquitous hackman, and none took a greater pride in the fact that the small group of Islands was the centre of international dispute and the subject of important diplomatic negotiations.

"I was the first man that busted in the door of the Government building," one announced to me as I was driving about the second day after my arrival. He stated the fact with all the pride that Winkelried or Leonidas might have shown. Then he gazed triumphantly at the American flag floating over the Government building, adding, "And I helped put that up there."

At another time I was discussing the Hawaiian race problem with a friend, entirely oblivious of the gentleman on the front seat. He turned round and announced solemnly, "My wife is seven-eighths." By this mathematical assertion he meant that seven-eighths of the blood in her veins was white, and the saving remnant Hawaiian.

However, with all his revolutionary predilections and his somewhat abnormal conversational powers, the Honolulu hackman rarely overcharges, and he is the soul of good nature.

Everywhere, even in the smallest grounds, there are lawns of thick Bermuda grass, which in the rainy season is of velvety greenness. It should be explained that there is not a definitely marked rainy and dry season. The trade winds blow nine months in the year; in December, January, and February they cease, setting in again in March. The first week after their arrival seems to be devoted to a general clearing up. The trades come with a terrific roar, and blow day and night without ceasing for a week, or a little less. People prefer, then, to remain in the house with the doors and windows closed. When the wind calms down to a normal velocity, it is seen that dead leaves, dead branches, and even dead grass have been blown away, and the effect is something like that of the vernal equinox in the temperate zones. There are frequent rains throughout the summer, but the rainfall is heavier in the winter, although there are many fair days. Thunderstorms are so rare as to be phenomenal. There are no extremes of heat and cold such as prevail in the United States, when the torrid summer, relaxing and enervating, may be followed by a winter of arctic severity; the maximum heat is 74° Fahrenheit in the winter, and 84° in the summer; the lowest winter temperature is 56°.

The houses are built with verandahs in the front and in the rear, and frequently upon all four sides. On these verandahs or in the *lanai* the family practically lives. The front door stands wide open from morning until night, and there is a Chinese or Japanese servant waiting about to announce you when you arrive. Sometimes the servant is dispensed with, and, if a door-bell is lacking, you may find a small hand-bell placed within convenient reach, and this you will gently tinkle and put back in its appointed place. The grounds about the houses on the main avenues are extensive, and are filled with many varieties of palms, tropical ferns, crotons, lilies, and masses of tuberoses. Notwithstanding the dense masses of foliage there is no undergrowth, and no litter anywhere from dropping twigs or withered leaves; the marvellous luxuriance, with the apparent absence of all fading and decay, forms a part of the wonders that constantly confront one.

Honolulu has a population of thirty thousand, and in his handbook Mr. Thurston states that there are sixty-seven miles of streets and drives, of which twenty miles are macadamised; it has five public parks and squares, private electric-light systems, and thirteen hundred telephones, for which a very low rental is charged, are in daily use. The city is very efficiently governed and policed. Honolulu is the paradise of the Chinese, and furnishes a sharp contrast to their status in San Francisco and elsewhere on the Pacific Coast. It is a pleasant sight to see them about their shops fondling their little children. It is a still pleasanter sight to see these same children, of a little larger growth, flocking home from school, playing by the wayside, and exercising their lungs in the manner of healthy and untrammelled childhood, their pigtails lengthened by strands of bright pink cord which end in a tassel that strikes their little heels as they run. The more tidy and thoughtful gather up the queue and carry it over the arm, as a fine lady carries her train. But the native dress, which they all wear, the queue, and the manila bag full of school books are an Occidental and Oriental combination which it would be difficult to find outside Hawaii. It gave evidence of a healthy democracy and a cosmopolitan broad-mindedness among the white children who had not been biassed by acquired or inherited prejudice.

The servants are almost exclusively Chinese or Japanese, usually Chinese. In well-to-do households four or five are employed — the cook, the house-boy, the "yard-boy" and his assistant: "yard-boy" being Hawaiian for gardener. They are usually model servants, obedient, industrious and clean, excellent cooks and incomparable house servants, doing their work without fuss or noise, and doing it quickly, systematically, and thoroughly. A Honolulu house

NUUANU AVENUE, HONOLULU.

seems, apparently, to keep itself; one hears and knows nothing of the friction of the domestic machinery.

There are of course exceptions. Shortly after my arrival I saw the housekeeper in the hotel shaking a rebuking index finger at an abashed "boy," who bore her high-pitched tirade in French very much as a spiritless dog might have submitted to a shower of kicks and blows. Inquiring into the nature of his misdeeds, I was told that he had exceeded his instructions in the matter of dusting, and had *washed* a costly gilt clock with a very wet towel. My own especial "neat-handed Phyllis" was a smiling, pock-marked creature, who drifted into my room and drifted out again without leaving much evidence of his labour behind him. One morning he voluntarily and unassisted removed a withered bouquet from my dressing-table, flourished his big dust-brush like an amiable demon in an incantation scene, waved his hand, said "Velly nice," and then stood with his arms folded, waiting my official approval. An uninvited caller shortly afterwards invaded my verandah, and left behind him the abomination of the tobacco chewer. When I called John's attention to it, he came with his mop, remarking, with the fadeless smile of his race, "Some man spit velly bad."

The Chinese servants employed in Hawaii rarely live in the house; they have their own lodgings elsewhere, coming early in the morning, and leaving in the evening after dinner has been served. This

is inconvenient, as it leaves no one to attend the
door unless this office is performed by some member
of the household, as it usually is, with that kindly
informality which is half the charm of Hawaiian life.
The only holiday the Chinese servant expects is
the week of the Chinese New Year — in February.
Then preparations must be made for his entire and
continued absence. The cook usually prepares a
supply of bread, cakes, cold meats, and like food,
enough to last several days; and the ladies must
then allot the work amongst themselves and manage
it until the domestic staff return. Prior to their ·
departure there is a formal presentation of gifts
to "mamma," as they invariably call their mistress.
These gifts consist of flowers, Chinese sweetmeats,
nuts, embroidery, and gaudy, cheap vases. "Mamma"
usually gladdens the heart of her servitors in return
with something which she knows is especially desired.

The streets are a perpetual panorama, full of life
and colour. In the Chinese quarters are rows of
small shops. It is like a lesser China-town, except
that here in peaceful Honolulu the industrious
Mongolian is not molested. In these tiny shops
there are no show windows, the entire front being
open to the street, and closed with heavy, wooden
shutters at night. There are a great many tailors;
and the Chinaman in his native dress and queue
running a sewing machine, making cotton *holokus*
for native women, is one of the curious mixtures of

Orientalism and "modern improvements" that flourish
on every hand.   There are coffee-houses and laundries
innumerable.   On the narrow side-walks Hawaiian
women spread their mats and set out their baskets
of flowers, alternately stringing *leis*, smoking, sleeping,
and gossiping.   They bring their pets to bear them
company, — disreputable, repulsive little dogs, with
weak eyes and the mange; or young pigs, a favourite pet which they thoroughly domesticate and
eat unflinchingly when he "comes of age."

These women literally "come and spend the day;"
and the men, who have even more leisure, stop
and chat, so that the young and handsomer women
hold informal "at homes" on the side-walk all day
long, with the privilege of their favoured class the
whole world over, and certainly to the inconvenience
of ordinary pedestrians.   Occasionally they make a
pretext of offering their wares for sale, but not
always; even keeping up the pretext is too much
of an effort.   One woman, who especially interested
me, began the day with a stock that consisted of
three oranges and two lemons, and complacently
strolled away in the evening with this stock intact:
a little thing like this does not trouble them.   *Poi*,
their staple diet, is cheap and fattening.   It is made
of the *taro*, — the *kalo* of Samoa and *koko* of West
Africa; botanically, the *Colocasia antiquorum*.   It
has a thick, fleshy root, which in a natural state
is said to be poisonous.   It is therefore boiled and

7

kneaded into a paste, greyish pink in colour, with a slightly sour flavour, something like buckwheat batter. It is of varying consistency, and is eaten without ceremony out of a common calabash, around which the family squat. Each dips into the mass, and dexterously rolls a ball of the paste on the tip of his index finger, which he still more dexterously conveys to his mouth. It is called "one-finger," "two-finger," or "three-finger *poi*," according to its consistency. A very small patch of *taro* will support a family a year; and if the head of the household can have with it a limited supply of *squid*, his physical wants are satisfied.

Therefore, with sufficient *poi*, clad in the airy and flowing *holoku*, or cotton shirt and trousers, according to their sex, with the mercury rarely falling below 60°, they are spared many of the ills that human flesh is heir to in other less-favoured quarters of the globe.

It takes very little to support life, and the Hawaiian is usually happy, apart from the natural aids to contentment. With the yellow-skinned Chinese, the dusky Hawaiians, there are numbers of swarthy Portuguese thronging the streets, and, added to these, seamen from the English, American, and Japanese men-of-war. The latter — the able seamen from the *Naniwa*, probably one of the best crews in the Japanese Navy — were slender, delicate-looking fellows, but there was about them a suggestion of the pugnacity of wasps. They have proved their courage

since in the war with China, and verified the opinion
of an American officer who said, "They fight like
ants, without regard to the size or strength of their
enemy, and hold on till death."

The Japanese officers, in their white duck trousers,
blue caps, and blouses heavily trimmed with gold
braid, were elegant and graceful. They wore a small
sword, like a carving-knife, in a sheath attached to
the belt at the left side. So closely did these short
swords resemble the familiar piece of table cutlery
mentioned, that the eye instinctively ran round the
belt in search of the accompanying fork and steel.
One evening the officers dined in a body at the
hotel, which was magnificently decorated with
American, Hawaiian, and Japanese flags, and with
the greatest profusion of flowers, which they must
have considered barbarous. They were guests of the
Japanese Consul, and I could not resist the temptation of watching them file through the corridor,
dignified, handsome, self-possessed — like gentlemen
of any other civilised race.

Too much cannot be said of the American and
European society in Honolulu. Almost all the
younger generation among the former, identified with
the business or politics of the Islands, have been educated in the best American universities, and have
been liberalised by European travel. Many of the
women also have been educated in the United
States, a few in England, and they too have had the

advantages of travel and of the essentially cosmopolitan life of the Islands. They are thoroughly
well-informed, and talk well, and their culture is a
good deal more genuine than I have found it in other
countries where the opportunities are supposed to be
greater.

Oahu College, which is permanently and liberally
endowed, was founded by the missionaries more than
fifty years ago; and it seems strange to recall that
the early settlers in California sent their children out
to the Islands to be educated there.   This college as
well as the other schools even then were co-educa-
tional, and were considered excellent, besides being
much more accessible than the educational institutions of the Eastern States, in those days of overland
travel, or when the voyage had to be made round
the Horn.

At the time of the Revolution — and it is hardly
probable that it has altered since — the honesty of the
people was remarkable.   There were no locks on
the doors or bureau drawers, yet nothing was ever molested.   Stealing was almost unknown, and no pre-
cautions were taken against possible theft.   I left
some coins upon my bureau for several days.   The
doors and windows were open, servants came and went,
and flower-dealers loitered about the verandahs.   I
was away for hours at a time, yet the money was not
disturbed, nor would it have been had not the "boy"
considered it necessary finally to return it to me.

CHAPTER VI.

THE last Sunday in February I received an invitation to visit Mr. Cleghorn's grounds, and to go through the new house which he had just completed for the occupancy of his daughter, the Princess Kaiulani, who was then absent in England. Mr. Cleghorn was of Scottish descent, a prominent personage in Honolulu society. He was a man of considerable wealth, and president of the British-American Club. He apologised for receiving me on Sunday, and explained that it was his only day of leisure. We drove up the winding carriage road to the house, halting under the shade of a giant banyan tree — one of the most magnificent of its kind. It recalled my geography days, — the spreading branches, with their thick, dark-green, glossy leaves; the heavy boughs, with their smooth bark, not unlike our birches, these boughs sending roots down into the earth like pillars, their spreading branches making a canopy under which a caravan might have found shade. A carpenter's bench was strewn with chips and shavings, and there were other evidences of incompleted work, which, however, was progressing rapidly towards completion.

Mr. Cleghorn's place was one of the most beautiful in the Islands. The spacious grounds were ordinarily closed to visitors, with "Kapu" ("No Admittance") over the gate at the entrance. The new house was a white frame structure, of two storeys, with wings at either end — the favourite form of Honolulu architecture — with a wide verandah extending across the front. The shrubbery had been cut away for several yards in every direction to allow the free circulation of the air, and just beyond the main entrance stood the one incomparable banyan tree, which the owner presently informed me was the handsomest thing he had. He was not visible when we arrived, and I was helped from the carriage and sat down upon the carpenter's chest among the chips and shavings while a Chinese servant went in search of him. After a short interval he came — a tall, handsome man, erect as a field marshal, as dignified as a Spanish grandee, and altogether an impressive figure, with his keen black eyes, white beard and hair. He had been out amongst his flowers, he explained, and in proof of this he dropped a pair of pruning-shears into the pocket of his loose alpaca coat. It was not every day that one met the parent of royalty so occupied.

"The house is nearly completed," he said, look-

ing up at the closed windows with a wistful expression. "I built it for the Princess, and expected
to have it all in readiness, and now this overturn
has come."

It was a little difficult to reply to this remark. I
could not assure him of any honest belief in the
re-establishment of Hawaiian royalty, which I did
not think would ever be accomplished. So I
gently turned the conversation upon other and
impersonal subjects, and told him how glad I was
to see a banyan tree, and one so beautiful as the
fine specimen which he had raised. This evidently
gratified him, and after pointing out its various
beauties he invited me to come into the house.
The key was brought, and I was shown into the
hall, then into the grand drawing-room, where the
young heir-apparent would have held informal
receptions. It was a stately apartment, probably
forty feet in length and thirty feet in width, with
many windows looking out upon the velvet lawn.
The panelling was in beautiful native woods highly
polished, and the decorative tiles in the corridor
had been brought from Chicago. At one end there
was a large room enclosed with Venetian blinds on
two sides, the windows extending from floor to
ceiling, and being provided with screens. This
was the "mosquito-room," in which the Princess
and the English companion whom she was to have
brought back with her had expected to sit and

sew, read and talk.   Much was made of the screens, so universal in the United States, but which, strangely enough, were not in ordinary use in that mosquito-ridden land.   On the upper floor I was shown the Princess's private suite, the bedchamber corresponding to the drawing-room below, with a boudoir at one end and a dressing-room at the other.   The Hawaiian coronet, and the *kahili*, the ancient symbol of Hawaiian royalty, recurred at intervals in the decorations of the ceiling.

Long experience had made me very expert in the use of my crutches, and upon getting up the gangway of the *Mohican*, a few days before, I had boastingly remarked to Captain Ludlow, her commanding officer, as he expressed some fear for my security, that I felt certain I could climb on to the roof of a house, if an opportunity were given me.   As frequently happens, I had been taken at my word.   After we had gone through all the rooms on the upper floor Mr. Cleghorn wondered if it would be possible for me to get out on the roof.   "There is a beautiful view," he added, by way of additional incentive.

I wanted to see the view; but, apart from this, I had said that I could walk onto a roof on my crutches, and now that the occasion, so little anticipated, had come I must make good the assertion or be considered thereafter a vain boaster and a person altogether over-imaginative.   So I replied, without an instant's hesitation, though I did not in the least know how it was to be managed, that nothing would be easier.

He opened a door, and there was a staircase as nearly perpendicular as a staircase could be, with the narrowest of steps, and lighted by a trap-door, which he ran up and opened.

I looked at this arrangement dubiously; I could have hopped down with a little help on one foot; but I could not hop up. However, a gallant escort came to the rescue and steadied me, while another followed to catch me in case I lost my balance and toppled over backwards, and the thing was done. The roof was flat, and once reached there was no further difficulty; the descent of the staircase was comparatively easy — comparatively, not altogether.

The view certainly was most beautiful — worth even more than the effort I had made to see it, and it remains vividly in my mind.

Below us were acres of rice field, the most vivid and tender green; there were the solemn mountains, with great ragged masses of cloud floating down their summits and across the valleys; there was the sea, blue as sapphire, with the white surf tossing along the curve of sunken reef; there was the harbour with its shipping; the shady streets, the blossoming hedges, and gardens crowded with palms and algaroba and mango trees.

The air was damp and soft and sweet, reminding me of an April day at home when the apple blossoms were in bloom, the gentle trade winds blowing across the Pacific and passing onwards to other islands whereof they knew.

Near the house was a bungalow — a long, low building, the roofs sloping on the sides from an elevation in the centre. It was provided with a *lanai*. The floor of the main apartment was covered with matting, and it was very simply furnished, to secure coolness and space.

The bungalow showed evidences of the Revolution, and was crowded with relics of Hawaiian royalty, evidently hastily gathered together—feather coronets, shell necklaces, pieces of furniture, and in a large box was one of the celebrated feather mantles like those worn by the nobles. Then the portraits were pointed out of the Princess Like-Like, the mother of the heir-apparent, and of the Princess Kaiulani herself. The mother had a pleasing face of the native type, while the portrait of the Princess Kaiulani showed her to be a very handsome girl, with large, dark eyes and the more regular features of the Caucasian race, inherited from her father. There was one pretty picture of the young girl sitting in the garden under a tree; another which was painted at the age of twelve; and another, the most interesting of the collection, in Japanese dress.

"When will your daughter return to the Islands?"
I asked the father.

"Not until she has completed her studies," he
replied. "This is some of her work," he said,
pointing at two little copies in oil; they were
specimens of her first painting. "That is a later
work," and he showed me a copy of Landseer's
"Challenge," taking evident pride in this latter
specimen of the young Princess's skill. Truth compels me to state that the pictures had no more
merit than other examples of the work of royalty
which I have seen since in other countries.

After exhausting the interests of the bungalow my
host walked through the lovely grounds with me
to show his cocoanut trees, which were bearing
profusely.

"When I bought this place a few years ago,"
he said, "there was nothing here. I have planted
everything myself, and have seen it come to
maturity."

It seemed incredible, for the trees that towered
above us, throwing their cool, dim shade down across
the long avenue, might have been of a century's
growth. He stopped to show me some fine specimens
of the croton. This curious plant is almost number-
less in its varieties, both in the colour of its foliage
and the shape of the leaf. It is yellow, green, dark
maroon, crimson, and mottled yellow and green.
The leaves on some are ovate, and others are a

perfect lanceolate. My host told me that frequently plants would send out a shoot differing in colour and form from the foliage of the shrub. This, broken off and planted, produced an entire shrub of its own kind.

"I am very much interested in their propagation," he said, "and I have already forty varieties."

A peculiar purple black bumble bee flew past — not at all like our brown bee, with its fuzzy body and its dark velvety stripes. This was a metallic-looking insect, with a vicious way of darting about. I was told that it was a great pest, from its habit of boring into wood, and that the heaviest timber was frequently honey-combed by it and destroyed. It had been imported into the country in cedar brought from Oregon.

CHAPTER VII.

AN OSTRICH FARM.

THROUGH the kindness of Mrs. C. A. Brown
I had the pleasure of visiting an ostrich farm,
where a resident of Honolulu was experimenting in
raising ostrich feathers for the market.   The industry
was yet in its infancy, but it will doubtless be a
success. Everything thrives in this wonderful climate
except frogs, snakes, and a natural enemy to the mosquito.   As we drove along the fine road to Waikiki
we passed the park with its many verdant islands,
the neat gardens of the Chinese, the vegetable beds
separated by narrow canals of flowing water.   Along
the roadside at intervals, on the outskirts of the
city, were Chinese shops, the proprietors at the
doors, usually caressing a child picturesquely clad
in white drawers, a green undershirt, a little scarlet
cap and jacket, as impassive and outwardly emotion-
less as its parent.   I also saw two Hawaiian firemen
mending a hydrant in the streets; they were barefooted, clad in blue cotton trousers and scarlet shirts;
one was hatless, but he wore, instead of the usual

head-covering, a gay wreath of scarlet hibiscus; the other retained his hat, but he had concealed the crown, except the top of it, with a wreath of orange marigolds. The vision of a Chicago or a London fireman similarly decorated makes one smile; here it seemed eminently fitting.

The ostrich farmer received us kindly, having evidently grown accustomed to tourists and their teasing, if not foolish, questions. He had grown patient under affliction. In a paddock near the road were a dozen birds, two years old, standing herded together in the shade of the algaroba trees. They were probably six feet in height, with grey, furry necks, which they writhed and twisted like serpents. Their fuzzy heads seemed ridiculously small in proportion to their size, with so much of the available space devoted to mouth and eyes: as the owner quietly observed, "there was n't much room left for brains." The eyes of these young birds reminded me, in their colour, size, and softness, of the eyes of a heifer — the softness being contradicted by the powerful hoof, like that of a camel, ending in a terrible claw, and a savage, muscular leg that could disembowel a man at a stroke. The birds yawned a great deal, and in the operation the head seemed almost to part in two. They had altogether the most bored and indifferent air I have ever seen outside of a London drawing-room at the end of the season. The little covering of feathers that scantily protected their backs only emphasised their nakedness, and they fanned themselves continually with their small, useless wings, in the ends of which are the feathers most valuable in commerce. As we approached they came to the edge of their enclosure, looked over, retreated, and yawned again.

"What do you feed them on?" I asked.

"Alfalfa, cabbage, and a little grain. They cannot endure the least overfeeding; it is fatal always."

He kindly offered to show us the incubators. The birds were then laying, and produced from fifteen to eighteen eggs. These were removed at night, and were not left to be hatched after the natural method. They had to be stolen after dark, when the old birds are not on guard, from the shallow depression in the sand which serves for a nest. The parents are very fierce, and the owner keeps them at bay with a long pole, on the end of which is a fork, with which he holds them by the neck beyond kicking distance. As we passed through the house to the hatching-room the wife of the ostrich farmer sat at a sewing machine, with one pretty cat in her lap and another curled up beside her. She confessed to a love for cats, in which I ardently sympathised.

The incubator is a cylinder of galvanised iron, heated with kerosene lamps. The temperature of the bird's body, while she sits, is 105°; the incubator is kept at 95°. The eggs have to be turned four times a day and as often through the night, so that the owner has pretty well earned his money by the time the eggs are hatched, which does not occur for six weeks. The work of watching the incubator seemed almost as difficult and tiresome as managing an orphan asylum. When the first sound of a chick's chirping is heard, the thick shell is broken with a sharp instrument — an office the parent bird performs by striking it with her or his breastbone.

"What percentage of the eggs is hatched?" I asked.

"Well, it 's mighty small; out of twenty-nine eggs I had only two birds," the owner admitted with a discouraged air.

After the hatching is accomplished the young birds are removed to what looked like a refrigerator, from the roof of which depended many woollen strings. These were supposed to provide the protection that nature furnishes in the plumage of the parent's body. The young birds are fed upon a diet suited to their youthful appetites, into which glass and nails do not enter as largely as is generally supposed. The old ones *do* eat nails, I was informed, but only at long intervals and in limited quantity. But to suppose that they trot about with an internal rattling of scrap iron and broken crockery is most erroneous.

After exhausting our interest in the incubator we went through a narrow lane, not more than four feet wide, several hundred yards in length, with a high fence on either side. Up this lane the old birds were driven to the corral near the house. The ostrich farmer went to the end of the lane and whistled, and presently three huge birds came trotting from the depths of an algaroba grove with an ungainly, springy tread which was suggestive of the dangerous elasticity of their legs. They were introduced as "John Sullivan and his wife," who occupied the paddock to the left, and "Jumbo," who had the other, upon the right, for his sole occupancy. He was a giant, imported from Africa, fierce and untamable, and I instinctively moved away as he craned his long, pendulous neck over the high palings and eyed me with the most vicious and malignant expression.

In one paddock was a nest in which the eggs had been scattered about promiscuously in the effort that the bird had made to turn them. "They do not sit much at first until the laying is finished," said the ostrich farmer; "and then the male bird is on the nest whenever the female leaves it, and that is most of the time." This challenged my admiration, and made me regard the savage John Sullivan with a little more toleration. It was a division of domestic responsibility, which in the whole scheme of nature was as rare as it was beautiful. As we walked away the creatures followed us as if they regretted they could not have a final nip at us, and I left them with mingled alacrity and gladness.

8

CHAPTER VIII.

A VISIT TO CAMP BOSTON.

ON the morning of March 3rd I was invited by Captain Swinburne to visit the American marines at "Camp Boston," where they were quartered shortly after being ordered ashore.

By a strange irony of destiny the camp was established in what had been the old home of Mrs. Bishop. Here Queen Liliuokalani passed her girlhood, and it was one of those mysterious decrees of Fate that it should have thus been occupied by the troops of the United States Government. Her father, one of the chiefs of Maui, occupied the house in feudal state, with a guard of three hundred armed retainers. It was a beautiful old house, with verandahs above and below, and the grounds were kept with the utmost care, to the marines being assigned the duty of gardening, in which they took the greatest pride and interest.

The morning of the visit was like a day in mid-June, the palms and oleanders and algaroba trees waving in the soft breeze, their brilliant

foliage shining in the sunlight. The officers came out to welcome us (we were a party of four), as the sentry stepped aside to let us pass through the gateway. The flag floated lazily from the staff; the sentinels marched to and fro, their cartridge-belts girded around them, their rifles upon their shoulders, with all the pomp and circumstance of glorious war. We chatted a little, and then were shown about the house and grounds, everything being explained and every question answered with the characteristic willingness and courtesy of American naval officers.

The front hall was occupied by an imposing desk, upon which printed forms were arranged, which embraced all the routine of daily life and official duty in camp.

"Here's the daily menu," said Lieutenant Laird, handing me one of the printed slips. It was as follows:

"Camp Boston routine: 6, reveille; 6.10, roll call fatigue; 6.40, recall, surgeon's call; 7, breakfast; 7.30, assembly of trumpeters; 7.45, assembly of guard details; 7.50, guard-mounting; 8.15, company inspection; 8.30, battalion drill, fatigue; 10, inspection; 12, dinner; 4, drill; 5, band call; 5.30, parade; 6, supper; 9, tattoo; 9.30, taps. Saturday: 8.15, company inspection, fatigue, general police; 5.30, parade. Sunday: 8.15, company inspection; 8.30, review and inspection, church.

"And do you really have to go to church?" I asked.

"It is not enforced, of course; it is voluntary; but the men go — not so much now, however, as they did at first," he admitted.

It was religious retrogression that could very well be excused in that lovely place and in that heavenly climate.

In what had been the front of the great drawing-room — divided then from the rear by a partition — there was a splendid stand of colours; and the adjective is used advisedly. One large flag was of thick, fine silk, edged with gold fringe, the stars embroidered by hand in white silk, the work alike on both sides. With this handsome banner was a set of signals, also of silk. They were the gift of the city of Boston, after which the ship had been named. This is a pleasant custom, followed by all the states and cities after which the new American war-ships have been named; and the gifts are of various kinds — libraries, clocks, and colours; plate, however, is preferred, as it is more easily taken care of, and can be handed down as an heirloom, as is the custom in regard to the costly mess-plate of most famous English regiments. This has been done by the State of Indiana for her name-sake. San Francisco gave so generously to the ship which bears her name, that the subscriptions could not be expended wholly upon the service which was ordered, and the surplus was invested in small gold grizzly bears as handles for tureens and covers, the grizzly bear

being a conspicuous figure in the Californian coat-
of-arms.

"You have very regal quarters," I remarked, after
we had sufficiently admired the beautiful flags.

"In many respects, yes," Captain Swinburne
replied; "but I am afraid that it is more regal than
convenient — less convenient, at any rate, than ordinary barracks. There, for one thing, we had the
regulation bunks. Here, the sleeping accommoda-
tion is very inadequate; but we are getting everything shipshape as rapidly as possible."

On board the *Boston* the men slept in their hammocks; in the fine old Hawaiian house the hammocks
were spread upon the floor. The first few nights
after they came ashore they camped in the private
grounds of one of the wealthy residents of Honolulu.
They were nearly devoured by mosquitos — that
terrible pest of Honolulu — and suffered extremely.
In one of the rooms several of the men were lounging
about taking their ease — honest, wholesome-looking
fellows, all of them.   One was making a cord by un-
ravelling and twisting into strands a piece of white
braid — the same cord intended to be attached later
to his clasp-knife in sailor fashion. Another, stretched
comfortably upon his back, was reading a novel. The
guns, holding five shells each, were shown us, and an
attempt was made to convey to our bewildered intelligence some knowledge of their merits as explosives.

"War nowadays is not a matter of mere defence

or conquest, but extermination," I could not help
remarking, as I was told the incredible number of
shells that could be fired in a minute by one of the
large machine-guns in the grounds.

"Yes," said my patient instructor, "when we fight
nowadays we fight to kill.   But the very deadliness
of war makes nations to-day more careful in declaring it."

On the walls were arranged a great assortment of
pictures — cigarette cards, cuts from the illustrated
papers, and odds and ends in the way of prints and
lithographs.   The collections were vastly like those
that men, irrespective of class, colour, or previous
condition of servitude, seem to have a *penchant* for
posting up in their respective places of business —
such as one will see over a printer's case, or a
reporter's or even an editor's desk.

As I have said, the grounds were in beautiful order,
and several of the men had been hoeing and raking
the flower-beds, and were then at work weeding the
borders.   There was none of the trodden-down
appearance, or the barrenness that might have been
expected in a barracks.   In the basin, where the
fountain sent down a cloud of silver spray, was a
mass of luxuriant water-plants, and a number of
gold-fish were swimming about.

"The men put these in here," Captain Swinburne
explained, when I expressed some surprise at the
tidiness of the garden.   "They take great pride in

beautifying it and keeping it in order, and the garden really is in much better condition now than when we came."

As we returned to the house "Finnegan" was brought forward, and we were formally introduced. Finnegan had already passed into history, but he was one of those rare characters whom praise could not corrupt or over-attention inspire with too extravagant an opinion of his own merits. Misleading as his name might be, Finnegan was not a naturalised American politician — a transplanted Home-Ruler, who had been carrying on war against the British Government from the safe vantage-ground of the United States. He was the *mascot* of the *Boston;* to the casual and indiscriminate observer, a little mongrel dog, of a nondescript colour, with cropped ears, and one lame leg.

After the usual formalities he was arrayed in his blanket — a marvellous covering of dark-blue cloth, with the word *Boston* embroidered on one side, surrounded by stars, which were also embroidered in red, white, and blue silk. This gorgeous blanket was further embellished with a small flag on the other side, and was finished off with a voluminous sailor collar. It was put on Finnegan by one of his attendant marines, and he bore the inspection of our party with rather shamefaced meekness. The gallant tar upon whom devolved the pleasant duty of showing Finnegan off basked in the *mascot's* reflected splendour. He also modestly explained that it was his own expert fingers that had made that wonderful blanket, embroidered stars and all. Finnegan's history was briefly this: He appeared suddenly in the camp, shortly after the men came ashore, and was kindly fed and made much of. Neither man nor dog can withstand material blandishment of this sort. Finnegan had duties and affiliations elsewhere. He had a short, though doubtless severe, struggle with his canine conscience, and disappeared at intervals to make amends to his original benefactor. But these spasms of conscience became rarer and less imperative. His visits to his home grew briefer and fewer; he called at first semi-weekly, then weekly, and then, alas! not at all. He had had a fatal taste of martial life. He was ensnared by the position to which he had been so suddenly elevated, and he finally cut the civil service once and for ever, and enlisted for life in the navy.

"What will you do with him when you leave Honolulu?" I asked Captain Swinburne.

"Take him with us; Finnegan belongs to the *Boston* now, and whenever the ship goes, he goes too."

Thus it will be seen that while the residents of Hawaii were awaiting diplomatic and legislative formalities, Finnegan had quietly annexed himself, and was to be henceforth, for the remainder of his

life, an inseparable part of the American Navy. One
could easily imagine his future career. A sailor's
life on the high seas, a hero in port, a participant in
other revolutions, a central figure in State ceremonials, and finally burial with honours of war in a
neat little shroud in some calm sea under tropical
skies. A dog's life, like a man's, depends upon
who and what he is.

But to return to the needlework. Our expressions
of admiration over Finnegan's blanket encouraged
the men to bring forth other treasures, which were all
duly admired.

"A sailor can make anything if you give him a
needle, thread, and a bit of soap," said Captain
Swinburne, and one could easily believe it after
having seen what we were shown. Upstairs we were
taken through the officers' quarters, the tables were
spread for luncheon with some crisp young onions
already set out upon the board. We declined the
generous offer to share this part of the prospective
meal, and so said good-bye with a promise to come
again, an invitation that was gladly accepted several
days later.

CHAPTER IX.

KING KALAKAUA'S PALACE.

THROUGH the courtesy of Lieutenant Laird of the *Boston*, and Colonel J. W. Robertson, Chamberlain of ex-Queen Liliuokalani, I was permitted to go through the Palace, which was then closed to the public. It was rather a melancholy experience — one more reminder of the unstable nature of human institutions and of monarchical splendours. To Colonel Robertson had been entrusted by the Provisional Government the custody of the insignia of State, the crowns, robes, and jewels, and the valuable gifts of other governments to the sovereigns of Hawaii. All the personal effects of King Kalakaua reverted to the Queen-Dowager and to ex-Queen Liliuokalani, but the collection retained passed into the possession of the Government, and has been carefully preserved in the museum. The Palace was built by King Kalakaua, as has been stated elsewhere; it is a piece of modern French architecture, with Mansard roofs, balconies, and many windows, each of which commands a view of unimaginable beauty, — lofty mountain peaks, over which the clouds descend; green slopes and valleys, with masses of tropical vegetation at their base.

As we drove to the entrance a sentry from the native infantry opened the iron gates to let us pass, and Colonel Robertson met us on the steps at the entrance. We were conducted upwards first, and in the grand corridor on the second floor were shown an interesting collection of portraits — all the noble old Kamehamehas, Queen Emma, Kalakaua, and ex-Queen Liliuokalani. The most striking was that of the first Kamehameha — the greatest of the line, a warrior of marvellous power, who united the domains of rival chiefs on the other islands into the government of which he became the head. The face in the portrait was that of the best Hawaiian type, uncontaminated by alien blood, the dark skin and dark eyes of the natives, with short snow-white hair. Over the scarlet uniform he wore the yellow feather mantle of royalty. Another scion of royalty, the wife of the successful Kamehameha, wore a magnificent tiara of ostrich feathers like that in one of the familiar portraits of the Empress Josephine. The portrait, and that of her husband, had been painted in England. It was a most interesting collection.

A portrait of Louis Philippe, presented by the French Government, was also one of the chief objects of interest with a history. It was four months in its passage round Cape Horn, and was received with imposing ceremony the very day the monarch was deposed, an event of which the Hawaiians received tidings just four months later. The portrait of Mr. John Dominis, the husband of Liliuokalani, a man of Italian descent, was that of a delicate, feeble-looking person, and he was a striking contrast to his robust spouse, who has all the *embonpoint* of the Hawaiian.

Two empty gilt chairs stood upon the daïs in the throne-room, with a staff on either side surmounted by the Hawaiian coronet, and behind these two towering *kahilis* — the ancient emblem of Hawaiian chiefhood — huge plumes, made of the black feathers of the *oo*. On the walls, framed and protected with glass, were decorations received by royalty from the various European Powers.

On the floor above were the library and the private apartments of King Kalakaua. The King's chamber, with bath and dressing-room, was hung with pale blue; the furniture was of gold and ebony; but the place was dismantled, all his personal effects having been removed. The Queen's suite, in the wing opposite, was still more simply furnished. The hangings and curtains were of chintz, and the rug in the centre of the bed-chamber had a pattern of huge roses in which the primary colours predominated. The library contained some volumes of the *Edinburgh Review*, a number of medical works, a small edition of *Audubon's Book of Birds*, and the *Encyclopædia Britannica* — not a particularly interesting collection. In a cabinet was a modest service of plate — spoons, forks, and ladles — the property of the Government, which had been sent by France with the ill-starred portrait of Louis Philippe.

In one small room was a collection of curios, also to be turned over to the museum, a polished swimming-board, a native drum (a block of wood covered with pig-skin), vessels for holding *poi*, one or two baskets, and two wooden trenchers, one for serving roast pig, and another, smaller and deeper, in which that salient feature of a Hawaiian banquet, roast dog, was brought upon the table.

After exploring the State apartments we descended to the lower floor, and the rooms in which the State insignia were preserved were unlocked, and we were permitted to inspect them at our leisure. Although the Revolution had been precipitated in a few hours, the Provisional Government permitted no violence and no neglect or abuse of the national possessions which the Hawaiians held sacred. Chief among these were the crowns, sceptre, jewels, and the sacred *mamos* — the wonderful feather cloaks which none could wear but the highest chiefs. These had been placed in chests and kept under lock and key, and it was an extremely difficult matter to get sight of them, whatever influence might be brought to bear. The *kahilis* were ranged in frames against the

wall, looking like big dust-brushes with long handles. Some were made of yellow feathers, some
of goose feathers, others of hen feathers dyed pink.
These were carried in procession on all State occasions, and the *kahilis* preceded the Queen when she
came into the throne-room or legislative halls.
There were several chests filled with feathers tied in
bundles, ready to be made up in *kahilis* if upon
regal occasions the demand should exceed the supply
on hand. The handles of these big plumes were of
bone or polished wood.   I saw neatly pieced into one
— a very ancient heirloom — the white wrist-bone of
a chiefess, and in another the thigh-bone of a chief.
These had come down from the time of the first
Kamehameha, and from long usage had acquired a
polish like ivory.

It took much urging and entreating to get even
a glimpse of the beautiful *mamos*. They are as
much a part of the Islands as the great volcano, and
to miss seeing one is as great a misfortune as failing
to see the other.   In a large circular box of galvanised iron was a great number of small collars, with
patterns in black or scarlet feathers upon the dazzling
yellow ground.   These were worn by the nobles
in attendance upon the chief.   The larger mantles
were stored in long chests and kept under lock and
key.   They were wound smoothly, without a crease
or crinkle, round long poles, and then covered with
many folds of some sort of native cloth, and tied so

securely that it was a little difficult to unfasten them.
Like the *kahilis*, the mantles were made of the
yellow feathers of the *oo* (*Acrulocercus nobilis*).   This
is a bird which is extremely rare, and lives in the
mountains of the islands of Hawaii and Maui, but
is not found on the island of Oahu.   It is a small
bird, with a long, curved beak, and lives upon honey;
its plumage is black, changing to green, and under
each wing is a single small cluster of yellow
feathers.[1]   From these the royal mantles were made;
the birds were not destroyed, but were snared, the
costly feathers secured, and the bird was then set
free.   The foundation of each mantle was a lace like
net made from the fibre of the *olono*, or native hemp,
and upon these the tiny yellow feathers, no larger
than those of a canary bird's plumage, had been
fastened one by one, making a smooth surface, dazzling as cloth of gold.   The mantles of the chiefs
were several yards in length, and were carried by
train-bearers.   Lieutenant Laird said that even at
the low valuation of native labour each royal mantle
was worth over a million dollars, tribute being formally exacted in *oo* feathers, a few every year from
each subject.   The mantles were carefully sunned
and aired at short intervals, tobacco being sprinkled
over them to prevent the ravages of insects.   This

[1] Professor Alexander states that the feathers of another bird, the
mamo (*Drepanis pacifica*), still rarer than the *oo*, were also used in
the manufacture of these mantles.

periodical cleaning is a most tedious process, and must be done feather by feather. Among many other wild rumours that had kept the natives in a state of continual unrest — statements exaggerated and circulated by demagogues — was one to the effect that these *ahulas*, from time immemorial the possession of the chiefs and kings of Hawaii, were to become the property of the United States and be removed to the Smithsonian Museum in Washington.

"We have put our heads into the lion's mouth, and must abide the consequences," said one man, speaking of the prospective loss.

I assured him that I did not think for one moment that the United States would molest the Hawaiian people in a single right or privilege they now enjoyed, least of all would they be deprived of their State insignia and treasures — an assertion which I am glad to say that time has fully verified.

After the *kahilis* and *ahulas* had been shown — and in the collection I have forgotten to mention three dusty silk hats with wide crape bands, survivals of King Kalakaua's funeral — the chests were closed and fastened, and the doors were securely locked behind us.

We were then conducted to the ex-Chamberlain's private office. In the outer apartment were several glass cases containing quantities of royal stationery — cards, large and small — forms of invitation for royal entertainments. Two were presented me as souvenirs; the smaller, for less ceremonious occasions, had a narrow silver border, and the larger a border of gold. The lettering, surmounted by the Hawaiian coronet in scarlet and gold, was in gold script and old English text. The receptions to which these cards were an open sesame were a thing of the past — as much as the native feasts of Kamehameha. Upon the ex-Chamberlain's desk stood a large calf-skin case with the name of a London firm printed on one end. It looked somewhat like a commonplace steamer trunk, though not so long; it was unlocked, and lo! within were two crowns — that of the King and the Queen of Hawaii. They were the crowns that had been ordered by King Kalakaua and made for him in London, and worn on his coronation. The larger, that of the King, was handed me, and I took it with the natural interest one could not help feeling who holds in his hands for the first time the *bonâ fide* coronet of a king, though that king had been classified as a petty sovereign. There was a cap of crimson velvet with four converging bands of very thin gold, surmounted by a small globe and a Maltese cross. The band which passed round the forehead was studded with opals and rubies, and above this at intervals were crosses set with diamonds and other jewels. That of the Queen was of the same pattern. Colonel Robertson gave some order to his secretary which I

9

did not hear distinctly, and he disappeared and presently returned with the sceptre and King Kalakaua's sword in its jewelled scabbard. The young man was a native, and I fancied that there was an expression of stern disapproval on his handsome face when he surrendered the sceptre to me. I did not see him smile, and his gravity was melancholy. Not being of the Kamehamehas, as I have said, there had been some lack of sympathy for the ex-Queen; but the Hawaiians loved their country passionately, and these were its signs and symbols, spread out to the view of people to whom they had only an abstract interest, and in which one could feel only, perhaps, a passing curiosity.

When the coronets had been returned to the leather case and the sceptre removed, the combination lock of the safe was unfastened, and case after case of jewelled decorations were shown us. On each was the letter "K," surmounted by the Hawaiian coronet — the royal cipher. From Russia there was a dazzling star of diamonds; another from Austria; the gold cordon of St. Michael and St. George; the cordon of the order instituted by Kalakaua himself — a necklace of gold, the links interspersed with Hawaiian crowns. From Pius IX. there was another star, this of silver, with jewels set in enamel, bearing the legend around the rim in enamel letters, "*Virtuti et merito.*" This constituted the entire collection, which reverted to the Provisional Government, and was held by it in custody and carefully preserved.

We thanked Colonel Robertson and Lieutenant Laird and passed out of the portico, the young Hawaiian secretary amongst us. Perhaps if the young Hawaiian could have realised — as he may in the future — how sincerely we, and I believe Americans generally, hoped that whatever might happen should be ordained for the welfare of the people, the cloud upon his brow would have been less heavy and the fear within his heart dispelled. The Government of the United States had never dealt unjustly with the people of its acquired territory. It was hardly probable that an exception would be made in the case of Hawaii, should annexation become an established fact. The crowns and jewels, the sceptre and the feathered mantles, would no more have been taken forcibly from the people of the Islands than would the colonial relics of Massachusetts have been removed from the Boston Museum to Washington. They belonged to the country, and there they would remain.

As I drove down the main avenue to the gates the awkward squad of the volunteer troops was being drilled; they wore no uniform, and in their cotton shirts, trousers, and straw hats looked like a contingent of South American volunteers.

By a singular coincidence it was the 4th of March, noon, in Honolulu, and I reflected that, far away in

Washington, President Cleveland had taken the oath of office, and the inauguration services were over hours ago. The new administration, at whose hands Hawaii was destined to suffer much, had assumed control of political affairs in the United States. How much depended upon the justice and the wisdom of that administration all realised even then; but what was destined to befall no one could have imagined.

On Saturday evening, after this memorable visit to the Palace, I had the pleasure of meeting Mr. Francis Gay, who is the largest wool-grower in the Hawaiian Islands. Mr. Gay was a Scotchman, and was a member of the Legislature, familiar, as are all old residents, with the political situation past and present. When Mrs. Bishop was in Hawaii in 1873 she visited their estate on the island of Kauai, and gave a most interesting account of the family, whose head was named Sinclair. They were of the best, sturdy stock, and came from Scotland to New Zealand. After their arrival in New Zealand Mrs. Sinclair's husband was drowned, and she herself assumed control of the estate, which she retained up to the time of her death a few years ago. She was a woman of great intellectual and moral force, a student, a reader, requiring like application from all her children and grandchildren, and was a financier of marked ability. She would never consent to the separation of her family, and when they outgrew the

limits of their New Zealand estate it was sold, and
the indomitable woman embarked her possessions
and her descendants upon a ship which they owned,
and cruised through the Pacific in search of a new
home.   They first went to Oregon; but as, Mr. Gay
told me, the laws of the territory would not permit
them to purchase a tract sufficiently large they returned to the Hawaiian Islands, at which they
touched, and where some of the family had been
temporarily left.   King Kamehameha, recognising
their value as an accession to his people, offered
them the entire island of Niihau at a very moderate
price.   The island, of seventy thousand acres, affords
good pasturage for twenty thousand sheep, and is
managed by overseers, the family having their residence on the adjacent island of Kauai, putting up
wooden houses which they had brought with them.
Mrs. Bishop relates that Mrs. Sinclair was called
"Mama" by the natives, who gave their services
once a month as an equivalent for rent.   Here they
have lived, remote from the world, in this land of
eternal summer, embowered in flowers and the tropical vegetation about them, in the midst of their
books, enjoying the comfort and luxury of an ideal
if somewhat solitary life.   Mrs. Sinclair, the ven-
erated head of the household, was described by Mrs.
Bishop as a lady of the old Scotch type; very tal-
ented, bright, humorous, charming, with a definite
character which impressed itself upon everybody;

beautiful in her old age; "disdaining that servile conformity to prevailing fashion which makes so many old people at once ugly and contemptible; speaking English with a slight, old-fashioned Scotch accent, which gives naïveté to everything she says, up to the latest novelty in theology and politics; devoted to her children and grandchildren, the life of the family, and, though upwards of seventy, the first to rise and the last to retire in the house. She was away when I arrived," Mrs. Bishop continues, "but some days after rode up to the house in a large, drawn silk bonnet, which she rarely lays aside, as light in her figure and step as a young girl, looking as if she had walked out of an old picture or one of Dean Ramsay's books."

Although more than fourteen years had elapsed since Mrs. Bishop's visit, and the venerable woman had gone to her reward, the family remained unbroken, and its members were everywhere recognised and respected as people of superior character and attainment. Mr. Gay, the grandson whom I met, was a man in middle life, with a voice, countenance, and manner of great mildness, frank, unaffected, and straightforward in his conversation. He gave me an invitation to visit the family on Kauai, but this, with others of a similar nature, much to my regret, had to be declined, both on account of continued lameness and the unsettled state of affairs, not knowing what might happen at any moment, which made it impossible for me to go away from Honolulu.   Mr. Gay was an unqualified annexationist. He raised cattle as well as merino sheep, and had large interests in both industries.

"I was a British subject," he said, "and have a profound love for English institutions.   Personally, I would have preferred the protection of the English flag, but it is not practicable.   The Hawaiian Islands, by all the laws of right and nature, are in sympathy with the United States, to whom they owe their institutions and their civilisation.   People of other nationalities here simply reaped the reward of American enlightenment and Christianising.   With unrestricted commerce between the United States, her markets freely open to us, our commercial and national prosperity will be assured."

"What is your estimate of the Hawaiians politically?"

"They are unfitted even to govern themselves, still more to govern others.   I have lived all my life amongst them, have grown up with them, and speak their language as fluently as I speak my own. They are indolent; they are ease-loving, cheerful, generous, and amiable; but their judgment is very imperfect; they are irresponsible, and possess very little forethought.   If the wants of the present are provided for, even among the more intelligent, they put aside every care for the future.   They are the most pliant of tools, and fatally susceptible to political corruption. Last year we sent a man to the Legislature whom we believed we could trust implicitly, but he went over to the Queen's adherents, undoubtedly bribed. It is perfectly impossible that they should be able to form any estimate of the needs of an intelligent and civilised country; many of them, enfranchised citizens, privileged to vote under the old Constitution, still live in the primitive way, in huts, subsisting on fish and *poi*. It is true that the majority can read and write, but their education rarely progresses beyond this; they are too much indisposed toward any protracted or systematic effort. It is useless to talk of elevating them or fitting them for the exercise of authority. It has been tried patiently for years, and they are more incapable now than they were twenty years ago, being influenced by a class whose association has always been harmful, and never beneficial."

Reverting again to sheep-raising, Mr. Gay said that the mutton produced on Hawaii was of good quality, and the wool was such as is used in the manufacture of fine worsteds. There is so little fresh water on the island, that as the fleeces cannot be washed in salt water the wool has to be exported "in the dirt," as he expressed it. This increases the bulk, and proportionately the cost of exportation.

"The United States is our natural market," he said; "England has already an over-supply, and is too far away. By the time we send our products to

California, across the States, and the Atlantic, there is no profit for the ranchman. Last year we sent a good deal to Australia, and Canada is our best and largest market, by the way of Vancouver and the Canadian Pacific Railroad."

Mr. Gay was asked if wool-growing in Hawaii would not conflict with the industry in the United States.

"No," he replied. "Our territory is naturally so limited that we can never engage in sheep-raising on the extensive scale possible in America. We can never be, in any important sense, a rival. But," he said in conclusion, "the commercial aspect is the least consideration in the question. The people here have been very patient with a monarchy which has gone from bad to worse. We have given up all hope of improvement from this source, and we can only rely upon annexation, complete and absolute, either to England or to the United States, for stable Government. I think, personally, that your election methods are very bad; they cannot be compared to those that prevail in Great Britain, or the English Colonies; but, notwithstanding this, the fitting and natural disposition of the Hawaiian Islands is to make them a part of the United States. The Government cannot and will not remain as it is. If your country cannot take us, England will."

CHAPTER X.

O N Thursday, March 9th, the Senate held its second session, just five days after the inauguration of President Cleveland. They took immediate action upon a message in which Mr. Cleveland recommended the withdrawal of the Hawaiian treaty which had been approved by ex-President Harrison. Recommending is perhaps a misleading term, as Mr. Cleveland usually commanded, and his orders were carried out in a manner much more like that of an autocratic ruler than the representative of the people, in office by their concurrence and their suffrages.

Mr. Gresham, the recently chosen Secretary of State, informed the Hawaiian Commissioner, the Hon. L. A. Thurston, that, "with insignificant knowledge of facts and of details, they desired time for consideration of the subject, and the treaty had been withdrawn for that purpose."

Subsequent action contradicted this, which was a mere excuse to gain time. There was never a moment from the hour that they went into office when both the President and his Secretary of State were not bitterly hostile to the Provisional Government of the Hawaiian Islands and afterwards to the Republic, because they had secured the sympathy and co-operation of the ex-President, to whom both Mr. Cleveland and Mr. Gresham were unfriendly. The contemptuous setting aside of the testimony of the five Commissioners who had been dispatched to Washington at the time of the Revolution — five men of tested integrity, uprightness, and disinterestedness — was part and parcel of what was to be endured without cessation for the ensuing four years. No one in the Islands had dreamed that the Hawaiian Commissioners would meet with such a churlish treatment at the hands of President Cleveland and his Cabinet. Experience taught them, subsequently, that they need expect no other.

When, however, the five men realised that argument was useless they desisted, and Mr. W. C. Wilder, one of their number, returned to Honolulu. Before he arrived American newspapers were received, in which it was stated that the President was about to appoint a Commission of three men, who, it was thought, would be Judge Cooley, of Michigan, a high authority in international law; Admiral Brown, who had been for so many years a warm friend of the natives; and General Schofield, of the United States Army. It was supposed that this

Commission had been named by the President and confirmed by the Senate, in conformity to the law in such circumstances. Mr. Wilder returned on March 22nd, and there was much disappointment that he had no definite news, the suspense by this time having become most painful. He reassured the people, however, with every hope, which was corroborated later by the arrival of Mr. Marsden, another of the Commission, who saw no cause for anxiety in the withdrawal of the treaty. It was known that change of administration meant a change in a large part of the officials of the entire United States Government, and that Hawaii would have to wait, very naturally, until this had been accomplished. It was also believed that the President wished to act independently of his predecessor, which would necessitate the negotiation of a new treaty. The rumour of the appointment of three Commissioners, all known to be men of ability and without bias, seemed to corroborate this optimistic view.

In the steamer with Mr. Marsden were Mr. Paul Neumann, the Queen's attorney, whom she had dispatched to Washington on the heels of the Commission; Mr. John Bush, the editor of a native paper which had been suppressed at one time and had been particularly scurrilous in its attacks on the Queen — the editor now posing as her friend; with Prince David, a relative of the ex-Queen. The two latter accompanied Mr. Neumann as far as San Francisco, waiting the result of his mission to Washington, and returning with him to Honolulu. All three seemed well content with what they had accomplished, no details of this, however, being given to the public.

They were received upon the deck of the steamer, after she had been docked, with the wildest demonstrations, smothered with *leis* and driven to the ex-Queen's private residence. That evening there was an open-air concert in the hotel grounds, at which the Queen's band, the members of which had refused to take the oath of allegiance to the Provisional Government, appeared for the first time since her retirement. The natives gathered from far and near, those of high rank in little coteries on the steps and verandahs of the hotel and in the *lanais*, while the humbler folk stood in solid masses in the deep shadow of the trees upon the lawn. All were in gala dress, and each man, woman, and child wore upon the hat and around the throat *leis* of marigolds and tuberoses.

At the appearance of the band, handsome, slender Hawaiians in suits of snow-white duck, shouts of applause broke forth that became almost uncontrollable, when the familiar notes of Hawaiian melodies filled the air. On the conclusion of the first number armloads of *leis* were passed up to the musicians, and a man pressed his way through the crowd loaded with more *leis* of tuberoses, some of them two yards in length. The musicians sat down, and were solemnly invested with these *leis*, which are in reality a national decoration. The picturesque ceremony proceeded in silence; and in the soft blaze of the coloured lights of the pavilion in which they were grouped, with the tropical surroundings, the dark-eyed, dark-skinned throng, clad in white and garlanded with flowers, formed a memorable scene.

When the investiture was concluded a mighty shout went up; the enthusiasm became overpowering, and when it lulled the concert proceeded. It was partly instrumental and partly vocal, the programme concluding with a number given by a native quartette known as "King Kalakaua's Singing Boys." Their contribution to the entertainment was a song in Hawaiian, written for the occasion, in which the missionaries and the Provisional Government were soundly rated. The reception of this song was also decidedly warm. The concert was followed by a ball, at which all the prominent royalists were present; it was pre-eminently a royalist evening, but there was no expression of ill-will from either Hawaiians or annexationists.

There was the same evening another native demonstration. Hawaiian women are famous equestriennes, and Mrs. Bishop describes processions of riders galloping along the seashore and up the mountain roads, wearing the native riding-habit of orange or scarlet streaming out on either side like wings — for all, as they do to this day, rode astride — barefooted and crowned with *leis*. These picturesque costumes had been abandoned for years, but on the night of the concert they were unfolded, taken out, and donned, and a company of riders dashed along the main streets of Honolulu at a wild gallop. It was the last flicker of the dying monarchy — probably the last time that foreign eyes were to behold a custom then in its decadence and soon to be abandoned for ever.

The day following both the adherents of the ex-Queen and the supporters of the Provisional Government were destined to have their sanguine expectations severely shaken; for up to this time each had been confident of triumphing. The natives construed — and rightly, as time proved — unfriendliness to the Provisional Government in the withdrawal of the treaty. On the other hand, President Dole and his associates regarded the appointment of the Commission, which they confidently believed had been named, as evidence of a desire to deal wisely and impartially with Hawaii in the consideration of so important a matter as annexation.

There is a telephone station on one of the headlands beyond the city, and when ships are sighted the news is immediately telephoned to Honolulu. At 9.30 on the morning of March 29th the Government offices and the American Legation were notified that the U. S. cruiser *Rush* had been sighted. As

if moved by a common impulse, the entire population
— at least the able-bodied portion of it — immediately resolved itself into a committee of reception,
and surged towards the wharf to watch the *Rush*
steam up the bay, and to be at hand when she came
up to the dock.

Every vessel in the harbour, which was crowded
with shipping, from the big *Naniwa* to the smallest
fishing-boat, suddenly displayed the American flag.
Nor were the streets of the city, business houses,
and public buildings forgotten; one could hardly
have imagined there was such a supply of bunting
in Honolulu. The annexationists, as soon as the
news of the *Rush's* arrival was confirmed, brought
out hundreds of flags, and, as if by magic, these
were grouped over doors and windows and wreathed
about the pillars of verandahs.

As the little *Rush* passed the *Naniwa* the latter
saluted, and the United States ship replied; it was
like the "yap" of a terrier echoing the deep bellow
of a stag hound.

The dock was thronged with Hawaiians, men,
women, and children, whose allegiance seemed
divided, for they wore both the American and
Hawaiian colours, and carried, of course, enormous
leis, white, red, and yellow, which made the whole
place smell like a garden. Along the edge of the
wharf was ranged a line of native women, representing the Hawaiian League; they were dressed in

white, and the passage way left open through their ranks for the guests, by which they were to reach their carriages, was thickly strewn with roses. The band, stationed on the deck of the mail steamer *Australia*, which was about to sail, struck up an American national air.

And *then* — then came an anti-climax that very closely approached the ridiculous. Instead of the dignified, affable, and courteous body of officials that had been expected — representing the army, the navy, and the judiciary of the United States — there stepped ashore a commonplace, rather sullen-looking man of sixty, clad in ill-fitting clothes of blue home-spun and a Panama hat. Public expectation had been roused to the highest pitch, and the revulsion of feeling was instantaneous and painful.

This new arrival was Mr. James H. Blount, an obscure Congressman from Macon, Georgia, who was scarcely known outside Washington and beyond the confines of his Georgian constituency. He had been a colonel of a Georgian regiment during the war, and in eighteen years of Congressional service had done nothing to distinguish himself. He was a man of upright life, but unpolished in manners; he had never been outside of his own country before; he knew nothing of people other than his own, except such members or attachés of the various legations in Washington as he might have met. He had not a single attribute that fitted him for the delicate task

which had been placed in his incapable hands —
work that demanded the wisdom and knowledge of
the highest statesmanship, and all the courtesy and
finesse of the skilled diplomat.   Mr. Cleveland had
made a wrong start from the very beginning, and he
was destined to go further and further astray, until
he should find himself in a political *impasse*, from
which he could only emerge — backwards.   Mr.
Blount had been made chairman of the Foreign
Affairs Committee of the fifty-second Congress, a
position he was about as competent to fill as a blind
man to hold a place where acute sight is a first
requisite.   He came, not in accordance with the
sovereign will of the people, but of the sovereign
will of the people's servant, Mr. Cleveland, indi-
vidually.   The manner of the appointment was absolutely illegal, and nothing could have been more
offensive, both to Americans and to the Hawaiians,
than the insolent wording of his credentials.   The
letter which President Cleveland sent to President
Dole, whom he was to address once more and with
even more irritating patronage, was as follows:

"GREAT AND GOOD FRIEND, — I have made choice of
James H. Blount, one of our distinguished citizens, as my
special Commissioner to visit the Hawaiian Islands, and
make report to me concerning the present status of affairs
in that country.   He is well-informed of our sincere desire
to cultivate and maintain to the fullest extent the friendship
that has so long subsisted between the two countries, and

in all matters affecting relations of the Government of the Hawaiian Islands. His authority is *paramount.* My knowledge of his high character and ability gives me entire confidence that he will use every endeavour to advance the interest and prosperity of both Governments, and to render himself acceptable to your Excellency.

" I therefore request your Excellency to receive him favourably, and to give full credence to what he shall say on the part of the United States, and the assurances which I have charged him to convey to you of the best wishes of this Government for the prosperity of the Hawaiian Islands. May God have your Excellency in his wise keeping !

" Written at Washington, this 11th day of March, in the year 1893.

" (*Signed*) GROVER CLEVELAND.

"*By the President:*
    " W. J. GRESHAM, *Secretary of State.*"

Mr. Blount also carried with him a letter to Mr. Stevens, the duly accredited United States Minister to Hawaii, who had been named by Mr. Cleveland's predecessor, and whose appointment had been properly confirmed by Congress. He was informed that, by a stroke of the pen, the Georgia Congressman had been invested with paramount authority, and that the individual will of Mr. Cleveland had superseded that of the Government — a high-handed usurpation of executive and judiciary authority that had no parallel in the history of the Government. He was named by the President personally to speak for the United States — without any more real authority, so to speak, than the humblest Government clerk in Washington. Even Mr. Cleveland's friends were aghast at such egotism and lawlessness, and acknowledged that "the President had gone a little too far."

The United States Consul, Mr. Henry M. Severance, with a party of representatives of the Provisional Government, had gone out in a launch to meet the *Rush*. Mr. Blount's treatment of the entire party was most uncivil. To Mr. Severance his manner was churlish. The Consul at once placed the documents in the Consulate at Mr. Blount's disposal, a polite offer which the Commissioner received by promptly turning his back upon the representative of the United States. Others were made to feel the great man's disfavour in a similar manner. The papers of the Consulate so obligingly offered to Mr. Blount were never examined; the Consul so ready to render him assistance was never questioned; yet the President's Commissioner quoted him in the so-called "report" which he afterwards returned to Mr. Cleveland — the *ex-parte* testimony he was sent out to collect. A great deal of the evidence like that relating to Mr. Severance was purely "hearsay," which would not have been accepted as credible in the most corrupt court in Christendom.

This was the beginning. The Provisional Government was quick to realise that Mr. Blount was no friend, and they were chilled and rebuffed. The American Minister and the Consul, Mr. Blount's official superiors, were openly humiliated and discredited. Mr. Blount was of the South, and he was one of the unreconciled advocates of the "Lost Cause," who had not been able to forget that, during the Civil War, the Islands had sympathised with the North, had opposed slavery, sent recruits to aid in the preservation of the Union, and raised supplies for the U. S. Sanitary Commission, in the ardour of their sympathy. The Americanism of the people rankled, and it continued to rankle to the last.

CHAPTER XI.

THE LOWERING OF THE AMERICAN FLAG.

THE demonstration of the Hawaiian League, apparently, was not altogether appreciated by the Commissioner. He gave no indication of being pleased either by the reception tendered him or by anything else. He drove at once to Snow Cottage, a bungalow attached to the Royal Hawaiian Hotel, which at the time was partially let to adherents of the Queen, and during the entire time of Mr. Blount's occupancy was a royalist rendezvous.

Along with the discourteous message which Mr. Blount was commissioned to deliver to the American Minister, whose authority the obscure Congressman had been instructed to usurp, one equally contemptuous was delivered to Admiral Skerrett, in command of the Pacific Squadron, whose flag-ship, the *Mohican*, with the cruiser *Alliance*, had been ordered to join the *Boston* at Honolulu. The old admiral, who had grown grey in the service of his country, to which he had given the best years of his strength and his youth, was notified that "he was to consult freely with Mr. Blount and obey any instructions he might receive from him regarding the course to be pursued in the Islands by the force under his command."

Professor Alexander in his official report to the United States Senate mildly observed upon this point: "The question whether the President had a constitutional right to clothe his private agent, appointed without the knowledge or confirmation of the Senate, with these extraordinary powers has been fully debated in Congress." And it might be added, it was one of the most stirring debates in which that body ever engaged, even in the troubled days of fugitive slave law agitation, or during the four years of the Civil War. It was boldly declared that the Executive Chief merited impeachment, which he certainly would have suffered at the hands of any other people less lenient than his own.

In the evening at eight o'clock the Annexation Club called upon Mr. Blount, and the Commissioner was informed that the organisation had a membership of two thousand, representing the respectability, intelligence, and material interests of Honolulu. The need of a strong, stable Government was pointed out as necessary to save the community both from internal discord and from foreign interference, and the time was anticipated when Hawaii would become a part of the Republic. Mr. Blount's appointment by President Cleveland was a matter of congratulation — a hasty conclusion which the Annexation Club was destined to reverse — and they felt confident that, upon careful inquiry into the situation, the fact would be disclosed that the establishment of the Provisional Government had been a matter of necessity, of duty performed in the interest of civilisation. The head of the recent Government had disavowed the obligations with which the Constitution of 1887 had invested her, and had announced her intention to rule by royal proclamation, and not by law. The establishment of the Provisional Government, therefore, was the only course that remained to the people. The speaker, Dr. J. S. McGrew, a resident of the Islands for more than forty years and president of the club, said in conclusion: "It is the hope of the members of this association that a treaty of annexation may soon be accomplished between Hawaii and the United States, which, while securing all the safeguards of a free and stable Government to all the natives — aboriginal Hawaiians, as well as to those of foreign ancestry — will bring no burdens upon the United States, but, on the contrary, be a source of additional strength and satisfaction."

Mr. Blount's reply to this dignified, straightforward, and truthful presentation of the situation was peevish and petty. He said impatiently: "Gentlemen, you will readily understand I can make no reply to this address. My negotiations will be conducted entirely with your Government." Then he added, as an after-thought, "I am pleased, however, to meet you."

He had listened with stolid indifference, and his manner belied the latter assertion. The Annexation Club departed in no very cheerful frame of mind.

The same evening the President was notified that the American flag, which had been temporarily raised over the Government buildings, would be lowered the following morning, at eleven o'clock. It has been said that the American Minister received no notification, but accidentally heard what was to happen from a neighbour, which, if true, was a gratuitous insult, from which his office, his long and honourable public service, his old age, and his grey hairs should have protected him.

There was just at that time a reason for especial sympathy and consideration. Mr. Stevens was a native of Maine; he had been a friend of Mr. Lincoln, and had held many important diplomatic posts in Europe. He strikingly resembled Mr. Lincoln, and with his knowledge of affairs, his liberal education, and his long residence abroad, he was a man of admirable manner and address.

He occupied a very unpretentious house on Nunanu Street with his wife and two daughters. One of these daughters had acted for many years as her father's private secretary. She was his almost inseparable companion, and he relied greatly upon her aid and counsel. The *Boston* was ordered to Hilo for target practice, and Mr. Stevens and his daughter went on the ship as the guests of the officers. They were entertained in Hilo by Mr. Luther Severance, a brother of the American Consul in Honolulu.

The Islands, in the country as well as in the towns and villages, are a network of telephone wires, and communication is maintained in this way between remote plantations.

As the Minister and his daughter were preparing to go on board the *Boston* to return to Honolulu some one called Miss Stevens over the telephone. It was a friend on a plantation on the opposite side of Hawaii, whom she had promised to visit, and she was reminded of the promise. Miss Stevens replied, asking to be excused, as she felt that she must return with her father, who could not spare her to make the visit at that time. The lady urgently repeated the invitation, and, contrary to the advice of the officers of the *Boston*, Miss Stevens decided to remain in Hilo and take one of the small inter-island steamers to Hamakua, where her friend resided.

She was reminded how dangerous the landing was at that point; but she still determined to remain, and the *Boston* sailed back to Honolulu without her. She landed in safety, but upon re-embarking for Honolulu the sea was unusually rough, but she was lowered into the boat below without accident, when the boat was caught by a wave, dashed against the rocks, and broken into splinters. It was thought that Miss Stevens died of heart disease induced by the shock, and not from being crushed against the cliffs. The body was recovered, prepared for burial, and reverently and tenderly laid upon the table in the saloon of the little steamer, and taken back to Honolulu. As there are no cables between the Islands it was impossible to inform the Minister of the terrible bereavement he had sustained. The revolution had come without any premonition upon the return of the *Boston* to Hilo, and he was harassed and anxious with the grave duty which he had had to perform. The sister, wholly unconscious of what had happened, went down to the dock with a party of friends to meet the steamer.

A messenger was sent ashore to inform her what had happened, and proper notice was sent to the family. The body was then taken home. All through the night, when the daughter lay in her coffin in the drawing-room, taken from him without an instant's warning, in the vigour of life and health, the heart-broken father sat writing the official dis-patches, which the steamer, sailing the following noon, must convey to San Francisco, for immediate transmission to the State Department. One can believe that it was no ordinary self-control and for-titude that enabled him to pass through such an ordeal. It was, then, this old and heart-broken man whom Mr. Blount had been commissioned to discredit and publicly humiliate. One would have thought that such sorrow would have been sacred to any one possessed of the commonest human instincts. Mr. Blount was accompanied to Hawaii by his wife, but neither was much in evidence that evening at the hotel where their meals were served. So far as the public was concerned there was not the slightest hint as to his proposed plan of action.

President Dole had considered it prudent to withhold the notification he had received from all but the Cabinet and the Advisory Council, as it was uncertain what might occur when the Hawaiian flag was hoisted. It was certainly a tempting opportunity for the natives, who greatly outnumbered the annexationists, to rally, and by a *coup de main* restore the monarchy in substance with the restoration of its symbol. I had gone to my breakfast in the general dining-room of the hotel, and saw in the morning paper, lying beside my plate, staring head-lines announcing the lowering of the American flag at eleven o'clock. I was thunderstruck; the entire city was in the wildest state of excitement.

If the rebuff of the five Hawaiian Commissioners; the summary withdrawal of the treaty upon Mr. Cleveland's succession to office ; the high-handed disregard of the Senate and their appointment of a proper commission of investigation for the United

States, had been condoned, this could not be considered other than a determination of the President
to refuse his support to the Provisional Government,
and eventually to withdraw American protection.
And this, time proved, was a correct estimate of his
course.

The feeling that prevailed among the annexationists in Honolulu could be compared to that felt by
the citizens of the North the day when Fort Sum-
ter had been fired upon — a day of lamentation and
anguish that tried men's souls. Those of the natives — by no means a majority — who sympathised
with the Queen were at first elated; but they realised the gravity of the situation, and made no open
demonstration.   The friends of the Provisional
Government were of two minds: one was still
bravely hoping for the best, and meeting the crisis
with an unruffled front; the other, less confident,
made but little effort to conceal dejection and
despair.

"Royalty shall not be restored," was the common
declaration. "We have tried it again and again;
we have nothing to hope from it, and the time has
now come when we will stand shoulder to shoulder;
the United States refuses to protect us, and we will
protect ourselves."

At ten o'clock the hotel was quite empty, and a
stream of people, very different in their uneasiness
and fear to the multitudes the day before, streamed

steadily in the direction of the Government buildings. There had been three hundred additional police sworn in early that morning, and there were many more volunteers than could be supplied with arms to aid in preserving order.

At half-past ten I called a carriage and drove to Camp Boston, to learn if it were true that Captain Swinburne and his company had been ordered on board the *Boston*. It was a beautiful day, the sun shining brightly, the blue sky without a cloud, the palms stirring in the breeze. Everything about the premises indicated immediate evacuation. There were heaps of baggage, beds, tents, and other portable property piled upon the verandah in charge of the Japanese servants. Sentinels were still pacing to and fro before the east and west gates; the marines were drawn up in line, along the front wall, while the officers were moving about issuing orders. I accosted one of the sentinels and asked to see an officer. The blue-coat saluted, and an instant later Lieutenant Laird courteously presented himself.

"Is it true that you are ordered to go on board?" I asked.

"Our orders are to march out of here promptly at eleven o'clock."

"Do you know the reason?"

"It is only another move on the chessboard. We are acting under orders, and have no further instructions," and he touched his cap and re-entered the gate.

At the Government buildings, a stone's throw beyond the camp, the stars and stripes floated from the staff on the tower, an added touch of colour in the tropical landscape, and vividly outlined against the sky.

A vast assemblage and a most characteristic one had gathered — Americans, Europeans, stolid Japanese and Chinese, Hawaiians — the women in *holokus* and loaded with *leis*. The native and Oriental population crowded the sidewalk across the road in front of the Palace; the Americans and Europeans were collected in the grounds or upon the pavement adjoining. All talked in subdued tones, and the most decorous order was preserved. Among the American women present was one who sat in her carriage looking on and weeping passionately. She exclaimed, —

"They may lower it from the tower, but it shall float over my house as long as I have life and breath to keep it there!"

As the minute hand of the clock moved slowly forward every eye was riveted on the flag, — the Hawaiians half exultingly, yet anxiously; the American and foreign Hawaiians (whites born in the Islands), and those who had cast in their lot with them, waiting with set lips and rigid countenances. By this time there was little talking, the silence increasing as the seconds slipped away. The flag tossed and fluttered from its height upon the tower, as if it were a sentient thing, realising that it was soon to be cast down, and with it the hope of thousands of anxious hearts who had placed upon it their reliance and their faith.

A detachment of thirty marines, under command of Lieutenant Draper, who for two months had been guarding the building, was still on duty. They had been completing their preparations for departure, and were fully accoutred in cartridge-belts, canteens, and knapsacks. It had been Mr. Blount's intention to haul down the flag with the same disrespect that he had shown in his treatment of the American Minister. President Dole, quietly, though quite unconsciously, defeated this intention. It became, instead of a shambling, furtive effort to display spite and contempt, a ceremonial so thrilling and dramatic that those who witnessed it will never forget it. At ten minutes to eleven President Dole, accompanied by S. M. Damon, Minister of the Interior, Robert Porter (Minister of Finance), W. O. Smith (Attorney-General), and General Soper (in command of the Provisional Government troops), descended the front steps of the building, and took his position immediately behind the statue of Kamehameha I. They stood with uncovered heads, and their faces and their demeanour were exceedingly grave. After the briefest interval of waiting there was a subdued stir in the street outside the gate; then the crowd gave way; there was a quick tread of marching feet, and immediately the sharp word of command, "*Forward, fours right, fours left into line, halt!*"

It was a company of volunteer soldiers called out to reinforce the Government troops.

The latter were placed around the circular drive to the right of General Soper (who was in command), the President, and his Cabinet, while the volunteers faced them. The battery, Company D, had previously taken its position so as to command the space in front of the building: this battery was largely composed of Germans, commanded by Captain Ziegler, also of German birth, as his name would imply. One of the Gatling guns was drawn by citizens, who had not taken up arms, among them a tailor, an apothecary, and a number of artisans and merchants. The volunteers marched into the grounds with beating drums and to the sound of the fife. While they stood waiting there was an ominous movement; the machine guns were shifted to a somewhat better position, and the gunners took their place in readiness beside them. All this had occurred in less than five minutes, for there was no dallying and no delay. At 10.56 a marine, stationed on top of the tower, approached the parapet and glanced down upon the scene below. Then he drew back and waited motionless beside the flag-staff. The hands of the clock moved forward relentlessly. The people stood in

11

silence like images of stone — the President, the Cabinet, the marines, and the Government troops all ready to anticipate the first sign of riot. The order was given, "Sound off," and as the notes of the bugle rang out the flag slipped from the fastening. For an instant the empty lines beat idly against the staff; then General Soper's voice broke the silence, clear and distinct, "Present arms!" There was another gleam of colour, and the Hawaiian flag crawled up the now taut ropes, and shook itself free, its blue, white, and crimson bars floating in their accustomed place. There was an unexpected pause; but the silence was undisturbed. The troops of the Provisional Government presented arms, but the American men-of-war in the harbour did not salute the restored flag, as they had their own.

Throughout the entire scene not a voice had been heard save that of the commanding officer; but when the Hawaiian flag first caught the breeze a grizzled native near my carriage, who had been watching with almost breathless intensity, broke into a hoarse cry. Quick as a flash a black, muscular hand seized him by the shoulder, and he was forcibly silenced — not by a foreigner, but by one of his own race.

The guns of the battery were left in position, and the marines, under command of Lieutenant Draper, marched down the street escorted by a detachment of Provisional Government infantry. They were not followed by a crowd such as would have collected in

London or in an American city, but, comparatively unattended, turned in at the east gate at Camp Boston, where they joined their comrades, who, still drawn up in a line, were waiting for them. Without a moment's delay they were ordered to "march," and at the word of command they faced about, passed through the east gate into the street, moving toward the dock to the familiar strains of "The Girl I Left Behind Me."

Thus Mr. Blount's first official order was obeyed, and the semblance of an American protectorate came to an end.

The day was naturally one of great anxiety and excitement, all the more intense because it was suppressed. I returned to the hotel, and visitors came and went all the afternoon; my piazza became a sort of Hawaiian forum for the discussion of what had just occurred and of what next might be anticipated from the Administration.

The known enmity between the Secretary of State and ex-President Harrison, growing out of years of political rivalry, was regarded as unfavourable to the cause of annexation; many incidents in the political career of both men were recalled which were considered sufficient grounds for apprehension, and it was afterwards proved that these anticipations were not imaginary.

Mr. Blount did not show himself at the Government buildings during the dramatic scene of the morning; he had the discretion and delicacy to remain in retirement — discretion and delicacy that might have served him to his great advantage, had he exhibited these qualities when they were subsequently required. All the afternoon he was visited by friends and adherents of the Queen, and presented with gifts of flowers, wreaths being thrown about his neck as he passed along the street — an attention, however, which I am forced to admit he neither desired nor relished.

Among his visitors in the evening was a committee from a body of Hawaiians known as "The Patriotic League," who presented an address, and of which Mr. John E. Bush, the partisan editor, acted as spokesman. Their reception was very different from that accorded the Annexation Club the evening before, and they were assured by Mr. Blount that the United States did not approve of its representatives "meddling in the conduct of the government of foreign countries."

The streets were practically deserted early in the evening, people remaining quietly within their houses.

CHAPTER XII.

VIOLATED CORONETS.

AFTER the removal of the flag from the Government building the people gradually settled down into a calm acceptance of the situation, hoping for the best. They had no intimation of their impending fate from the inscrutable Mr. Blount. He preserved a silence that ought to have become historical — it was so rare and phenomenal in the annals of loquacious politics.

The week following the flag episode I had a decidedly amusing experience. My newspaper correspondence had been finished, down to the recording of the latest scrap of rumour, and I was enjoying a well-earned hour of rest. A card was brought, and the bell-boy — a Portuguese product of the Azores — informed me that my caller was the ex-Chief of Police. I was prepared for anything, and so received my visitor with a composed mien, seated comfortably in my steamer chair on the balcony, with my crutches within reach. He was tall, red-haired, and most polite. He apologised for intruding upon me, but had been told that I had recently seen King Kalakaua's coronet, from which it had just been discovered that the jewels had been stolen. I admitted that this was true, and that the date was March 4th, which I remembered because it happened to be Inauguration Day.

"Were the crowns taken out of trunks, and were the trunks locked?"

"They were in small sole-leather cases, and, while I cannot positively affirm it, I think that both cases were locked." I had noted the extreme care with which everything had been put away and secured; the feather cloaks were packed in a chest securely fastened, the door of the room in which the chests were placed being also locked. The decorations, some of which were very valuable, were taken from a safe which was unlocked and locked again before us.

"What was the condition of the crowns?"

"One large stone was gone, I noticed, and two or three small ones."

"The large stone was lost several years ago," said the policeman.

Then he asked me if I was a judge of diamonds. I replied modestly that I was not a *connaisseuse*, but that those in the King's crown did not impress me as being of much value; the opals and the few rubies were rather good, and the metal-work; the gold bands in which they were set, with the ornamentation of taro leaves, were more pleasing than the jewels. The good-natured official then wanted to know if jewellers were in the habit of putting tinfoil behind diamonds when they were set, if the stones were good; and I replied gravely that I did not think so. Then he asked if I thought the jewels could be very valuable, when the entire crown, metal, filigree, workmanship, and all cost only $5,000.

"Besides," he said, "there was the maker's profits. He was a Hebrew, and he got all it was worth out of it, you bet."

It was rather an embarrassing statement, which I did not answer immediately, and the comment as to the maker's thrift I also prudently passed over.

"I am sorry that any reflection as to carelessness should have been cast upon Colonel Robertson," I said; "for both coronets were carefully cared for when I was permitted to see them."

Then I could not help reflecting that I had little expected ever to be called upon to testify concerning the exact condition of a king's coronet when I had last examined it; but that was only one of many unexpected things that happened after my arrival in Hawaii. I made some observation to this effect.

"Yes," remarked my caller, with an instantaneous appreciation of the humorous side of the case, "it is a queer country, hain't it?"

He admitted that it was a mystery which he could

not unravel, because the crown of the Queen-Dowager Kapiolani had been left untouched, but he believed that the thief had been some emissary of the ex-Queen, which proved to be an error. The culprit was subsequently found and arrested. He was a private soldier in the volunteers, a worthless character, who had hung about the town without any visible means of support. Dropping the subject, the ex-Chief of Police then politely inquired as to my health.

"I hated to bother you," he said apologetically, "because I know you are an invalid."

"No," I interrupted, by way of reassuring him and setting him at his ease, "only temporarily dis-abled — not an invalid."

He took his departure, expressing a hope that I might be able to walk within the near future, and he apologised once more for having intruded upon me. I again assured him that it was no intrusion, and regretted that I was unable to furnish him no better clue that might aid him in the recovery of the lost crown.

Within the past week a mongrel mastiff, literally a yellow dog, a trifle smaller than a calf, had taken up his abode in the Hawaiian Hotel; he fared luxuri-ously on tid-bits from the kitchen, and had two staunch adherents in the Portuguese bell-boys. He properly valued the good fortune that had befallen him, and jealously guarded the territory he had acquired. That evening a black dog, his equal in size and strength, invaded his domain, and there was such an encounter as the Hawaiian Hotel had rarely witnessed. The rivals met in the main corridor, and without a moment's hesitation fell upon one another furiously. There were yells and growls and roars, with clinching and biting that were terrible to witness. It sounded as if a menagerie had broken loose. It was a deed of prowess to attempt to separate the combatants, and most of the guests took refuge in the dining-room or on the stairs.

From a safe point of vantage one of the newspaper correspondents looked down upon the conflict and remarked, "That's the first real fight I have seen since the Revolution began."

The next morning at dawn I was awakened by the chattering of two Chinamen, fruit-vendors, who had seated themselves under my window, waiting for the cook to make his appearance in the kitchen. Their thin, high-pitched voices disturbed me, and I rang for the night clerk, Wing — also a Chinaman. As he rapped against the venetian blinds of my door I rose and went to speak to him. Turning the blind, I looked out, and there stood the "boy" with the yellow dog standing demurely by his side; the brute had a rope, something smaller than a hawser, around his neck, the loose end trailing on the floor of the verandah. After giving my orders as to the talkative Chinamen I asked Wing, "What is the

matter with the dog?   Have you had to tie him up?"
Wing smiled pensively, and replied with significant
terseness, "He go for milkman!"

The following night we were treated to one more
of the many studies in ethnology which we had
already enjoyed.   The band was giving a concert in
honour of the departure of the *Mariposa* in the
pavilion on the hotel lawn.   In the midst of the
"Miserere" the sound of a drum was heard in
the distance, and there was an evident commotion
down the street!

"Another crisis!" was the unanimous exclamation.

But the crowd advanced without any hostile
demonstration, sweeping up the drive, passed the
verandah, out again into the street.   The band
ceased playing, then recovered itself, and as they
departed with commendable delicacy and feeling
struck up a Hawaiian march.   It was a company of
Samoan dancers *en route* to the World's Fair.   They
carried the paddles with which they navigate their
canoes, and were clad in *tapa* robes, their heads
covered with white cloths, in lieu of the application
of lime, which is the Samoan method of hair-dressing
for State occasions.   They were to give a national
dance at the Opera House, and public entertainments were so rare that there was a general stampede
of guests to the place of amusement, the ladies not
taking time even to put on their hats.   A *bonâ-fide*
theatrical company at that time was very rarely seen

in Honolulu, although a number of companies have since stopped and given performances on their way to and from Australia. At the time mentioned, however, the advent of any sort of show was an event. A negro minstrel troupe had arrived a short time before in a ship *en route* to Sydney from San Francisco, and remained in harbour for one day. In the afternoon they gave a performance, and there was a general suspension of business. The shops were closed, and everybody went to the show, except of course the ultra-religious missionary element.

CHAPTER XIII.

THE PRINCESS KAIULANI.

WHILE all this had occurred the Princess Kaiulani had not been a disinterested looker-on.
The ex-Queen had never been well-disposed towards
the young girl whom she had been forced to name
as her successor.

Kaiulani had lived for some time in England in
the family of Mr. Theophilus Davies, an English
merchant who owned large estates and warehouses
in Honolulu, where he resided only a part of the
time. The young Princess had received the education of an English gentlewoman; young, graceful,
refined and attractive, during the monarchy her
rank was properly recognised by Queen Victoria — a
recognition, however, which of necessity ceased
with the possibility of her succession to the Hawaiian
throne.

Parliament almost at once announced its intention
not to interfere in Hawaiian affairs, considering the
interests of British subjects in the Islands quite safe
under the protection of the Provisional Government
and the United States. This, no doubt, was a blow

to the English guardian of the Princess, and, finding it useless to expect support at home, he proceeded to Washington with his Hawaiian ward, ostensibly to appeal to Congress and the President.

It was in reality an opportunity for an effective theatrical pose which would catch the fickle sympathy of the ignorant, and furnish some sort of an excuse to the Administration for the discreditable course it had elected to pursue.

Personally, the young Princess was a charming and interesting character; she gave a certain picturesqueness to the little drama, appearing upon the scene just at the proper moment, as the conventional heroine should, gently appealing to the American people for redress and protection in the maintenance of her rights.

The American, it is well known, is easily moved by any appeal from womanhood wronged or distressed. That the presence of the young Hawaiian girl in Washington made no impression on the public mind was proof that the people were not disposed to take seriously her demand that the monarchy be restored, and that she should be placed upon the throne as the successor of the ex-Queen Liliuokalani. In the first place, whatever the views of the President might have been, it was believed that a government pledged to the maintenance of democracy could not consistently lend its aid to the building up of a fallen monarchy; and, in the second place, however pure and disinterested her motives might have been, no human power could have prevented the Princess Kaiulani from being a helpless tool in the hands of men who had controlled King Kalakaua and abetted the ex-Queen in her conspiracies against the Government.   Men like President Dole, like the Attorney-General, Mr. Smith, born and reared in the Islands, who had strenuously advocated their autonomy as long as there was any hope, saw no advantage to be gained in the proclamation of the Princess as Queen, nor any immunity in such succession from the inherent evils of a thoroughly corrupt system.   A Regency with Mr. Dole at its head had been proposed for the three years that must elapse before Kaiulani attained her majority.

She left Liverpool with Mr. Davies, February 22nd, and arrived in New York a week later, where she at once published in the daily newspapers an appeal to the American people.   It was known that, with many graces and accomplishments, the young Princess had not the pen of a ready writer.   The composition of the address, as sentimental as a school-girl's essay or an elegant extract from an old-fashioned three-volume novel, was therefore supposed to be the work of her guardian.   At any rate, it was couched in the following remarkable language:

"To THE AMERICAN PEOPLE, — Unbidden I stand upon your shores to-day, where I thought so soon to receive a royal welcome on my way to my own kingdom. I come unattended, except by loving hearts that came with me over the wintry seas. I hear that Commissioners from my own land have been for many days asking this great nation to take away my little vineyard. They speak no word to me, and leave me to find out as I can from rumours in the air, and they would leave me without a home or a name or a nation. Seventy years ago America sent over Christian men and women to give religion and civilisation to Hawaii. They gave us the Gospel. They made us a nation, and we learned to love and trust America. To-day three of the sons of those missionaries are at your capital, asking you to undo their fathers' work. Who sent them? Who gave them their authority to break the Constitution which they swore they would uphold?

"To-day I, a poor, weak girl, with not one of my people near me, and with all these Hawaiian statesmen against me, have strength to stand up for the rights of my people. Even now I can hear a wail in my heart, and it gives me strength and courage, and I am strong — strong in the faith of God, strong in the knowledge that I am right, strong in the strength of seventy million people, who in this free land will hear my cry, and will refuse to let their flag cover dishonour to mine.

" (*Signed*) KAIULANI."

Very pretty; but not susceptible of careful analysis. The Constitution which Mr. Davies, over the signature of the Princess, charged the Hawaiian Commissioners with violating had been already abrogated by the Princess's relative, the ex-Queen; there was no Constitution to violate, except such remnants as the "sons of the missionaries" had managed to preserve. Furthermore, the fact that there "was not one of her people near her" was a self-ordained bereavement on the part of the young Princess. She had voluntarily separated herself from them: she had gone away and remained away for several years wholly of her own volition, and the loneliness which she lamented appealed more to sentiment than to common intelligence.

She was in Washington on the 4th of March, a pretty and graceful figure in the heterogeneous multitude drawn together by the Inauguration. Mr. Cleveland was doubtless glad that she had come; she was of herself, as I have said, a partial reason and excuse for his subsequent conduct. She was warmly received at the White House by Mrs. Cleveland, in whom she found something more than the ordinary sympathetic hostess. She played her part like a pretty marionette, directed by her guardian, keeping silent or speaking when and as he advised, and following his guidance implicitly in all matters. He had never been credited with profound intellectual force, and the real intelligence that had planned the little side-play was probably that of the ex-Queen's attorney, Mr. Neumann.

At any rate, having delivered her "appeal" through the medium of the press, having been introduced to the President and Mr. Gresham, and having won the confidence and enlisted the sympathy of Mrs. Cleveland, she returned to England over the same wintry seas and accompanied by the same loving hearts. Before her departure she issued another, and this time a "farewell," manifesto. Of this, unfortunately, I have no copy; but as it no doubt emanated from the same facile hand, the redundancies of metaphor and "its pathos that was not pathos," to quote Robert Louis Stevenson, can be readily inferred.

The matter created no interest in Honolulu. The "appeal" was laughed at because the authorship was guessed, and the only comment was, "Kaiulani never wrote it; she could n't" — which, whatever interpretation might be put upon the declaration, was a compliment to her intelligence.

12

CHAPTER XIV.

THE CHINESE POPULATION.

HONOLULU, as I have said before, is the Paradise of the Chinaman. Here he has his little shop, his own quarter, his laundry, or he works upon the plantations, the stolid image of patience, with no one to molest him or make him afraid. No one tweaks his pigtail, stones him, or knocks his hat over his eyes, and he is altogether a respectable member of society. I was invited to lunch with Mr. and Mrs. F. W. Damon, both of whom have been identified with the Chinese missionary work here for many years. Mrs. Damon was a woman of unusual loveliness of mind and character; she was the daughter and granddaughter of a Chinese missionary, and was born in Canton, where she lived until her removal to Honolulu fifteen years ago. She spoke Chinese fluently, and this accomplishment had given her great influence among the people to whom both she and her husband had devoted their lives. Their home was one of the most picturesque in Honolulu — the old Damon homestead, which is situated in a narrow winding street, overhung with palms and other tropical trees, the balconies on the ground floor paved with huge unglazed tiles that were brought from China years ago.

The tour with Mr. Damon through the Chinese quarter was most interesting, and it was pleasing to see with what affection and deference he was treated wherever we went; every hand went up to the hat-brim and every countenance was lighted with a smile of recognition as he passed. Even in the temple, which we visited first, we were made welcome, and the custodian showed us about while the worshippers were crooning and mumbling before the shrine of their hideous gods. As a structure the temple was not so imposing as a new joss-house which I had seen in San Francisco. But I was much impressed by the entire unanimity of the worshippers. A man was kneeling before the altar, upon which frowned a grotesque bewhiskered figure. He struck the floor with his forehead in his genuflections, and tossed a vaseful of sandal-wood sticks toward the idol. One dropped on the floor, and was picked up and compared with a scrap of red paper, one of many such suspended along the wall, which bore a corresponding number and an oracular inscription which decided his luck for that day. There were sandal-wood tapers and wax candles burning near at hand, and, in one corner of the altar, votive offerings — small silken banners, which were emblems of special gratitude for divine favour. We walked all about the place, watched the burning of the silver-paper propitiatory offerings, and inspected the carving and tinsel with the amiable acquiescence of the priest, who left the worshippers to talk with Mr. Damon in Chinese, and answer any question of an enlightening nature.

I was particularly attracted by the god of filial piety, the rude wooden image of a boy, whose story had come down through the ages as an example of devotion to his mother. One tradition of this youth was related to me; the mother had been exceedingly afraid of thunderstorms throughout her life, and after her death the son was accustomed to sit beside her grave, during their prevalence, to calm and reassure her spirit. As we strolled about, children came and went at will, one girl of eleven carrying on her back a big baby that cried astonishingly for a Chinese child; but the little nurse herself, the worshippers, and the priest all seemed entirely unconscious of this. We had been joined by a young man who had cut off his queue, having adopted Hawaii as his permanent residence. He was beautifully dressed in fine, dark-blue cloth, with a sort of womanly daintiness of manner, and spoke wonderfully pure English.

From the temple we went to the schools, which were charming. There were in attendance about one hundred and forty pupils—the largest Chinese school outside the empire. The pupils were instructed in English and in their own language, it having been found that they show a disposition to forget Chinese when they once acquire English. I found, to my great surprise, a perfectly appointed kindergarten in charge of a trained and competent teacher. The kindergarten was a most attractive place — a big, airy apartment, with glimpses of tropical landscape from every window. The room was supplied with all the usual appointments — charts, pictures, blackboards, and tables. The little children were unique — Chinese, all of them, in their native dress. One little girl wore a wonderful costume of cotton cloth, a pattern of polka dots on a fawn-coloured ground. Their little queues had been lengthened, as usual, by braiding into them strands of pink cotton cord. The funny, black-eyed babies stood in the circle singing, each with a coloured worsted ball in its hand. The child in the centre would make a gesture, selecting the one to take his or her place — for the pupils in the primary schools were of both sexes. The child in the circle advanced, made a curtsey, and shook hands with the other, who took its place, while the singing went on. The curtsey was a little difficult, and Mr. Damon's daughter, a beautiful little creature of seven, a perfect type of the fair-haired, blue-eyed Anglo-Saxon, offered to show the Chinese how to do it correctly. She stepped into the ring accordingly, and took the little Oriental woman by the hand, made a deep obeisance, like a *grande dame* in a minuet, and, still clasping her hand, the Chinese child gracefully repeated the curtsey. The American child, with her fleece of golden hair, was a strange and striking contrast to the other, almond-eyed, olive-skinned, with a dangling queue, two bracelets on one slim wrist, an anklet above the little unbound foot, made still more picturesque by her pea-green drawers, pink blouse, and the outer blouse of dark blue. Another child was called up to receive the ball, when all the others stopped and exclaimed, "Ah Bow did not bow!" and every small, slim hand went up to the mouth, and the class broke into a very natural human laugh as they were struck by the odd play upon words. I was much impressed by their English, which was excellent, and by their sweet voices, which, in speech and in singing, were clear and tuneful, unlike the harsh cries that pass for music among their elders.

In the next room were boys only — no girls. They all rose as we entered and stood until we were seated. Most of them were recently from China, and displayed an eagerness to learn in their rapt attention and their patience in repeating a word over and over again until the pronunciation was acquired. The instruction was entirely by what is called "the natural method." On the second floor were the young men, who constituted the boarding school over which Mr. Damon presided. They were studying from

Chinese textbooks, as one of the pupils told me, "about the animals." They also rose and stood respectfully while the schoolmaster cordially welcomed us. He was an odd-looking man in his native dress, to whom his big Chinese spectacles imparted a scholarly air. After he had shaken hands with us his pupils reseated themselves, all studying aloud, a sort of wild chant, in a dozen different keys. Chinese words are susceptible of many variations of meaning, which depend upon pitch and inflection. A word in one key means an entirely different thing from the same word pronounced in another. The master's quick ear caught an incorrect tone now and then, which he instantly noted — a miraculous keenness of hearing, it seemed to me, in that babel. As the studying progressed, pupils in turn came out from their desks, and stood with their back to the master, repeating what they had learned by rote. Much of their study is simply the committing to memory words which are entirely meaningless to them at the time, the definitions being acquired subsequently.

There lived in the rear of the school a woman whom we endeavoured to see, and whom Mr. Damon told me was one of the finest examples of the Chinese peasant woman he had ever known. She was uneducated, a widow, but possessed remarkable common sense and excellent business qualifications. She had reared a family of four children, all of whom did her great credit. One daughter was happily married, and the other was devoting her life to teaching among women of her own class. One of the sons was the handsome young man whom we had seen at the temple. Chinese women, when they are mothers, in Hawaii as in China, are accorded great respect and wield much influence in their families.

From the schools I went with Mrs. Emory, a friend of the Damons, to call upon the wife of one of the leading Chinese merchants. I was received with the utmost cordiality and courtesy by both the husband and the wife. They had a suite of tiny rooms in the rear of the second floor, above their fine shop, one closet-like apartment being occupied by two large white parrots. In their own small parlour there was an odd mingling of orientalism and civilisation — Chinese mats, lacquer and embroidery, American lamps, a clock, and a rocking-chair. The hostess wore wide, dark-blue trousers of fine cloth, and over them a garment of bright-green velvet. Her wrists were covered with jade bracelets, and in her ears were rings set with large green stones. She was a woman of the better class, and her poor crippled feet were just four inches long. They resembled wrists, from which the hands had been amputated, thrust into shoes. She was making a new pair of shoes of fine silk, upon which she had drawn a pattern which was to be embroidered.

When we expressed our admiration, although she could neither speak nor understand English, the ruling passion was manifest, and she tottered into an outer room and returned with two more pairs which she had just finished, quite as an American or English lady might show her best bonnet to her dearest friend. One pair was scarlet, with birds embroidered in gold thread. The others were yellow. She then pointed with great admiration to a photograph of her mother, an elderly matron of much dignity, who still lives in China. Her husband, who was present throughout the call, also showed us a photograph of himself, in which he wished us to observe that he was arrayed in the attire of a mandarin, which he was entitled to wear. His wife, posed beside him, was also resplendent in garments befitting her rank. I asked the man his opinion of annexation, upon which he talked very intelligently. "I would rather the island belonged to the United States than to Japan," he said, "if the authorities would treat us fairly and protect us, as the Hawaiian authorities always have done. We have nothing to complain of now, and have prospered here under Hawaiian rule." His statement was true.

One merchant, Ah Fong, who married a woman half American and half Hawaiian, has amassed a large fortune, and both he and his family are people of social distinction in Honolulu. He has a family of thirteen daughters and four sons. Four of the daughters are married to Americans, one of the latter a naval officer, all being intelligent and well-educated girls of charming manners.

There is also in Honolulu a well-equipped and well-disciplined Chinese fire brigade, which raised the fund by subscriptions among their own countrymen exclusively to buy their engines and uniforms and to build their own engine-house.   At the funeral of a member of the Hawaiian Fire Brigade, on the Sunday after my arrival, the Chinese firemen marched in procession, and had evidently never been taught that they were under a race ban in other parts of the world.

CHAPTER XV.

THE QUEEN-DOWAGER.

SHORTLY after this visit to the Chinese school,
Mr. C. A. Brown called and informed me that
the Queen-Dowager, Kapiolani, would be pleased to
receive me at two o'clock that afternoon. The visit
had been arranged upon my arrival; but a number
of unforeseen circumstances caused its postponement
from week to week. Kapiolani still owned large
estates, and was a woman of great wealth. She
suffered from rheumatism, which the moist climate
seemed to aggravate, and as a consequence lived in
comparative retirement. She occupied a villa on
the Waikiki Road, between Honolulu and Diamond
Head. Opposite the entrance to the grounds was
the beach and the sea, with a perpetual dash of the
surf against the reef, which could be seen as well
as heard through the dense growth of date palms and
algaroba trees. The house was approached by a
circuitous drive. Over the entrance to the gate
was a board with a notice, " Kapu " (" Keep out ").
The grounds were planted with date palms, algaroba

and cocoanut trees; but there is a lack of that care which most estates here receive. I was told that this was in accordance with the old Queen's wish; that she had the labour of a retinue of natives whenever she saw fit to command it, the people still paying their rents in this manner — a survival of the old feudal system which prevailed under the Kamehamehas. In front of the house was a low edge of *ti*, the tree whose leaves are used for wrapping up almost every article bought in the market, and which is also wrapped about fish and pork, which the natives roast in the ground.

The villa was characteristic — a sort of bungalow, the entire front covered with lattice-work, a door leading to the *lanai* in the rear of the vestibule, over which was a single window. The drawing-room in front, which was lighted by windows in the rear of the apartment only, was approached by a flight of stairs on the outside. In the lower vestibule on the ground floor were two large divans of wood, inlaid with mother-of-pearl — former possessions of King Kalakaua, and evidently souvenirs of his travels in India. As we approached, one of the Queen's ladies came out of an inner apartment, and met us upon the threshold. She ushered us into the drawing-room, and said she would inform the Queen of our arrival. She was a Hawaiian, dressed in a trained *holoku* of blue-and-white check silk. Before the Queen appeared, I had an opportunity to look about the drawing-room, which, like all Hawaiian houses, was a combination of American and native taste.   There was a set of brown rep furniture, such as was in fashion twenty years ago; over one large armchair was thrown an *ahula*, made of the feathers of some sort of sea-bird.   Upon the floor was a Brussels rug, with a pattern of mammoth red and yellow roses; and upon this, in the very centre of the room, stood a towering *kahili*, which almost touched the ceiling.   This had a wooden handle five feet in length, from which was a spreading base of soft scarlet and yellow feathers, surmounted by a structure composed of the greyish black feathers of a gull.   Over the windows were lambrequins of flowered chintz, ornamented with bows and loops of scarlet ribbon; while the doorways were draped with splendid Oriental brocade, scarlet interwoven with gold.   There were a great many portraits of King Kalakaua — one in oil, another in crayon, and a fine water-colour.   These portraits represented a man of a decided negro type rather than Hawaiian, with thick lips, flat nose, hair less wavy than that of the pure-blooded Hawaiians.   A bust in clay stood on an ebony pedestal.   There were many vases of flowers standing about — not on tables, as we should have arranged them, but upon the floor: one at the foot of the pedestal which held the bust, one beside the *kahili*, and another near the armchair.   They were oppressively fragrant, gardenia, stephanotis,

and roses.   Presently I saw, halting hesitatingly at
the doorway of an inner room, a tall and commanding figure clad in black.   She approached, then apparently retreated, and then finally entered with two
Hawaiian ladies in attendance.   It was Kapiolani.

Her manner was somewhat shy, but at the same
time extremely dignified.   I was presented to her,
and she received me with unaffected cordiality and
great kindness.   She must have been much past fifty
years of age — a perfect type of the Hawaiian woman,
very tall, with a massive frame, swarthy skin, and
rather irregular features.   Her hair was intensely
black, long, wavy, and silken, and was arranged in
a lofty coil on top of her head, which added to her
stature.   She wore a *holoku* of rich stiff black silk,
and around her neck a *lei* of the feathers of the *oo*,
the bird which furnished the plumage of the royal
mantles — a symbol of rank forbidden the common
people.   She wore no jewels — not even a ring —
her only ornament being a brooch with a portrait of
King Kalakaua in mosaic with a heavy setting of
gold.   It was a marked peculiarity of the Hawaiian
women of rank that they wore few jewels, preferring
wreaths of flowers instead.   Queen Kapiolani shook
hands in the American fashion, and then seated herself in the red armchair.   While she understood
English, she did not speak it, and the conversation
had to be carried on through the medium of inter-
preters.   Her manner was exceedingly pleasing, and

the Hawaiian — always a most liquid and musical language — she spoke with peculiar sweetness of tone and inflection.

The Queen-Dowager and the ex-Queen were not on friendly terms; and I was told that the same strained relations existed between Liliuokalani and the Princess Kaiulani, the young heir-apparent, who at the time of the Revolution was living in England. The Queen-Dowager, however, was exceedingly popular among the people of all classes. I should infer that she and the young Princess were friends, for I saw upon the wall a pretty portrait of Kaiulani, though none of Liliuokalani. After she had seated herself the Queen-Dowager politely expressed her regret at the many things which prevented her seeing me sooner, and wished to know if I were well pleased with the Islands. There was but one answer to this question, and I expressed my pleasure in the beauty of the scenery, the wonderful flowers and vegetation, and the enchanting climate. I told her that I had left Chicago buried in snow and sleet, that I had dreaded winter, and was glad to escape from it. All this was rapidly interpreted to her, and she replied through the same medium that she, for her part, would be greatly pleased to see an American winter, and that she thought snow "was most interesting."

She then made many inquiries concerning Admiral Brown, and said that she would always remember

with the greatest gratitude his kindness to the
King. Kalakaua had been deeply attached to him,
and he had a strong hold upon the affection of the
Hawaiian people. While he was here she had
greatly enjoyed his visits, and he had come to see her
many times.

It was very warm, and at this interval in the conversation she asked one of the ladies to get me a fan.
She sat fanning herself with one of native manufacture woven from the *ti* leaf, which she used with
much grace. She then had the various portraits of
the King pointed out to me, and explained which she
liked best. The clay bust, she told me, was modelled from life. There was a cylinder of highly
polished *koa*, or some other native wood, in a curious
frame. It had a lid, and was encircled with two
narrow bands and one broad band of chased gold.
It resembled a small cannon with its muzzle turned
to the ceiling, and was furnished with a lid.
Through the interpreter she told me that it had been
found during the King's reign in a cave where the
ancient chiefs were buried. It was supposed to be
a repository of the winds. When the priests wished
to rouse a tempest, they did so by simply removing
the lid. King Kalakaua had had it mounted as a
memento. The World's Fair was to open the following month, and I asked her if she would visit it.
She smiled and said that she had not yet fully decided. She could not make up her mind whom to

take, she said; then added with a laugh, "I should have no women with husbands; the husbands are too much trouble." All the ladies present, to whom she pleasantly referred, laughed with the Queen at this sally. I regretted that the Islands would have no exhibit, and told her that I had not realised until I came to Honolulu what an extensive and interesting show they might have made. She fully agreed with me, but said that the matter had been deferred until it was too late.

Politics were not mentioned, nor even indirectly alluded to. Being women, we also very naturally talked of dress, and I could not refrain from saying that I thought the simple, graceful *holoku* much more becoming to the Hawaiians than the modern corsets and tight-waisted gowns which they were adopting and which were painfully unsuited to them. The Queen agreed with this thoroughly, and then I told her that women in the United States were endeavouring to simplify their mode of dressing, so that they might achieve some such degree of comfort as the women in the Islands enjoyed. She was very much interested, and asked many questions, admitting frankly that she did not think one could feel very comfortable in a fashionable Parisian costume. It will be remembered that when she made her tour through the United States in 1874 the Queen adhered rigorously to the *holoku*, which, as on the occasion of my call, was always of very rich material.

13

When we finally rose to take our leave, my royal hostess kindly asked me to visit her again before my return to the United States.   She then extended her hand, with the national "*Aloha, aloha,*" which is alike greeting and farewell, and which means "My love to you."   She impressed me as a woman of exceedingly liberal and generous mind, and I could well believe, what I heard many times, that during Kalakaua's reign at all the Palace functions she was always a most impressive and queenly figure.

CHAPTER XVI.

THE LEPER SETTLEMENT.

WHEN you arrive in Honolulu, you are warned and with no apparent reason, that leprosy is a word not to be mentioned in polite society. Leprosy exists, as is well known, though almost exclusively among the natives. The whites occasionally contract it, it is supposed, by inoculation, where there is abrasion of the skin; but only those whose systems have been vitiated by dissipation seem susceptible to the taint, although there are again exceptions where the apparently healthy are attacked. The latter instances, I have been told, are exceedingly rare. Leprosy seems to defy all ordinary rules, both in the manner of its appearance and development. Leprous parents have children who are free from the disease and in whom it never appears. A man on Molokai married in succession two leprous women, both of whom died and both of whom bore seemingly healthy children. The husband did not himself contract the disease. I had a conversation with an intelligent young physician connected with the Hawaiian Board of Health relative to the Receiving Station which is located at Honolulu. It can always be visited by special permit from the Board of Health, which is not difficult to obtain. There were eleven hundred cases then on Molokai, and probably a few among the natives on the other islands which had not been apprehended. The most careful surveillance was exercised, and every precaution was taken to isolate patients as soon as the disease presented itself. This it had been difficult to do. The Hawaiians are a peculiarly affectionate race, and the removal of the sick to Molokai is a parting which must be as final as the death which it foreshadows.

It is one of the sheriff's official duties carefully and regularly to inspect the natives and report to the Board of Health those whom he believes to be suffering from the disease. To facilitate this work each island is divided into Sanitary Districts, which are carefully patrolled. When cases are apprehended, they are taken into custody and brought to the station. They are then examined by the surgeons in charge. This is a delicate task, for occasionally the apparent symptoms are deceptive. If the board of five examiners are all of the opinion that the patient is a leper he is sent to Molokai. If there is doubt he is examined at intervals until a decision is reached.

"The natives are seemingly without the slightest fear of the disease," said my informant. "I have seen the sound eating out of the same bowl of *poi* with a leper who had lost two or three fingers. The evidence of leprosy did not excite their fear any more than it affected their appetite. They will hide the sick in their huts, or take them up into the mountains, where they can be kept out of the way and more securely concealed for many months. When they are taken into custody and sent away, their friends gather at the dock to bid them farewell, and it is a heart-rending scene. They express their sorrow in poignant lamentation — a national wail which is so harrowing that I avoid hearing it whenever it is possible. No matter how far the disease may have advanced, though it may have attacked the nose and lips, it sometimes requires official interference to prevent the friends and relatives kissing and embracing the lepers who are to be sent into banishment, and whom they know they will never see again."

"How does the disease first show itself?"

"By discoloration — white spots on the lower limbs usually. Then there is a depression of the muscles between the thumb and index finger — a wasting that continues until all the fingers bend backward, shrivel, and drop off. The face also takes on a bluish pallor. Blotches appear upon the forehead above the eyes, which assume an abnormal appearance. The lobes of the ear are frequently much elongated until amputations are necessary, the diseased portion being sometimes four or five inches in length. Eruptions that do not heal are another form, and the lips become drawn and pitted, with hard swellings over the brows, and the nose is reduced to a shapeless mass; it is often eaten entirely away. This also happens to other portions of the face. Strangely enough the patient does not always suffer, and there are many instances where the terrible disease is said to be entirely painless. The lepers are maintained on Molokai at the expense of the Government. Comfortable houses have been furnished them and unlimited *poi*, and apart from the separation from their friends and families, to which in time they become reconciled, their lot is not considered one of unmixed misery."

The Hawaiians are a light-hearted people, and find amusement in every diversion that offers. Their songs and their love of flowers are a natural instinct, and they are like children in the simple joyousness which evinces itself in their manner and in their smiling countenances. Grief does not rest heavily upon them, and the bereavement which follows everlasting separation from home and friends finds speedy consolation in the formation of new ties. Their friends, in turn, similarly console themselves when they are bereft. Upon arriving at Molokai the lepers are permitted to found new families — dreadful as it seems. Leprosy is a statute ground of divorce. And in this land of death there are speedy betrothals, marrying and giving in marriage, and some births, although not many, as leprous women seldom have children. The children remain in Molokai unless there is reason for the authorities to believe they are free from the taint, when they are permitted to go to any one of the other islands or are cared for at government expense at the "Kapiolani Home" in Honolulu, until they become of age. I have characterised these leprous marriages as dreadful, but in reality they are little worse than the perpetuation of vice and hereditary degeneracy and physical disability which is permitted without restriction in all civilised countries. Dr. R. Oliver is now the resident physician — a terrible existence, one may well believe, in this literal Valley of the Shadow of Death. The presence of disease, however, does not affect the inhabitants, who are well fed and well clothed, and who here, as elsewhere, crown their disfigured and ghastly heads with flowers. Dogs and horses are allowed them, apparently, without limitation. They take no thought for the morrow, and they have no cause to feel anxiety as to wherewithal they shall be fed and clothed. Food in abundance and clothing and shelter are theirs as long as they live; and, although doomed, they probably reason logically enough that, even in this event, their lives may be extended beyond that of the apparently sound and able-bodied whom they have left behind them.

Some years ago an Englishwoman, professedly a trained nurse, went out to Molokai with much theatrical demonstration, ostensibly to emulate the self-sacrifice of Father Damien, who lived for years amongst the lepers and died there. She reached Honolulu, but soon afterward married and went to the United States. In any event it would have been a work of supererogation, since there is a little band of Catholic nuns who remain with the lepers constantly, quietly performing their duty, ministering to their comfort, nursing them in their last illness, sitting beside their beds at death, in the quiet obedience and the devoted courage of their order. They went to their terrible post of duty unheralded, and remain there, shut away from the world, without considering that they have done more than that which their religion and humanity require of them. They have a convent which receives the few strangers who are permitted to set foot upon the shores of the settlement.

The plan of isolating the infected was first discussed in the Hawaiian Legislature in 1865; but, as might be imagined, it was violently opposed by the natives, who resisted the enactment of the law, and it was not carried into effect until 1873. At this time it was estimated that there were some four hundred leprous persons living with their families upon the various islands. The first attempts to apprehend and remove these unfortunates were savagely resisted. No discrimination was shown, and among the first exiles was William Ragsdale, a cousin of Queen Emma, an able lawyer, a man of wealth and influence, who afterwards devoted himself to the comfort and well-being of his fellow-sufferers. The whole of Molokai is not, as is erroneously supposed, given over to the habitation of the lepers. The name, in Hawaiian "*Molokai Aina Pali*," means "The land of precipices." This describes the formation of the island, which rises almost perpendicularly from the sea. The lepers occupy a plain of twenty thousand acres, which faces the roaring surf, and which is cut off from the remainder of the land in the rear by a precipice two thousand feet in height. Up this cliff there is a steep zigzag bridle-path which it is difficult and dangerous to traverse, even upon the back of the most sure-footed horse. Between the sea and this dizzy precipice the settlement is virtually a prison from which there is no escape. Mrs. Bishop has been charged with greatly exaggerating the misery of life in the settlement, but it is just to explain that great improvements have been made within the past twelve years, houses having been built for the reception of the lepers, and many accommodations provided them which were lacking at the time of her visit while the colony was in the experimental stage. On the contrary, apart from the hideousness of the disease, the loathsome spectacle of decaying flesh animated by the breath of life, the ever-present odour of decay, Robert Louis Stevenson has pronounced the provision made for the lepers by the Hawaiian Government both comfortable and humane. He was impressed with the contentment and cheerfulness of the people, who did not seem to dread in the least the death ordained them. He said that, had he been set apart from humanity by any ban that made him unsightly to his kind, he would have sought refuge in Molokai, where, in the common lot of affliction, he would find security and peace, and so pass out of life unmarked, and spared the suffering that aversion and loathing add to the pangs of dissolution.

I did not visit Molokai, although permission would have been given me. I had been warned by Mrs. Black, of San Francisco, then on the staff of the San Francisco *Examiner*, not to do so. She had gone to the island a few years previous, and she said, " I shall never be able to banish the recollection of that terrible experience from memory. Do not fill your mind with images that will make you shudder when you think of them, as long as you live, and that you will inevitably carry with you to the grave."

EX-QUEEN LILIUOKALANI.

CHAPTER XVII.

AN audience with the ex-Queen at eleven o'clock, a reception on board the *Mohican* at 3 P. M., a call upon the Minister-Resident, Mr. Stevens, and a most delightful dinner with the President and Mrs. Dole at seven o'clock, completed the programme of my last day's memorable sojourn in Honolulu, on the occasion of my first visit. The hour fixed for my call upon the Queen was eleven o'clock, and at the appointed time I was received upon the piazza by Colonel Robertson, who was then still acting as her secretary. Washington Place, as the Queen's town house was called, was a delightful villa, with wide verandahs above and below on all sides. It was painted white, contrasting pleasingly with the heavy foliage which overshadowed it. The doors and windows were standing open, and there was a suggestion of patriarchal custom in the retainers about the grounds and upon the verandahs. Men arrayed in cool suits of white duck came and went, and a group of women sat together in the shade, wearing the native dress, loaded with the usual garlands of tuberoses, waiting until they could be admitted to the ex-Queen's presence. When I arrived, Liliuokalani was conferring with Mr. Paul Neumann, her attorney, and Mr. Harold Sewell, recently arrived from Samoa, the present Minister to the Hawaiian Republic. I was therefore shown into the reception-room to wait until the ex-Queen was at leisure. A young Hawaiian, with a bright, intelligent face, sat at a desk writing. At his elbow was a photograph of a member of one of the royal family, over one corner of which was lightly thrown a *lei* of tuberoses. Near this was a larger photograph of Commissioner Blount, Mrs. Blount, and the Commissioner's private secretary, Mr. Mills. There was a polished calabash and a towering *kahili* in the hall just outside the door. With the books upon the table were heaped other *leis* of tuberoses, which filled the air with their heavy odour.

Mr. Neumann withdrew, and I was then informed that the Queen would see me. She was sitting upon a sofa, but rose when I entered the apartment and extended her hand, greeting me with the utmost informality. There was an undefinable unlikeness in the portraits that had appeared in the public press, and I do not think that I should have recognised her. She requested me to be seated, and as the conversation progressed I had an opportunity of studying her face. It was strong and resolute. The

features were irregular, the complexion quite dark;
the hair was streaked with grey, and she had the
large, dark eyes of her race.   Her voice was musical
and well modulated, as is the case with all Hawaiians; and she spoke remarkably pure and graceful
English.   Her manner was dignified, and she had
the ease and the authoritative air of one accustomed
to rule.   A strikingly handsome young Hawaiian sat
near by, listening with interest and attention to all
that was said.   She told me that she had learned of
my visit shortly after I arrived in the Islands, but
was at the time in the midst of political trouble
which forced her to deny herself to visitors.   She
then kindly inquired as to the cause of the accident
which necessitated the use of crutches, and expressed
her regret that my recovery had not been more rapid.
She also inquired after Admiral Brown, and talked
of an accident which had befallen him during his
stay in Honolulu the previous summer.   She wished
to know if I had been pleased with my visit, what I
thought of Honolulu and of the Islands, and she
seemed sincerely gratified when I told her that it
was one experience of my life when the highest anticipations had fallen far below the reality.   I spoke
of the beauty of the country, the charm of the
climate, and the cordial hospitality which I had received from all classes of people.

"Yes," she said, "we love our beautiful country,
and we love to hear it praised."

Like all other people of all other countries, she wished to know what impression the Hawaiians and their institutions had made upon me, and I told her of a visit I had recently paid the Royal School for Hawaiian Boys and the Kawaiahao School for Girls. She asked if the girls had sung for me, and I replied that they had, and that it was a great pleasure to hear them.

"People from the United States are surprised at the excellence of your schools," I added.

She replied, "And it is very gratifying to me when foreigners are able to see our schools for themselves. The Hawaiians are a well-educated people; there are few, if any, who cannot read or write."

I spoke with especial praise of a recitation that I had heard in the Royal School, the pupils giving evidence of excellent training and of natural intelligence. She then reverted to Admiral Brown and the affection that was felt for him by the Hawaiian people.

"He was very kind to our King," she said. "He was with him during his last illness, and brought the body back to Honolulu for burial. The Hawaiians have never forgotten this; they were deeply disappointed that he did not come at the time they expected him. We have great *aloha* for him — that is our national term for affection."

It was quite true that Admiral Brown had been a warm friend of the ex-Queen and of her people, but I had reason to know that he sternly disapproved of the unlawful course she had pursued in the abrogation of the Constitution which she had sworn to support at the time of her accession. I could not refrain from giving her an intimation of his real opinion. I therefore said that, personally, I was greatly relieved that he had not come; that his relations with the people, and his official responsibility as a Commissioner, had he been chosen, would have made the situation most embarrassing; that it was better that the kindly feeling which had so long existed should be spared so great a strain, and remain undisturbed.

"That is true," she admitted after a moment's hesitation, "but we should have been most happy to welcome him back, for whatever he might have said or done we should still have believed him to be our friend."

Neither the name of Commissioner Blount nor his errand to the Islands was mentioned. When I rose to go, both the Queen and the young attendant also rose, and she again extended her hand, holding mine in a strong, warm clasp while she bade me good-bye.

"Give Admiral Brown my *aloha*," she said again; "and I hope you will return when you are recovered and able to visit the other islands; they are all well worth seeing, and all as dear to us as this." She bowed gracefully, and with an added good-bye I left the royal presence.

As I stepped out upon the piazza the company of

native women who had been awaiting my departure rose and passed into the house toward the drawing-room with their wreaths, which I learned were daily offerings, and which left a waft of overpowering fragrance as they passed. There had been the utmost informality in the reception and in the conversation which followed, and the deposed Queen, in her severely plain gown of black and grey serge without a single ornament, still evinced in her speech and bearing much of her former state and dignity. She was an accomplished musician, fairly well read, and was at that time devoting a good many hours a day to the study of German. She lived in extreme simplicity, with the smallest practicable staff of servants, driving out regularly, going backwards and forwards from her town house to her villa on the seashore. She was apparently peaccable, and resigned to her fate; no one, except the closest of her confidants and advisers, knew that she was simply biding her time.

The interview occasioned a good deal of comment and some amusement among the Americans and Europeans in Honolulu. I had certainly no wish to be impertinent or disrespectful, but I felt that the ex-Queen should be undeceived as to the position of the Rear-Admiral, whom she really respected and trusted, and I took it upon myself to tell her the truth. But my Hawaiian friends assured me that I should never make a courtier.

CHAPTER XVIII.

THE CLOSE OF THE BLOUNT ADMINISTRATION.

DURING the remainder of the time which Mr. Blount devoted to his official inquiry he saw very little of the people, except the natives, who had access to him at all times to the last. Those who were qualified to speak on behalf of the Provisional Government were still given the briefest and most reluctant hearing; there was no change in his partial and unfriendly attitude. His witnesses, as the Congressional investigation subsequently showed, were many of them disreputable fellows, entirely untrustworthy — one especial source of his information having been arrested and imprisoned in China for forging passports for coolie emigrants. An attempt had been made to prove that the Revolution was a conspiracy of the annexationists, who had perfected their plans in a series of meetings held secretly at the residence of the American Minister. When Congress finally succeeded in forcing Mr. Cleveland to submit Mr. Blount's report, which he refused to do as long as possible, and it was published and sent back to Honolulu, one witness was made to retract this statement. He did so in one of the daily newspapers over his signature, saying that "he did not personally know that the charge was true, but he had been informed that it was by some one else" — rather shadowy evidence, one would conclude, to be incorporated into an official report of the gravest importance, not only to the Provisional Government of Hawaii, but to the Government of the United States. Having finished my work, and there being no indication that the Provisional Government was not perfectly stable and secure, I returned to Chicago to be present at the World's Fair, and to preside over the Women's Branch of the Press Congress, the first of a series of Congresses held in connection with the Exhibition. There was no news of any consequence from the Islands throughout the summer, and I was occupied with my professional and official duties.

Mr. Blount had succeeded Mr. Stevens as American Minister, but by this time, having become emphatically *persona non grata* to the entire Hawaiian Government, he felt his position not only embarrassing but difficult, and asked to be relieved. He was succeeded by Mr. Albert S. Willis, of Louisville, a man of very different calibre. Mr. Willis was sent by the President with all professions of good-will to President Dole, who had no suspicion of his mission. When it was learned, steps were immediately taken to resist the restoration of the Queen by force of arms, if necessary. Mr. Willis, being a man of far greater intelligence and prudence than Mr. Blount, saw that his instructions could not be carried out without bloodshed, and waited for further advice from the State Department in Washington before resorting to extremes. The plan of restoration was furiously opposed by the people of the United States, irrespective of politics, as un-American and undemocratic, and Mr. Cleveland, dogged and stubborn though he was, was forced to yield to public opinion. It is doubtful if there was ever a more ridiculous fiasco. The President of the United States was so absolutely certain that he would carry out what he had undertaken that he evidently notified France that it had been actually accomplished, and that government sent out a successor to its consul, who had asked permission to resign his office. When the successor arrived, he found himself accredited to a non-existent monarch, and his rage knew no bounds.

When the news of the Willis episode was received, I was ordered to return to Hawaii at once, and left Chicago January 2nd, arriving in Honolulu within a fortnight. We were detained in San Francisco several days waiting for the European mails, that had been belated by storms in the Atlantic. The Mid-Winter Fair, an after-thought of the Chicago Exposition, was in progress. Among the exhibitors was Harriet Hosmer, the sculptor, who contributed the fine model of her "Isabella"—a heroic figure intended for the World's Fair. She was occupied with putting the model in place; but we managed between times to have several outings and visits together. One incident of the week was a Spanish dinner, which was given in her honour at a Mexican restaurant, and which induced the first attack of sea-sickness I had ever had—for I sailed the next day. The dinner consisted of red pepper *au naturel* and in various disguises—chicken tomates, frijoles, and other unnameable things, with a variety of fiery wines. We felt in duty bound to taste a little of everything, and we repented at leisure—a leisure in my case necessarily and unduly extended.

We landed in Honolulu under very different conditions from the year before. It was pouring down as if the fountains of the great deep were broken up. The first pilot who came out to meet us searched for hours without finding us, and we were forced to wait until it cleared somewhat before we could enter the harbour. At the quarantine we learned that the town had quieted down, and it was thought that the worst was over. My friends had not been notified of my return; so I drove to the hotel, which was crowded with naval officers and their wives, and I had assigned to me a very damp, earthy, cave-like room in the basement. The next day I was given an apartment on the second floor adjoining the kitchen, where I was wakened at four o'clock by a

protracted and violent grinding of coffee and beating
of eggs — cheerful reassurance as to breakfast, but a
dreadful interruption to one's slumbers.

On Monday a piece of great good fortune befell
me. My friend Mrs. W—— came in her carriage
and carried me off, and I quitted with joyful alacrity
the cave-like room in the basement and the chamber
over the kitchen. It seemed blissful to be removed
from the noise and smells and bustle of the hotel to
the great, airy, peaceful chamber which was given
me in my friend's beautiful house, with the mountains and valleys on one hand, and the sweep of the
sea stretching away for leagues beyond my windows
on the other.

I could now walk short distances with comparative
ease, and this greatly simplified my work, and, in
spite of everything, added greatly to my renewed
pleasure. My special mission was to investigate the
sources of information from which Mr. Blount had
made up his report to President Cleveland, which
was soon accomplished. Much of my writing was
done in the throne-room of the Palace, where I had
been given a desk by the Vice-President, and which
was used as a Council Chamber by the Advisory
Council. It was an instance of the meeting of extremes to sit writing reports for a Chicago daily
newspaper confronting the empty throne of the deposed Queen.

The weeks slipped away pleasantly, the President

and Council drafting the new Constitution and deliberating over it, which was to be submitted to the Convention that was to assemble the last day of May. There were the customary entertainments — dinners and "at homes," and receptions on board the U. S. S. *Adams*, which had been sent out when the *Mohican*, *Alliance*, and the *Boston* were ordered to other stations.

CHAPTER XIX.

HAWAII, from which the entire group derive their name, is the largest and southernmost of the Hawaiian Islands. Like the others, it is a barren lava plain on the leeward side, while to the windward there are vast plantations of sugar-cane covered by myriads of unfailing streams. These not only furnish power for electric motors, but supply the mills which, though driven by steam, require a great water supply, and also feed the conduits which cross the fields, sometimes for miles, in which the cane, after it is cut and stripped, is sent down to the mills.

The approach to Hawaii on the windward side is of unsurpassed loveliness. The shores are a mass of verdure, with the still greener plantations in the distance; and down the lava crags of the coast, through clefts and over precipices, pour a thousand leaping watercourses — sometimes a tiny rivulet that scarcely stirs the ferns that overshadow it, sometimes a rippling and dancing brook, and again a rushing torrent churned into foam white as the surf into which it falls and melts. Far away, if the sky is clear, may be seen the peaks of Mauna Kea and Mauna Loa, rising out of the dark forests interspersed with patches of the grey-green *kukui* which girdle their lower slopes — cones of purest crystal, covered with unmelting snow.

On my first visit I had been unable to accept kind invitations that were sent me to visit Hawaii from friends living in Hilo; but having now partially recovered, I considered myself extremely fortunate that the opportunity — a most unlikely thing to have happened — should have been thrown in my way a second time. There had come a lull in affairs in Honolulu, and I was assured that there would be no new revolution, no attempt to restore the Queen, and no invasion by the Japanese during my absence; so that I felt I might venture to go away for a fortnight's holiday. I left Honolulu the first week in February on the *Kinau*. She was a tiny craft to brave the rough seas.

It is two hundred and seventy-five miles from Honolulu to Hilo, and it is here that the tourist takes the stage for the Volcano of Kilcauea, which is still thirty miles distant. The channels between the islands of Oahu, Maui, Molokai, and Hawaii are said to be the roughest waters on the globe; and whether his experience be limited or extensive, the tourist will at once admit that it is true. If he has travelled much, his experience will bear out the truth of the assertion; and if he has not, his natural intel-

ligence will still lead him to the same conclusion.
To me the voyage is a blurred memory of remaining
on deck, the solitary watcher there, until the stars
came out, of retiring to my cabin, and emerging
no more until the afternoon of Wednesday — one
day of dreadful qualms and two nights of spasmodic
clutching at any support that presented itself to keep
me from being tossed from the berth. Among the
passengers who had come on board at Honolulu was
an American physician and his ward, who had taken
cabins on the upper deck. It was found, upon inspection, that they were separated only by a curtain
over the connecting doorway. When this was discovered, the physician asked me to exchange cabins
with him, which I willingly did. After this was
agreed upon, the steward came into my room to make
up the berth, and placed in it a wide mattress, which
he squeezed down until it formed the half of a
cylinder. I looked at this arrangement with great
disfavour, but had reason afterwards to thank myself
that such support had been supplied me.

We stopped the next morning to take on board a
load of sugar at Mahukona, which was brought out to
the steamer in flat boats attached to a cable connecting the vessel and the shore. This place is the
terminus of the railroad which runs up to the plantations beyond the arid ridge facing the sea. Near
the beach was a cluster of bungalows embowered in
algaroba trees — that blessing which brightens the

desert wastes throughout the Islands. Beyond this bit of greenery there was not a trace of vegetation upon the lava-strewn hillside, which, however, was crossed by that evidence of civilisation here omnipresent and indispensable — the telephone. There was a broad road winding up the steep ascent along the ridge, leading down to the hidden plantations beyond. Over this highway we could see the natives riding on horseback, four abreast, the women in *holokus* and flower-wreathed straw hats. Far away rose the snowy peak of Mauna Kea, the highest peak on the island, volcanic, like all the mountains throughout Hawaii; and in every direction stretched the sea, blue as sapphire, and flecked with white caps.

When we reached Hilo, we crawled out, limp and disconsolate, made an impressionist sort of toilette, and buttoned two buttons on each boot. Then we huddled together on the deck, surveying the shore through the fast-descending rain, which came down, not like ordinary rain, but after its manner in Hilo, a solid deluge. There were great stretches of yellow-green cane-fields, the graceful cocoa-palms lifting their plumy branches along the edge of encircling forests. But to see the shore and to reach it were two widely different matters. We were anchored in the harbour, and went over the ship's side to drop into the tossing boat below at the word of command. This required steadiness of nerve and extreme carefulness and calculation, but it was accomplished.   The boat was wet, not only with the rain, which continued to pour, but with occasional waves that broke over it.   We were rowed across the bay, then up a wide inlet to a pier, up which we were pulled by main force.   The twenty unfortunates who were to go on to the volcano that morning, exhausted as they were by the rough voyage, were loaded into stages waiting for them and driven away. My host, who was awaiting me, took me at once to his house, and I spent the remainder of the day in resting and convalescing.   One meets here people from every quarter of the globe.   In our little passenger list there were two young girls from New Zealand, the physician and his ward from New York, and a fat priest from Lisbon, who had come out to do missionary work among the Portuguese.   The father of my host had been a political exile from Germany.

At the house, after my wet clothing had been removed, an appetising luncheon was brought to my room by Mademoiselle, the governess, a charming young Swiss girl, who had left Lucerne only the year before.   The next morning overshoes and mackintoshes were donned, and we made an expedition to see a rushing river, which had been greatly swollen by the rain, dashing over the black volcanic rocks in its bed with tremendous noise and velocity. Its steep banks were matted with ferns and ginger, and here and there cascades leaped through the greenery, to fall into the larger torrent below.   In the afternoon the sun came out for a little while, and an expedition was planned to Rainbow Falls.

There are very few good roads in Hilo, so that exploring must be done either on foot or on horse-back; consequently we arranged a riding-party, with rather lamentable results. There was my host on a clay-coloured mule, named Bella; his son, Bert, upon another; I upon a tame old horse; while Mademoiselle had borrowed Billy, the family horse belonging to Mr. Severance, the postmaster. I knew nothing whatever of horsemanship, but once mounted soon became accustomed to the snail pace of my steed. The road was something indescribable. We climbed what was apparently an endless causeway, layers of volcanic rock like paving-stones — proceeded over stones and boulders, through sloughs and boiling streams, swollen by the rain to unimaginable depths. We rode single file, following the narrow trail, and then dismounted to walk the last half-mile through a jungle of matted grass, waist-deep and dripping. But the falls repaid us — a great stream foaming and roaring and dropping one hundred feet in a sheer descent into a frothy pool, and rushing down to the sea in a succession of cascades.

When we reached the uplands, we found the grassy plain intersected by many small streams. These wound through their narrow channels some thirty or forty yards and disappeared, to reappear twenty yards or more away in a direction that could hardly have been guessed. The subterranean channels had been hollowed out in the buried lava which underlay the entire region. In other places there were deep, clear pools, ice-cold, but bubbling up like cauldrons. We walked back to our tethered animals and re-mounted. Mr. L——, on Bella, the yellow mule, led the cavalcade. The lava above Hilo is the sur-vival of the great flow of 1881, which poured down a molten river from the summit crater of Mauna Loa, burning all vegetation in its path, and threatening to destroy the town. Fortunately, however, it stopped within a mile of it, and the black and con-gealing mass, which still has a perceptibly sulphur-ous odour, was one year in cooling. Disintegration has already begun — ferns taking root and lifting their delicate fronds in the crevices, and insidious lichens aiding the work of decomposition. There were acres of this lava — black and shapeless masses, poured down in a thickening liquid that had hard-ened, coil upon coil. In other places there were solid blocks, and again little jutting crags and smooth slabs fitted together like paving-stones.

As a horsewoman I am entirely unskilled, and when Mr. L—— proposed to ride across this Titanic highway I looked at it a little dubiously. But as Sam Patch remarked, "Some things may be done as well as others;" and as I had successfully climbed the causeway, scaled the stone-heaps, forded the river, and traversed the sloughs, it seemed inconsistent to refuse the lava-bed. I said I could manage it, and up we went, Bella again leading; Bert on Dandy; then myself, and Mademoiselle bringing up the rear on Billy.

There is said to be an amiable cherub who sits up aloft looking out for the welfare of poor Jack. I think the same protecting genius must have an eye also to the preservation of foolhardy women, and confidently believe that I have had my own share of his good offices. We really got along admirably — for a time. My horse dexterously picked his way along narrow ridges a foot wide, and slid down the inclines in a way that might have excited the envy of a coasting schoolboy. With equal skill he climbed the slippery slopes, winding in and out like a cat. I knew but one rule, so far as riding was concerned; this was, "Hold a tight rein," and I observed it punctiliously. Mademoiselle, much more experienced, followed me. We had nearly crossed the dangerous stretch in safety when I heard a crash and a shriek behind me. Billy was down, and Mademoiselle was trying to get her foot out of the stirrup; she finally succeeded; but alas for poor Billy! he floundered a moment, and then lay helpless, his leg broken below the knee. I rode off the lava down to the grass, Mademoiselle following on foot, crying and wringing her hands. But nothing could be done until help could be had. Mr. L——

dismounted, climbed the lava, put his hands over his mouth, and gave a loud halloo. Then a party of Japanese came to the rescue. There were eight of them, carrying pieces of timber, out of which they improvised a litter, and poor old Billy was lifted down to the grass, laid on a heap of fern, and covered with a blanket. The broken leg was put in splints, and it was hoped that he might be saved; but he was too old, and the next day it was agreed that he must be shot to put him out of his pain. Mademoiselle and I left Mr. L—— and the Japanese at work, and started home alone — two decidedly dejected-looking women. My costume was a dark-blue divided skirt, a peacock blue blouse, a cap that shed the water from its peak in streams down my nose and cheeks (for it was raining again), a pair of wet, bulging gloves, wet, muddy gown, wet boots, and over this array the wet and mud-stained mackintosh. Mademoiselle's habit was less composite, consisting of a broad-brimmed straw hat, that flopped down over her eyes, a dark-blue serge riding-habit, covered completely by a big, yellow, muddy oilskin coat. After we had proceeded some distance we heard Mr. L—— shouting to us. We thought it was hope for poor Billy, and Mademoiselle exclaimed with fervent piety, "Oh, t'ank God!" But we were mistaken; it was only a signal of distress and a call for additional help. We did not return as we came, but went round three craters beyond the

lava flow by a bridle-path.   It was called a path;
but it was a sluggish, moving stream of mud and
water, into which the horses sank to their haunches.
They would plunge in and withdraw their hoofs with
an explosion that was like the crack of a whip-lash.
As we started Mr. L—— had said of my mount,
"That 's a splendid little mud horse."   And I found,
before the ride was finished, that his virtues in this
direction had not been exaggerated.

We passed numbers of interesting Japanese houses,
neat as the houses of a toy village, each with its bit
of garden in which tapioca and ginger were growing
and thriving.   Portuguese, who are even more successful farmers than the Chinese, were standing in
the verandahs of their small houses, and smiled
affably at us, surrounded by swarms of young children.   If they had been encouraged and could have
obtained land, the Portuguese would long ago have
redeemed the waste places of Hawaii, and made the
desert place blossom as the rose.   Removed from
the tyranny of a State religion, they become liberal
and progressive, no longer the servile tools of the
priests.   They are a most temperate, industrious,
and peaceable people, prizing above all things the
little home which each aspires to acquire and hold;
and they are in every way most desirable as colonists.
At the end of one long and unutterably boggy lane
we met a handsome Hawaiian boy carrying home a
sackful of grass.   He wore the usual white cotton

shirt and blue cotton trousers, both soaked with rain. He was barefooted, and round the crown of his hat was wound a small American flag, the blue of the ground faded into the white stars which the running dye had completely blurred. Portuguese, Japanese, and Chinese we had passed in that melancholy ride; and here, at the parting of the ways, stood youthful Hawaii pensively surveying us, his black eyes looking out from under that little wet flag above his hat-brim. Somewhat later I crawled off my saddle at the verandah steps of Mr. L——'s house, muddy, drenched, and stiff, grateful for a hot bath and a dry gown, but with no appetite for dinner. During the night I could hear the rain falling in sheets. I thought of poor Billy lying out on the hill-top on his bed of fern with his broken leg, and it troubled my repose. And this is a true chronicle of my first ride in Hawaii.

Mrs. Bird Bishop has written with pardonable enthusiasm of Hilo and Hawaii. I have heard her charged with exaggeration; so it is pleasant to state that the account of her perilous adventures, fording torrents, scaling precipices, and making her way through pathless forests, is fully corroborated by the people of Hilo among whom she lived, and who still hold her in affectionate remembrance. During the latter half of my visit it was my good fortune to be entertained in the same delightful home, that of Mr. and Mrs. Severance, where Mrs. Bishop and Miss

15

Gordon Cumming had been received. They spoke of Mrs. Bishop with the greatest admiration and affection. She had been an ideal guest, readily adapting herself to the ways of their household, anxious to avoid giving trouble, waiting upon herself, and lending her assistance in household matters whenever she could. She would sit and write in the drawing-room with the family and the guests seated about her talking, not in the least disturbed by their conversation. It was in this hospitable home the interesting reception was given King Lunalilo in 1875, which Mrs. Bishop has described with the amusing difficulty of procuring materials for a feast of sufficient magnitude for his entertainment. Such a drawback would not be encountered to-day, as Hawaii is now in comparatively close touch with the world, which brings all its luxuries, and fortunately but few of its discomforts, to her door.

It is difficult to make the people of the United States or England realise the refinement and culture of the people of these remote Islands. Even at the risk of violating the sacredness of hospitality, I feel that I must describe this beautiful house and its surroundings, that unenlightened Americans and English may comprehend what the life is like. It was a bungalow, with sloping, picturesque roof and verandahs on every side. The rooms opened upon the verandah with glass doors, which were seldom closed. They were connected and separated only by *portières*, ceiled with wood, panelled, and painted in delicate, warm shades of cream with pale-blue ceilings. The floors were covered with fine mattings and rugs. Upon the walls were good paintings in oil and water-colour, with photographs of famous pictures. There were luxurious lounges and easy-chairs, heaped with beautifully embroidered silken cushions; tables covered with books; and there were flowers in bowls and vases everywhere. There were more books in the cases and shelves, and with them the American magazines in their familiar covers. There was a copy of Clytie in Parian marble standing upon her pedestal, with a background of maroon velvet; while there were table-covers and draperies decorated with the most exquisite needle-work. The glance could turn in no direction but that it rested upon dainty bric-à-brac — harmony in form and colour that is only possible to perfectly cultivated taste.

People lived much in their verandahs, and my favourite lounging-place was a capacious hammock slung across one corner, where I could lie and read and dream, looking off across the blue Pacific, over the tops of the palm-trees, for miles away to the dim horizon line. In front of the verandah was a semi-circular rose garden, around which ran a narrow, limpid stream, with smooth, thick turf clothing its shallow banks to the water's edge. In the centre of the garden was a stately traveller's palm, while the walks were thickly bordered with splendid tropical ferns, varieties which we can scarcely coax to grow in the artificial warmth of our greenhouses. The roses were magnificent, white, pink, and crimson, and they filled the air with their fragrance. They had not yet been attacked by the beetle, supposed to have been imported from Japan, which had utterly destroyed all the roses in Honolulu, a strict quarantine being maintained against all plants imported into Hawaii from the island of Oahu. In addition to the little stream which encircled this lovely rose garden was another which babbled under my window, dropping down in a foaming cataract. In the moonlight this cataract, with its overshadowing cocoanut-palm, beneath the great, luminous tropical stars, which here seem so very close to earth, was a bit of fairyland. Across the steep street, surrounded by a moss-grown wall of volcanic stone, were the grounds of the court-house, also crossed by a running stream, with a shaven lawn, palms, giant bamboos, flower-beds, and fern-borders. I thought of the tobacco-stained corridors of the Chicago City Hall, and could not help reflecting that, if annexation came, perhaps it would be the mission of our Hawaiian foster-brothers to teach us the fundamental principles of real civilisation. The court-house was an unpretentious wooden structure, and amazingly clean, considering that its verandahs were the favourite congregating-places of the natives.

I attended a meeting of the Ladies' Shakespeare Class during my visit to Hilo, and listened with interest to the reading and the very animated, intelligent discussion of *Henry IV.* To give an idea of the progressive spirit of the place, it need only be stated that there were two women physicians in Hilo, each having an extensive practice, and one woman lawyer, who had graduated with honours from Michigan University and was then practising in Maui, having married a physician there. The deputy sheriff was a woman. During the temporary disability of the pastor a woman had been asked to take charge of the Congregational Church, and women were at the head of both the Government School and the Boys' Boarding School. A permanent resident laughingly warned me "not to put any more notions in the women's heads, or," he said, "the men will have to emigrate." From my observation, however, there appeared to be a very hearty acquiescence and co-operation on the part of the husbands and fathers and brothers, who were not at all cast in the shade by the clever, energetic wives and sisters who had been given so prominent a place in public affairs.

The village of Hilo is quaint and fascinating, with its stony streets and beautiful surroundings. It is girt by tropical forests, with miles upon miles of sugar plantations, the snow-clad peaks of Mauna Loa and Mauna Kea looking down upon it and across the bay, one of the most beautiful sheets of water in the world. A single island breaks the regularity of its surface — a small mass of volcanic rock, which is covered with venerable cocoanut trees and screw palms. A picnic was given there during my stay. We drove to the bungalow on the shore, where we left the phaeton. Others of the party, being on horseback, dismounted, and we were rowed across to the island. Some repaired to the cottage which had been erected as a shelter, put on their bathing-dresses, and plunged into the surf. I stood upon the lava and watched them swimming about in the clear, blue water like mermaids, my attention distracted by the wonderful blue and brown and scarlet gold-flecked fish which had been stranded in the pools left among the rocks by the recession of the tide.

One of the most interesting social events during my visit was a *luau* (a native feast), given by Mr. L——, the Government surveyor. It is customary, when the weather is favourable, to hold a *luau* in an arbour constructed of bamboo, thatched with palm leaves and festooned with garlands. The weather prohibited the arbour, so the feast was served in the long verandah. A screen of the branches of the magnificent ginger plant had been arranged to shut out the rain, while ferns and flowers were fastened against the opposite wall. The floor was also thickly strewn with ferns, with a broad band of crimson pandanus leaves down the centre of this green carpeted space. On this were arranged bowls of *poi* of all sizes and conditions. There was no tablecloth, ferns being the substitute. Over the ferns were scattered young onions and heaps of water-lemons — a delicious, juicy fruit which, outwardly, resembles a small gourd. No plates were used. The pork, taro, chicken, and mullet, of which the *menu* consisted, were cut up and wrapped in young taro leaves, with a covering of banana and an outer wrapping of ti leaf. The latter was given a deft twist which left the long stem as a sort of handle. This food had been cooked for many hours, a hole being dug in the ground and lined with heated stones. This primitive oven was then filled with taro leaves, in which the fish, pork, and chicken were placed; a little water was added, then the whole was covered with earth to cook slowly and gradually. It was the native method of preparing food, and the flavour was certainly delicious. In point of excellence we have hardly improved upon it. The guests were assigned their places and sat down on the fern-covered floor, and the viands were passed round. The leafy wrappings were opened, and the savoury morsels inside were eaten with the fingers. The juices had been confined in the wrappers of leaf, and the taro, which is the *luau* that gives the feast its name, imparts to the meat its own delicate flavour. Between bites of pork or fish those to the manner born dipped their fingers into the bowl of *poi* which stood

before each plate, drew out a sticky wad, and trans-
ferred it to the mouth with astonishing dexterity.
Those not to the manner born clumsily imitated their
example, but made rather a dribbling, messy failure
of it.   Onions were eaten liberally, and also sweet
potatoes, with salted shrimps, which are placed
upon the board alive by native Hawaiians at their
luaus, and so devoured.   It was a gay little entertainment, accompanied by laughing and hilarious
conversation, all the guests talking at once, the
residents finding much amusement in the heroic
efforts of the visitors to eat with their fingers and
swallow the *poi* without a grimace.   It will be
remembered when more ceremonious and pretentious
functions have long been forgotten.

Among the guests was Professor Albert Koebele,
formerly of California.   He was well known throughout the United States as an entomologist of the
highest attainments.   He had been formerly employed
by the Agricultural Department in Washington, and
in his professional capacity had travelled all over the
world.   The stories of his experiences in Tahiti and
elsewhere in the South Seas were as marvellous as
romance; for, though naturally diffident and retiring,
he talked extremely well, with the encouragement
of an appreciative audience.   His greatest work was
the introduction of the *Vedclia cardinalis* from
Australia into the orange and lemon orchards of
California.   This "lady-bird" preys upon the para-

site known as the "scale-blight," which is so destructive to the orchards, and which it completely destroyed. This was an experiment of his own, and its success was due to his individual effort. He gave me an interesting account of it, having proceeded upon the theory, well known in natural history, that all living creatures have their enemies in parasites, and that it was only necessary to discover the natural enemy of the scale-blight. This he found in the lady-bird, of which there are many hundred species in Australia. It is a tiny beetle which hides in the bark of trees, and must be collected, a few at a time, so that the search for an ordinary supply is long and laborious. He told me that he shipped five thousand in one box; they were frozen until they became torpid, and a small supply of scale-blight was placed in each box, for food in case the insect revived. When they reached their destination, they were simply turned loose in orchards where their services were required, and they fell upon the affected trees at once and rapidly cleared them. As Professor Koebele was a scientist, and not a politician, he was not able to cope with his political rivals, who conspired to prevent the success of his discovery. He left what was supposed to be a trustworthy agent in California, with implicit instructions as to the disposition of the beetles when they should be received. Instead of obeying orders the jealous agent permitted the entire first shipment to die, and then reported in Washington that the experiment had been a failure.   Fortunately Professor Koebele had sent a number of the beetles to friends who were fruit-growers, and these being saved proved the truth of his assertions.   However, as is usual, while it has saved the Californian fruit-growers thousands of dollars, the discoverer did not profit in any way by his labour.   He was a slight, delicate-looking man, only forty-one years of age, with a clear olive complexion, fine regular features, and dark-brown eyes, refined in manner and appearance.   He was subsequently employed by the Hawaiian Provisional Government at a salary of $5,000 per annum, and was about to set forth on an expedition to discover an enemy of the coffee-blight, which he felt sanguine that he would be able to find. I met him subsequently in Sydney, and went with him on one of his beetle-hunting expeditions in an orange plantation near Paramatta.   His method there was to find a tree covered with blight upon which the beetles were feeding.   An open umbrella was placed under the lower boughs, which were beaten with a walking-stick, shaking the insects into the receptacle below.   They were then scooped up, and placed in wide-mouthed vials, ready for the process of freezing.   From Australia Professor Koebele expected to visit Ceylon, India, China, and Northern Africa.

CHAPTER XX.

A LITTLE JOURNEY TO KILEAUEA.

THE very first question put to the tourist returning from the Hawaiian Islands is, "Did you see the volcano?" A reply in the negative is always disappointing, and the questioner invariably wonders why any one should have taken so long a journey only to miss its most interesting feature. It is consequently almost a matter of self-respect to be able to answer "Yes." I had had the first experience the previous year; now I should have the latter, and felt that fate had made amends.

Formerly the ascent was made by a rough trail on horseback; but within the past three years the Government has completed a fine road from Hilo to the crater, so that the journey, once so fatiguing, can now be made comfortably and conveniently in a day's time. Before the road was finished tourists were forced to carry with them not only food but bedding and fuel, spending the night at a rude half-way house, which furnished shelter only. The narrow track over the lava was so steep and rough that horses had to walk at a snail's pace the entire distance.

My friend Mrs. L—— and I visited Kileauea in the month of February. We left Hilo immediately after breakfast upon a lovely tropical morning. For once the incessant downpour of rain had ceased, and we had a fine view of the snow-covered peaks of Mauna Loa and Mauna Kea — peaks of dazzling crystal softly outlined against the deep-blue sky. We had booked our seats in the stage-coach, a dilapidated vehicle drawn by four gaunt horses in rather rusty harness, and driven by a bashful, good-natured Scotchman. In addition to taking charge of the luggage the driver obligingly distributed along the entire thirty miles of the route newspapers, letters, and parcels, and he was also the custodian of a good-sized box of joints and steaks, sent by the butchers in Hilo to their customers in the upland plantations. The steaks were deftly hooked to a crane by the roadside, or, with the joints, deposited upon a shelf in a box out of reach of hungry animals. Occasionally the black-eyed Hawaiian cook, displaying two rows of white teeth in an amiable smile, would suddenly appear out of the bush, attracted by the rattle of our wheels, and take the driver's supplies herself. As she usually wore a wreath of flowers on her head or about her throat, her sudden appearance out of the dense greenery gave her some semblance to a modern variety of dryad, perverted to the utilitarian uses of a prosaic age.

Few bungalows could be seen, or the plantations

about them, those on the highlands being devoted to the cultivation of coffee. A narrow path was cut through the thick undergrowth, which rose almost like a wall on either hand, and at the end of the path a glimpse could be had of sloping roofs and pretty gardens.

The road from Hilo is a gradual ascent, and the change in vegetation, as we left the lower lands along the sea, gave one the impression of having passed from summer to autumn within the lapse of a few hours. As we ascended it grew perceptibly cooler, the face of the landscape altered, and there was in the air the chill and pervasive melancholy of an October day. We left Hilo, driving through the Chinese quarter with its picturesque shops, tiny children playing about in their familiar little costumes of pink, blue, and yellow, the boys' queues lengthened as usual by interwoven threads of rose-coloured cords.

Just beyond these Chinese huts were the cane-fields, an intense yellow-green, the long, slender leaves tossing in the breeze like a maize-field before the harvest. There were great bands of Japanese at work in the field. They are labourers who can endure the heat and dust of the cane-field, and they work with incredible rapidity, the line of men crossing a field, levelling the cane with a stroke of the sharp knife which they use for the purpose. As they return, they collect the cane, tie it into bundles, and load it on the cars of the little narrow-gauge railway, a temporary, movable line being laid between the mills and the fields, and shifted as occasion may require.

Some distance beyond the cane lands we plunged into the depths of a marvellous tropical forest. Through this forest the coffee plantations multiplied, the young plants growing either in cleared spaces or in the midst of shrubs and bushes. Beyond the first forest was a wide expanse of sloping plain covered with ferns of the most extraordinary hues — pink, green, rose-coloured, and purple. From this point there was a fine view of the sea surrounding three sides of the island, and Mauna Loa and Mauna Kea reappeared, their lower slopes covered with rich vegetation.

We passed many native houses. These, alas! are no longer the beautiful grass houses of the old Hawaiians, but rude wooden cottages with a broad verandah in front. Upon this verandah the family was usually assembled, sitting indolently about on mats. The women were clad in *holokus*, and were stout to unwieldiness from the consumption of *poi*. Occasionally a group would be seen enjoying a social pipe, men and women passing it from hand to hand, each taking a temperate whiff. Even in the poorest cottages servants seemed to be employed for the more menial work, while the mistress lolled at ease upon her cushions. Upon the fences here and there patchwork quilts were hung out to air, and they were of startling design and colour. The grounds about these native houses were, as a rule, untidy and dirty, strewn with worn-out kitchen utensils, rags, sticks, and straw, with perhaps a flower-bed, the drooping plants fighting for existence in a wilderness of weeds. The fencing most used was sections of the trunks of tree-ferns; these have a wonderful tenacity of life, and had sent out young shoots until it seemed to be a hedge of matted fronds.

Much of the land in this region formerly belonged to the Crown, and could be neither bought nor leased; it had therefore remained unproductive. Under the new Government it has been surveyed, placed upon the market, and sold, freehold, in small tracts, thus enabling the natives to own their homes. Much of it is being rapidly brought under cultivation and planted with coffee and pineapples.

At noon we stopped for luncheon at the new half-way house which has supplanted the old structure, a comfortable little inn on the edge of the second forest, reached either by the winding drive or a flight of steep wooden steps. From the verandah, where our coffee was served, we looked down on the forest, in which we heard for the first time the delightful singing of birds. That which we had first crossed was absolutely silent, the only living thing we had seen being a mongoose, which ran across the road, plunged into the thicket, and disappeared. The birds were of the most brilliant plumage, delighting both the eye and the ear. We had with our coffee an appetising luncheon of new-laid eggs and bacon, which we ate in leisurely fashion, enjoying the hour of rest which we had been allowed. The trees were quite different now, and we saw nothing more of the strange *ié-ié*, a huge vine with brilliant scarlet cones; instead, there were clusters of giant bananas, with the grey-green and jaggy-leafed screw palm, and the *kukui*, or candle-nut.

When we resumed the journey we presently came upon a crowd of convicts working on the new road to the volcano, of which at that time there were three miles still to be constructed. The men were oddly uniformed in a combination suit of cotton, one side brown and the other blue. The prison was a flimsy affair, and the routine of locking up the men at night must have been a mere form; there were few guards, and the door would have yielded to very slight pressure. The convicts were chiefly Japanese and Chinese, convicted of violating their contracts with the planters, gambling, smoking opium, or petty theft. They seemed very mild and tractable, and were well fed and kindly treated. It might be said, parenthetically, that the entire population of the Islands, native and immigrant, though extremely heterogeneous, is most peaceful and law-abiding, violence and the graver offences being extremely rare. The road to the volcano was an elaborate piece of engineering, and, owing to the peculiar character of the soil, its construction was labour of the most difficult nature. In many places the solid lava had to be blasted by heavy charges of dynamite; here a yawning gulch had to be filled, and there a shelving ridge cut away. At one point a causeway was thrown across the crater of an extinct volcano sixty feet in depth, its sides covered with moss and trailing vines, while within the hollow cone was a wild tangle of ferns and bananas.

The hotel at the volcano is an excellent one, with good service and palatable food. I had imagined that it stood on a plateau of naked lava, and was unprepared therefore for the thick growth of *koa* and *lehua* which clothed the entire outer ruin. By the roadside as we approached was the richest grass with clusters of pale-pink eglantine. As we neared our destination the steep wall of the crater, a circular sweep of nine miles, became perfectly distinct. At one point it was broken away, and we drove through the cleft into the hotel grounds, alighting under the *porte-cochère* at the entrance. Trees grew upon the inner as well as the outer wall of the crater, and the hotel stood upon a grassy shelf some three hundred feet in width. The contrast between the blooming garden and the neatly shaven lawn, with the barren waste of the yawning lava-strewn gulf below, was very strange.

The floor of the crater is three miles in width, and
16

is reached by an almost sheer descent of twelve hundred feet. The only path down this precipice is a bridle-track, but the sure-footed horses that have grown accustomed to it make no difficulty in picking their way through the yielding earth and stones. The lake of fire, the core of the volcano, is at the farthest side of the bed of the crater, and the guests can stand upon the verandah and watch its crimson billows rising and falling like the surges of a stormy sea. When I went to my room I raised the window-blind, and by the light of the dancing flames three miles away could see distinctly the hands of my watch. We spent the evening, a very contented and congenial trio, around a wood fire which was blazing invitingly in a big open fireplace in the billiard-room. This was the favourite rendezvous of the guests, who usually deserted the more pretentious and modern drawing-room. It was a relic of the old hotel, and its homely comfort was very alluring. Mrs. L—— had arranged to meet her brother, an artist who had just returned from Paris, where he had been studying for several years, and who was then at the volcano making studies of Kileauea. He was a young man of decided genius, an interesting talker, and beguiled the time with amusing stories of his life in the American art colony in the French capital. He had painted a study of the volcano above the fireplace, as a contribution to the various

sketches and autographs that had been left by distinguished travellers.

Kileauea has been visited by tourists from all
parts of the world. Among them were Lady Franklin (who was carried to the volcano by relays of
natives), Miss Gordon Cumming, and Mrs. Bishop.
Many distinguished people have written their names
upon the pages of the hotel register, and have added
reflections and comments that were occasionally in
keeping with the sublimity of the scene that had
moved them out of their prosaic and every-day mood.
Taken altogether, however, it was a sort of gamut
of the human emotions, from awe and wonder to
frivolity and drivelling idiocy. I found two apos-
trophes in verse which did fitting honour to this, one
of the greatest spectacles of Nature. Of the rest,
the less said the better, for many of the notes were
a painful commentary upon the limitations of human
intelligence. Two gifted creatures had written respectively, "O me!" and "O my!" There were
several clever pen-and-ink sketches and semi-
amusing caricatures of tourists. Among the collections was a "Vision" by Mark Twain, written at the
time of his visit in 1866. It was republished in one
of the Honolulu papers, and a copy was sent to him.
When he was living in Hartford, Connecticut, he
acknowledged the authorship, but explained that
he "must have been pretty young then, or sick, or
something," and asked that it might be taken out

of the record, or, by way of atonement, the letter of explanation pasted beside it to keep it company, which has doubtless been done.

The next morning there was a heavy hailstorm, an almost unheard-of phenomenon, which delayed our descent into the crater until the afternoon. The delight and wonder of the natives as they collected the big hailstones, crunching them with their white teeth, were very amusing. They had never seen such a thing before, and, still extremely superstitious under the thin veneer of their Christianity, they ascribed the storm to a supernatural cause. In the interval of waiting, the sun having come out again, we explored the place about the hotel. A few yards away were some very interesting sulphur banks, the scalding steam escaping through crevices, the openings being thickly coated with yellow crystals. Here, strangely enough, the nasturtium grew luxuriantly, and the *ohelo*, a low shrub whose delicately flavoured berries were once sacred to Pelé, the deity supposed to preside over Kileauea. Almost immediately after luncheon the horses were brought round, mine a stupid, hard-mouthed steed, whose anatomy presented an array of angular bones.

In the Sandwich Islands everywhere — in the cities as well as in the country — ladies universally ride astride. The habit consists of a graceful divided skirt pleated very full over the hips, so that when the rider alights it falls together like the folds of an ordinary kilted gown. Not having the conventional costume, I managed a rather shabby substitute, a green Newmarket coat with longish skirts, which separated and hung down on either side; my appearance was not improved by the battered cap and bulging gloves that completed the dress.

We rode away in single file, the proprietor of the hotel (the most loquacious of landlords), H——— (the young artist), myself, and a motley company of Hawaiian guides.

The path, at all times uncertain, had been badly washed by the rain of the previous morning, and as my horse floundered and scrambled in the mud I expected every moment that a land-slip would precipitate us over the edge of the cliff into the abyss below. But the animal was experienced and sure-footed, and he leaped across boulders and fissures like a goat; it was a special good fortune, not good horsemanship, that enabled me to keep my saddle. Once upon the solid floor of the crater I looked about me, and surely nowhere upon the globe is there a spectacle more grim, forbidding, and awe-inspiring. The black cliffs, with their nine miles' circumference, as clearly defined as walls of masonry, rose almost perpendicularly, to a height of from five hundred to twelve hundred feet. No stratification was apparent, but the elevated masses were heaped together in confusion, while in the bottom of the crater successive floods had poured from the lake and spread themselves in myriad fantastic forms. There were what seemed to be heaps of stained and blackened sail-cloth, twisted strands of giant cable, shapeless mounds, and here and there apparently the perfectly outlined remains of animals thinly covered with mud.

As we moved slowly along we had to halt now and then, as blinding clouds of steam strongly impregnated with sulphur completely hid us from each other. In order to keep the file of horses on the trail in such circumstances, a low, irregular wall had been loosely thrown together along either side of the faintly defined path; the surface beneath, while the heat of subterranean fire could be felt, was sufficiently thick to be quite secure; outside this walled track the crust varied, and it was the part of wisdom to keep in the path. The volcano is not always active; it has irregular periods of quiescence, when the lake is simply a great empty basin some two hundred feet in depth. There is then not a vestige of heat, and not even a fissure has been discovered after the molten mass has escaped into the fathomless and unexplored depths beneath its bed, which closes completely. After a time smoke appears, the lava flows in again from below, rising higher and higher, until the bed is quite full, and a rim some five feet in height, which cools and hardens, is deposited around the margin of the lake.

One may make the long journey comparatively in

vain, since, without the burning flames, interesting and impressing as Kileauea must always be, the final touch of weirdness is wanting.

At the time of my visit, fortunately, the volcano was more active than it had been for many years, and as we approached the lake the heat became very intense. In our slow progress through steam and stifling gas over the lava, we crossed a bridge which spanned a chasm some twenty feet in width. Mr. H—— said that he had been down in the crater when this chasm had opened. It was late in the afternoon, and he was alone. Suddenly the cliffs trembled; there was a noise like muffled thunder, and the chasm opened at his feet; he followed it to its narrowest point, leaped across, and ran up the path along the cliffs, escaping without accident; but he met a company of guides hurrying to his rescue, greatly alarmed for his safety. A few months before my visit a hut had been destroyed by the lava, which had been erected near the fiery lake for the convenience of tourists who came down into the crater at night; after this it was considered prudent that night visits be discontinued.

We dismounted near the ruins of the hut, leaving our horses, and proceeded to the edge of the lake on foot. Every moment the clouds of steam seemed to grow more dense, and the gas which we inhaled became so oppressive that breathing was difficult, and we were forced to cover our mouths with our handkerchiefs. Fortunately a favouring wind lifted the heavy vapour and carried it away, and the scene that revealed itself was indescribable. Before us stretched a sheet of molten lava one thousand feet in length and six hundred in width, the surface covered with a greyish film, which was crossed with a thousand white-hot seams; from these leaped innumerable flames, waving and bending and dancing like goblin torches. Near the centre rose and fell two mighty fountains of fire fully forty feet in height, leaping into the air and subsiding with a terrific roar. The mass was comparatively still near where we stood, but now and then the grey surface would wrinkle ominously, lift slowly, and sink, with little jets of smoke breaking out here and there. It was a grim intimation that it was a calm not to be trusted — a reminder that the molten mass might at any moment stream over the margin upon which we had a precarious foothold, and over which, indeed, through field-glasses, we saw the grey, smoky cascade pouring the next morning.

While we were watching the tremendous spectacle our Hawaiian guides were unconcernedly making what they called "specimens," dipping coins into the lava from the point of a cleft stick, which smoked and burned in the process.

The awful lake was never calm for a moment; the white-hot seams in the bubbling mass opened and closed, the flames leaped up and died away and leaped up again like flaring flambeaux, and over all shone the fierce light of the two appalling geysers. It was little wonder that the natives formerly believed that it was inhabited by Pelé, the most cruel of their deities, whose wrath could be propitiated only by frequent offerings of living sacrifices. We stood watching the impressive spectacle in silence, fascinated by its unearthly grandeur, until a guide reminded us that it was growing late, and that we must retrace our path across the lava before nightfall. We walked back to the ruined hut, remounted our horses, and returned to the cliff, up which the horses carried us in safety. Evening was closing in, stormy clouds floated across the sky, and over the scene of desolation below us, the rising mist and smoke and the glow of the lake of fire, hung the pale horn of the crescent moon.

CHAPTER XXI.

SOCIAL LIFE.

THE excellence of the servants, the perfection of the climate, the absence of many of the ills against which house-keepers wage ceaseless war in England and the United States, as well as of the varied amusements which are offered the public in American and European cities, have brought the art of entertaining, as it is understood in Honolulu, very nearly to perfection. People have been thrown upon their own resources, and, there being neither theatre nor opera to distract their attention, have made their dinners and luncheons and picnics a compensating substitute.

The reciprocity treaty with the United States, which has been already mentioned, and which, it will be remembered, was negotiated in 1876, revolutionised the commercial and social status of the Islands. Up to that time, while there was no oppressive poverty, neither was there any very great wealth, except among a few of the highest chiefs and chiefesses; and their possessions were mostly in land, much of it uncultivated, so that they had no great excess of ready money, and lived simply and unostentatiously.

When Mark Twain visited the Islands in 1866, Honolulu contained, as he states, "between twelve and fifteen thousand inhabitants." He found "a place of contrasts, with dwellings built of straw, *adobe*, and cream-coloured coral cut into oblong blocks and laid in cement; also a great number of neat white cottages with green window-shutters." There were none of the "flat front yards like billiard-tables with iron fences around them," such as he had seen in San Francisco. "I saw these houses," he writes, "surrounded by ample yards, and shaded by tall trees, through whose dense foliage the sun could scarcely penetrate . . . huge-bodied, wide-spreading forest trees, with strange names and strange appearance — trees that cast a shadow like a thunder-cloud, and were able to stand alone without being tied to green poles. In place of fish wriggling around in glass globes, assuming countless shades of distortion through the magnifying and diminishing quality of their prison, I saw cats — Tom cats, Mary Ann cats, long-tailed cats, bob-tailed cats, wall-eyed cats, cross-eyed cats, grey cats, black cats, white cats, yellow cats, striped cats, spotted cats, tame cats, wild cats, singed cats, individual cats, groups of cats, platoons of cats, companies of cats, regiments of cats, armies of cats, multitudes of cats, millions of cats, and all of them sleek, fat, lazy, and sound asleep. I looked on a multitude of people, some white, in white coats, vests, pantaloons, and even white-cloth shoes, made snowy daily with chalk laid on every morning; but the majority of the people were almost as dark as negroes, — women with comely features, fine dark eyes, and rounded forms, inclining to the voluptuous, and clad in a single bright-red or white garment that fell free and unconfined from shoulder to heel, long black hair falling loose and encircled with wreaths of natural flowers of a brilliant carmine tint; plenty of dark men in various costumes and some with nothing on but a battered stove-pipe hat, tilted on the nose, and a very scant breech-cloth; certain smoke-dried children were clad in nothing but sunshine — a very neat-fitting and picturesque apparel indeed."

The changes that have taken place since this was written have been remarkable. A city with tram-lines, electric lights, water-works, police, well-filled shops, with handsome residences and villas, has entirely effaced the old town of thirty years ago. The native in his silk hat and breech-cloth has been gathered to his fathers long ago, and the single red garment of the women has been abandoned for the be-flounced, modernised *holoku*, or, worse still, for fashionable gowns and French corsets. The children who were primitively clothed in sunshine have grown up, and, after having been taught in the public schools, the Royal School for Boys or the Kawaiahao Seminary for Girls, are now influential members of society, and their children trot to school morning and noon in the neatest of print frocks and white pinafores, or cleanly coats and trousers. They have kept nothing but their love of flowers, their dark hair and eyes, and their dark skin, and even the latter has seen several variations in tint from infusion of alien blood in later generations.

The men of the lower classes are labourers, preferring employment on ships or about the docks to tilling the soil; or they are mechanics. Those a grade higher are clerks, a few have gone into the professions, and others have been employed in the Government offices. Mr. Thurston in his handbook has called attention to the fact that the Speaker of the House in the last Legislature was a native. Education has had the same effect upon the Hawaiians that it has had upon the natives of India and the Maoris of New Zealand. It has made them unwilling to work at manual labour; and the law, which they prefer to follow, with the limited number of clerkships at their disposal, is hopelessly overcrowded.

The admirable Manual Training School, founded and endowed by Mrs. Bishop, may afford some relief, since upon the farm connected with it and in the workshops excellent instruction is given under competent and well-trained teachers, most of them from institutions of technology in the United States. Scientific farming on the allotments which the natives can now purchase at low rates ought to be very remunerative; for, where it is fertile at all, the soil is extraordinarily productive, and almost everything except cereals and the fruits that are indigenous to colder climates can be produced.

The effect of the reciprocity treaty was immediate. Plantations were multiplied, the old improved, the cultivation of cane being carried on after the best methods, and the mills being not only furnished with all the newest improved machinery, but the American managers in several instances having invented labour-saving appliances of the greatest value, like the ingenious "shredder," which rapidly tears the cane to pieces, simplifying the work of extracting the juice, patented a few years ago by Mr. John A. Scott, of the Hilo Sugar Company. Indeed, a list of inventions made by practical sugar manufacturers in the Islands would be as surprising as it is interesting.

The industry not only doubled but trebled, and the sugar-planters made great fortunes — a state of prosperity in which their employés shared. They built fine houses, which were luxuriously furnished and supplied with all the accessories — baths, electric lights, telephones, and electric bells — that one would find in a modern mansion in Chicago or New York. My friends the W——'s, whose guest I had

the privilege to be for three delightful months, had
their own dynamo, which furnished the light for the
house, the stables, and the billiard-room.   Their
grounds were finely cultivated, the main avenue
being planted with rows of royal palms — a long
remove, all this, from the little white houses with
green blinds of Mark Twain's memory.

The usual breakfast-hour in the Islands is eight or
half-past eight o'clock, and the meal is American
rather than English.   Like the Americans, the
people are coffee-drinkers, not tea-drinkers.   There
are very few houses in which five-o'clock tea is
served.   Breakfast begins, as in the United States,
with fresh fruit, oranges, guavas sliced and served
with sugar and cream, or delicious strawberries,
which ripen all the year round.   There are the same
varieties of hot cakes that are included in an American breakfast *menu*, and one at least that is not.
This is the very dream of a hot cake.   It is made of
the root of the *taro*, boiled until it is quite soft,
then it is mashed and beaten into a light batter, a
little salt added, and nothing more, and baked in
muffin tins in a hot oven; it is eaten with butter,
and with a cup of the incomparable *kona* coffee —
the indigenous coffee — it would satisfy an epicure.
With this are served steak, chops, or salt fish, eggs
and toast, with potatoes cooked in various ways.
For luncheon there are usually cold meats, cold
bread, or hot biscuits — biscuit as the term is used

in America — with a compote of stewed mangoes, which is very delicious, potatoes again, with cake, fruit, and tea; the tea, as it will be observed, being taken in the middle of the day, one o'clock being the ordinary luncheon hour. A dinner is like the ordinary dinner anywhere, with soup, joint, entrées, sweets, dessert, and coffee, claret being the wine in common use, with champagne for more festive occasions.

Ladies have their day at home, and are punctilious in the matter of returning calls, keeping a conscientious account of their visiting list. An "at home" in one of these delightful houses is certainly a very satisfactory form of entertainment; it has neither the exaggerated show and parade of an American reception, nor the stiffness and formality that frequently attend the same function in England. In what constitutes society the ladies are all acquainted, not only with each other, but with all each other's kith and kin, like old county families in England. But, unlike old county families in England, they are so accustomed to strangers in their midst, that the peripatetic tourist, who always comes bristling with letters of introduction, is received with an unfailing kindness, although their boundless hospitality has been sorely taxed for the past twenty years and grievously abused times without number. Unlike the old county families again, these globe-trotters are received into full communion, and it is a point

in Honolulu etiquette that no subject shall be introduced or discussed in their presence upon which the
visitors are not at least moderately well informed,
and upon which they too cannot freely talk. You
never hear any of that "Yes, dear Julia is still
frightfully ill, poor thing; the Smythes think she
will not recover in time to go with them to Norway,"
or "Sir Reginald came home yesterday, and Lady
Ellen with him. Fancy!" which echoes through
London drawing-rooms during the season, and makes
the outsider feel as if he were an atom on the outer-
most rim of the universe. To discuss dear Julia or
Sir Reginald or Lady Ellen before strangers who
had never heard their names before would be considered ill-bred, and in this Honolulu etiquette is
American rather than English. At these entertainments, where every one talks with animation and
amiability, where the less well-known guests are
carefully introduced, there is usually a musical programme, and cakes, fruits, and ices are served in the
lanai or on the verandah.

Swimming and riding are two favourite amusements, and in both accomplishments women, foreign-
born Hawaiians (those born in the islands of
American or European parents), with the new-comers
and natives, are experts. Every one rides astride.
There are no such horse-women in the world; they
sit perfectly erect, and go like the wind over the
roughest roads and the wildest, steepest bridle-paths

17

up the mountains. One of the most accomplished riders in Honolulu at the time of my visit was Miss G——, the daughter of the German Consul. I remember an amusing circumstance. She was calling at the American Legation, and when she rose to go one of the American naval officers who happened to be there at the same time escorted her to the gate, where her horse was tied. He looked at the saddle dubiously, then at the pretty rider in her kilted habit, and said hesitatingly and much embarrassed, "I would assist you to mount, Miss G——, if — if — if *you were using an ordinary saddle.*" "Thanks," she replied, smilingly comprehending his dilemma, "but I do not require any assistance." And she sprang upon her horse and dashed away with the grace of a young centaur. The bewildered sailor looked after her much as he might have watched the rapid flight of a strange but interesting bird.

On seeing the security and ease with which these Hawaiian women sit in their saddles, one wonders that there ever could have been any prejudice against women riding in a manner that, like most other comfortable and sensible fashions, has been monopolised by men. Certain it is no man could be induced to twist his knee round the pommel and balance himself in a side-saddle, as is considered the fit and proper thing for women. One needs only to see the ordinary and the Hawaiian fashion contrasted —the rider in her divided skirts seated on her horse as if she were a part of it, and the woman in the conventional habit, more or less insecure and a good deal more ungraceful — to realise how much the first is to be preferred.

Women of all classes and conditions swim as well as they ride.   The warm climate is partially accountable for this, with the perfection of the bathing. Outside the reefs the sea swarms with sharks, which infest the entire Southern Pacific.   But the reefs form a barrier which they rarely ever cross, so that the lagoon is not only an ideal but perfectly safe bathing-place.   One swims in Honolulu as one walks or drives elsewhere, quite as a matter of course.   At a luncheon given at a seaside villa, where the *lanai* frequently fronts the sea, its steps leading down into the water, the first question is not "Would you like to walk about the garden?" but "Will you have a swim?"   The question is almost invariably answered in the affirmative, and the guests go to their rooms, put on the bathing-dresses that are furnished them, return, pass through the *lanai*, have their swim, and a comfortable lounge afterwards before luncheon is served.   Usually no men are present at these luncheons; but it would make no difference if there were, for, after the American fashion, which seems so shocking to English prudery, men and women bathe together.

Frequently riding and swimming parties are combined.   Riding out to Waikiki on a moonlight night on horseback, the entire party take a dip in the warm lagoon, which is followed by a gay little supper and the ride home afterwards, frequently long past midnight.   Balls and swimming parties are also much in favour, and I had the good fortune to be present at one such entertainment during my first visit.   It was given in the villa at Waikiki to the officers of H.M.S. *Garnet*, and some of the officers of the American cruisers, by an American gentleman and his wife.   There were a number of handsome Hawaiian girls among the guests, almost all in white gowns, which contrasted pleasingly with the blue and gold of the officers' uniforms.

The music was furnished by the King's Singing Boys — Kalakaua's quartette.   They played upon a very sweet-toned native instrument somewhat like a mandolin, and not only played for the dancers, but sang.   The waltzing went on until midnight; then the entire company suddenly dispersed to rooms set apart for them; ball-gowns and uniforms were changed for bathing-dresses, and after a short interval they returned to the *lanai*, thence to a narrow quay jutting far out into the water.   The Singing Boys, all uniformed in white and wearing *leis*, left the verandah where they had stationed themselves, came out upon the quay, and to the sound of their singing and playing, which still went on, men and women leaped into the sea and swam to the strains of music.

The moon was full; in the distance rose the mountains, cloud-veiled and mysterious; the palms along the beach rustled in the night wind; and with the foam of the surf breaking upon the reef, with the shimmering waves stretching to the horizon, the tropical sky studded with stars that even the full moon could not quench, the wild melancholy voices of the singers blending with the lap and beat of the waves, it was all Hawaiian — a characteristic bit of the poetical and fascinating life.

When they were tired of swimming, mermen and mermaids came out upon the quay and became ordinary human beings once more; they returned to the villa, resumed uniforms and ball-dresses, and the dance went on.   Dawn was breaking over Diamond Head when the King's Singing Boys dismissed them with the enchanting "*Hawaii Ponoi*," which is the Hawaiian substitute for "God save the Queen."

The arrival of American or European cruisers is always the beginning of a special season of festivity. This is peculiarly true when the ships are American, not only because of the natural affiliation of the foreign-born Hawaiian, who is usually of American descent, with his countrymen once removed, but because there is generally a renewal of old acquaintance among the officers and residents.   There is hardly one of the older officers in the American Navy who has not been in Honolulu once or oftener, and in Honolulu albums there are series of photographs of these gallant sailors, taken at various ages during their recurring visits. I was shown one photograph of a dashing and handsome young lieutenant who had been there in 1868, and had returned during the Revolution grey, grizzled, and taciturn, his face roughened and furrowed by the gales of more than twenty years — a man whom Time had sobered as he sobers the best of us.

American naval officers, though perhaps possessed of less private means than many English and European officers, are liberally paid, as public service goes. At any rate they are liberal and hospitable to a fault. There is always on board a succession of entertainments of greater or less elaborateness, with officers' receptions. One very splendid ball was given on board the *Boston* when political matters had quieted down somewhat, and before the arrival of Mr. Blount. The decks were covered with awnings of flags, and the sides screened with palms; there were garlands of the fragrant stephanotis and *mailé*, and the supper-room was beautifully dressed with flowers and ferns. In the centre of the supper-table was a mirror, and upon this a beautiful model of the ship, made by one of the seamen, while the cloth was bordered with more of the waxen clusters and wreaths of stephanotis.

The guests were brought out to the ship in launches, and the excellent band of the flag-ship furnished the music. I had a stately armchair at the upper part of the deck, where I looked on enjoying the picturesque scene intensely, and where I had no less than seven separate relays of cake and ice cream offered me by my attentive hosts. One of them, more courageous than the rest, if that were possible, insisted on carrying me down the gangway that I might see with my own eyes the glory of the supper-table. He assured me that his wife was an invalid, and that, when he was on leave, he was accustomed to carry her all about the house. I did not doubt it, but nevertheless would not consent to put his gallantry to such a test, though I managed the descent after another fashion.

The English and Japanese officers — the latter talking French very fluently when they could not speak English — were resplendent in showy uniforms, besides which those of the Americans looked modest in the extreme. Yet I preferred my own countrymen, who, if they were outshone in the matter of gold lace and brass buttons, were certainly not lacking in any of the essentials that are the characteristics, natural and acquired, of what the service terms "an officer and a gentleman."

CHAPTER XXII.

A FEW uneventful weeks slipped by upon my return from Hilo, and while deliberations were still going on concerning the new Constitution an opportunity was given me to visit New Zealand and Australia, of which I gladly availed myself.

Up to within a few hours of sailing, however, my departure was uncertain. I had written to my newspaper asking leave of absence, but had received no reply. The *Alameda* was sighted at ten o'clock, and having been detained by rough weather was to remain in port but two hours. The letters I had expected by her were not received, so I took the matter into my own hands and decided to go without permission. I had but two hours in which to pack my trunks, and was intent upon this when Mr. W—— telephoned that the captain had decided to remain until evening. That gave me an opportunity to breathe again, and to finish my preparations with some sort of system and deliberation. In the afternoon President Dole called personally, and brought me the passport which I was required to have — a courtesy and an honour which was thoroughly appreciated. At nine the W——s drove me down to the dock. There was the inevitable concert in the hotel grounds, the streets were flooded with moonlight, and the air was sweet with the fragrance of jasmine and orange flowers. There was a ball on board the U. S. cruiser *Adams*, which had succeeded the *Mohican*, the *Boston*, and the *Alliance*. The strains of the band came softly across the water, and the forms of the dancers could be seen floating along the brilliantly lighted deck. The steamer had been coaling, and when she was ready to cast off a solid line of natives extending from bow to stern pushed against her side, and so literally shoved her from the edge of the wharf.

Good-byes were exchanged again and again, the departing ones were smothered in *leis*, the last words were spoken, and we were off. The seas which we were to cross stretched out illimitable before us, a sheet of shimmering silver; the stars hung low overhead; and I sat upon the deck alone long after the other passengers had turned in, watching the lights of Honolulu fade in the distance, enjoying the rush of the waves and the enchantment of the tropical night. The *Alameda*, on which I had taken passage down, and the *Mariposa*, returning, both belonged to the Oceanic Steamship Line of San Francisco; they were clean and comfortable, the cabins large and airy, the service good, and the table excellent.

Both called at Apia in Samoa, and this was one of the most interesting parts of the journey, partly because of the loveliness of the shore, but most of all because I had the great good fortune to see Robert Louis Stevenson: this, however, was on the return voyage. Samoa from the sea is much more verdant than the Sandwich Islands. There is the same volcanic formation, and in profile the mountains are peaked and pinnacled, rounding here and there into domes and minarets, covered with banana, mango, bread-fruit, and the *ti* trees to their summits. When we woke in the early morning, the breeze blowing through the open port was like the moist, heavy, scented air of a greenhouse. I rose, dressed hurriedly, swallowed a cup of tea, and then went on deck to go ashore with Professor Koebele, who had also taken passage in the *Alameda en route* to Australia. He was familiar with Samoa as with all the other South Sea islands.

The deck was already taken possession of by the favoured few — natives permitted to come on board and offer their wares to the passengers, — wares that consisted of *tapa*, beautiful mats, shells, baskets, and the airy native dancing-dress that consists of a scanty fringe of green and scarlet wood fibre of some sort, and fragile little rings of horn beautifully inlaid with silver, which broke with the slightest blow. We were anchored about a mile out, and all around the ship the sea was covered with boats —

the narrow, apparently clumsy craft of the Polynesians, which are kept afloat only by the huge outrigger with its heavy, curved timbers. The natives
were magnificent creatures. We had grown somewhat familiar with them during the World's Fair
in Chicago, where a company of them — those we
had seen *en route* in Honolulu — formed an interesting part of the great ethnological exhibition in the
Midway Plaisance. They were big, burly fellows,
laughing and chattering like magpies; they had not
yet acquired the bad habit of wearing European
clothes, although I was told that the remarkble draperies that were a substitute — prints of gorgeous
colour and alarming designs — were a Manchester
product. It seems that the English cotton-spinning
town has a monopoly in the manufacture of these
prints, and drives a thriving trade, not only with
the natives of Samoa, but of Tahiti, the Fijis, and
other groups. Having long catered to the barbarous
taste of 'Arriet, the English manufacturers find in
these simple savages only wider fields where they
can carry their abnormal ideas in design and colour
to the last baleful extreme.

The outrigger boats were loaded with articles like
those that had been brought on deck — tapa, mats,
prints, mangoes, alligator pears, the most delicious
pineapples in the world, and big round oranges,
sweet as honey, with a thin greenish rind. We
selected our boat out of the dozens that offered

themselves, and were rowed to the little rickety landing-stage across the harbour. The rusting skeleton of the German man-of-war *Adler*, which lay high and dry on a sheet of coral, was a grim reminder of the great tidal wave of March 15th, 1889, when the American vessels the *Vandalia* and the *Trenton* were wrecked, and the English ship *Calliope* escaped by steaming out to sea in the teeth of the hurricane. Wreckage companies had collected all that could be saved of the American ships. There were on shore, however, many melancholy reminders in the way of broken masts and weather-beaten timbers. One wonders how the town could have escaped a general inundation, as the beach at this point is not much more than ten feet above the water at high tide. But while the great ships were wrenched from their moorings, and beaten and battered to pieces like egg-shells, in Apia but three or four signs over shop doors were blown down; there was no damage to property and no loss of life. The scene of the tragedy was the treacherous harbour, which had lifted its huge billows like a beast of prey roused from slumber; and those on land could only witness the frightful wreck, men torn by twos and threes from the rigging where they clung, some of them for hours, as the waters, rising higher and higher, swept them away. A survivor has related how the men in the lower rigging, biding their time, talked calmly and collectedly to those hanging to the ropes above them, leaving messages for families and friends, until they were washed into the sea, those to whom they had committed these last messages dying in their turn and in the same way. In Honolulu I heard a thrilling experience — a reminiscence of this terrible wreck. One of the men had been watching, with a sort of fascinated dread, how the water rushed into the hold of the ship, and then, as the vessel lurched, shot up into a great spouting geyser some thirty feet into the air. It occurred to him what an awful fate it would be to be sucked down into the darkness of the hold, and there battered to pieces: in the flash of an eye he was caught and wrenched from the mast where he thought himself secure, and, blinded, strangled, agonising, was swept into the dreaded gulf! Fortunately the wave in its recession carried him out again; he snatched at the ropes, caught them, and was saved.

To return to the Samoans. Both men and women wear the hair cut short; and either as a final touch of extreme elegance, or for hygienic reasons, they cover the head with a plaster of lime, which, when removed, has not only accomplished a good deal in the way of extermination, but has reduced the hair to a peculiar shade of reddish brown. Near the landing-stage, when we came ashore, were two youths who spoke excellent English — pupils, as they told us, in the Mission School, and, without being in the least obtrusive, they attached themselves to us forthwith, and remained with us the entire day. Their brown skin was like velvet in its softness and smoothness — a race characteristic intensified by frequent bathing and liberal use of palm oil. Like the Hawaiians, the Samoans have long straight hair — or would have, if they let it grow — and they resemble them in many ways. The Hawaiian language is perfectly intelligible to both the Samoan and the Maori, an ethnological problem that has never been entirely solved, as the islands are some hundreds of leagues apart. The difference in many of their terms is scarcely noticeable: for example, the Hawaiian greets one with the musical "*Aloha*," and the Samoan with the equally musical "*Telofa*." Both have the same knowledge of mat-weaving and tapa-making; their houses are unlike, the Hawaiian grass hut being much more artistic and beautiful than the Samoan hut, which is simply a sort of ellipse, the roof thatched with palm boughs supported upon timbers placed at regular intervals, the undressed trunks of small trees. The interior of the Samoan houses which I visited were much cleaner than the Hawaiian houses; the floor was thickly covered with pebbles, and over these were spread mats, which were frequently aired and sunned. In each was a sort of recess, wherein was piled the food supply — bananas, oranges, pineapples, bread-fruit, yams, and mangoes. There were curtains of matting that could be lowered to exclude the rain.

We walked through the village, following a road leading out to the residence of King Malietoa, an unpretentious bungalow, where he supported his royal state upon a stipend of $75 a month, which was allowed him by the triple protectorate. There was at that time one of the chronic outbursts of rebellion. The followers of the banished King, his rival, who had been deported to one of the other islands, had risen to strike a final blow for what they considered their rights. They had been furnished with rifles and ammunition by conscienceless white traders. We met a number of prisoners being brought in, prisoners and guards walking single file, bare-footed, bare-headed, with their cropped hair smeared with lime, only the scantiest bits of Manchester print about their loins, and their legs tattooed in a pattern of fine stripes to the knee: it gave them the appearance of being oddly but neatly clothed. The guards carried Winchester rifles over their shoulders, and each and every prisoner — a black cotton umbrella! It was like a scene out of a comic opera. They smiled and showed their white teeth, and greeted us with a wave of the hand and a musical "*Telofa*" as they swept past, tall, brawny, broad-chested fellows, walking erect and with the elastic tread of tigers. We also passed a comely little lady whose garb was a mongrel Samoan-American combination. "One of the King's women," was the information vouchsafed by the two boys, both of whom trotted at our heels like a pair of brown spaniels.

Malietoa is the most approachable of sovereigns, and there is little ceremony in securing an audience with his royal highness. He was not at home, and I am ashamed to confess that we walked in, nevertheless, and strolled about the house. One of the servants informed me that he had gone to take his morning bath. His breakfast was spread upon a verandah in the rear, and must have been quite cold by the time he returned. There was fish that had been cooked some time, with bread and fruit. The tablecloth was wrinkled and awry, and the breakfast service was thick, heavy, cheap stone-ware. In the main room the floor was covered with mats, and on the walls were coloured lithographs of the late Emperor William "der Grosse" and of the Prince and Princess of Wales, each surrounded by a border of Samoan fans. On the table in the centre of the room were a large kerosene lamp and a big family Bible, printed in Hawaiian and bound in scarlet morocco — a gift of King Kalakaua, who at one time had a consular representative (and a very bad one) in Apia. There was also a copy of "The Book of Mormon," presented by Gibson, Kalakaua's Mormon Premier — a curious jumble of religions certainly, underneath which the King no doubt retained a solid stratum of his aboriginal heathenism. In the royal bed-chamber, across the threshold of which we did not venture — our sole and saving qualm of propriety — we saw the King's bed covered with the most wonderful counterpane — great scarlet lions tramping along and thrusting out one paw, on a background of white. It was a canopied affair, and on one of the four posts hung his Majesty's embroidered smoking-cap, which was exactly like that which admiring female parishioners are supposed to embroider for the curate's birthday present. Had we been in England there would have been a register, and we could have left our autographs, thereby betraying ourselves as trespassers of the most shameless and boldest type. But you do not leave your autograph in Samoa — it is not yet sufficiently civilised — and so we escaped the righteous punishment for our misdeeds.

As we had approached the confines of the King's domain the force of heredity asserted itself in our two attendants. They said in unison, in an awed undertone, *"The King's!"* and would approach no farther. But we were deceived if we supposed ourselves rid of them. They simply fell back, and stretched themselves in the shade of a mango tree, kicking up their heels with the most amiable patience. When we reappeared they sprang up and joined us with beaming smiles and renewed ardour.

As we returned to the village we dropped into the native Roman Catholic church to hear the Mass. It was a queer sight — the worshippers were squatting about on the mat-covered floor, going through the

service with all the proverbial enthusiasm of prose-
lytes. The high altar was not completed, so the
priest was officiating at an improvised altar at
the entrance, stopping occasionally to rush down the
steps and whack an obstreperous dog over the back
with an umbrella, and then resuming the service
where it had been interrupted.   Two comely Samoan
nuns — and odd enough their brown faces looked
framed in coif and veil — were moving softly about
the chancel, which they were dressing with flowers.
As we came away a tall, burly man stopped to take
the holy water, and one of our lads mimicked him
rather rudely. I rebuked him, and asked, "Are n't
you a Catholic?" He drew the scrap of rag with
which his middle was girded a little closer about
him, and looked me in the face with as much of an
expression of scorn as the Samoan countenance was
capable, and replied loftily, "*I'm* Church of
England."

We made a little detour to call upon one of the
chiefs, an old friend of Professor Koebele. The hut
stood somewhat apart, in a grassy space shaded by
mangoes and orange trees. The chief, a noble old
man with an intelligent face and of great dignity, sat
just within the entrance of the hut. Opposite, two
women were making *kava*, a slightly intoxicating
drink prepared from the roots of the *awa*, in common use throughout Polynesia. The old process of
preparation was mastication, but fortunately for me

it was no longer in use. The women were pounding the fibres in a calabash, water being added at intervals. The hut was filled with people — many men who had been fighting, and whose wounded arms had been bandaged by the English surgeon. When we entered and I was introduced, the chief ordered one of the women to get me a seat, and she brought forward a little chest, upon which I sat during the call. She was also requested to procure me some refreshment, which was easily done. There was no ceremony about it, and none of the fuss of boiling a tea-kettle or cutting and spreading bread and butter and arranging a tray; the smiling handmaiden ran outside the hut, knocked some oranges from a convenient tree, returned, knelt, and sliced the fruit, which she presented daintily on the end of the knife. Professor Koebele and Dr. Casey, the ship's surgeon, who had joined us, presented both men and women with cigarettes, of which they are extravagantly fond, and which they carry over one ear until they are ready to smoke. When the *kava* was done, those who could clapped their hands three times; the chief waved the bowl toward me, and it was presented by one of the women in the most respectful way. The beverage is not agreeable to the untrained palate, having a smooth, soapy taste, and I quaffed it neither long nor deep.

In the *lanai* of the hotel I met Mr. Lloyd Osbourne and his sister Mrs. Strong — a very handsome, dark-eyed young woman, beautifully dressed in a white duck gown. They were both loaded with papers and letters, an enormous quantity, which the steamer had just brought. They were both lamenting the non-arrival of a certain hurdy-gurdy that had been ordered from Sydney, and which they urgently required for festival occasions.

Mr. Osbourne invited me out to Vailima; but as our stay was so short I was forced to decline, to my regret at that time, and my greater regret since. Mr. Stevenson was hard at work upon "Weir of Hermiston," and could not spare the time to come down to the ship, as he usually did. I did not see him, consequently, until I returned in May. Mr. Osbourne spoke with much indignation of the fighting going on among the Samoans. "They are like children," he said, "and are just about as fit to be trusted with firearms." And he described their strange manner of warfare — the belligerents declaring a truce, sitting down and eating together in perfect friendliness, then, after a rest and a smoke, exclaiming, "Now it's time to fight," and banging away again. It was not child's play, this part of it — for they fought to the death, and, until it was prohibited by heavy penalties, cut off the heads of their enemies as trophies for the King. The morgue at the time was filled with bodies, which I was invited to inspect, but which I need hardly say I had no desire to see. We sailed at one o'clock,

Samoa vanishing in a haze of silver rain, through which the beautiful Samoan doves darted and soared, their glistening plumage shining in the sunlight that presently broke through the shower.

New Zealand, with its incomparable climate, its wild and characteristic scenery, the high intelligence of its people, its well-built cities, with their schools, universities, libraries, and museums, and, above all, the justice which has given to women a share in the dignity of the State, seemed to me the flower of the Australasian colonies. I liked the country much better in every way than Australia, so far as I was able to judge during my brief visit. I made the journey overland through Rotarua to Napier, thence to Wellington, Christchurch, and Dunedin, meeting delightful friends everywhere, and crossed to Melbourne, and proceeded from Melbourne to Sydney by rail. There I caught the *Mariposa*, after a fortnight's rest and over six weeks of rapid and fatiguing travel. It seemed good to see the ship again. She was like home, the faces of the officers were like the benevolent countenances of near kindred, and whatever else might have been lacking the flag of my country was an evidence that her decks were virtually American soil.

We were uncertain as to whether we should land at Apia on the return; it depended on the weather, the captain said. Fortunately this was propitious, and the landing was made.

Among the passengers was Miss Ide, the daughter of the American Chief Justice of Samoa, who invited me to lunch when we went on shore. But she had been long absent from home, and I felt some scruples in intruding at this first family reunion upon her return.

Just as I was about to leave the ship a boat came out rowed by an unusually comely crew of Samoans. In the bow stood a tall, slender figure clad in spotless white from head to foot. It was Robert Louis Stevenson. He stood directing his men with the utmost gentleness, speaking so softly that he could not be heard at the ship's side when they approached the gangway. His face was swarthy and seemed greatly emaciated, and his large dark eyes were like two burning stars. The hands were thin, nervous, and expressive. Few faces have half the expression of those long, slender, delicate fingers. Stevenson was a great favourite with the ship's officers on both the *Alameda* and the *Mariposa*, and as usual he and his family lunched on board. There were no ice machines in Apia, and ices were always specially prepared on these occasions — a rare treat. With his great genius there was nothing of arrogance in his manner to the simple, warm-hearted officers; he was as unaffected and straightforward as they, and met their cordial advances more than half-way. His men rowed him to the gangway, and he sprang lightly from the boat and ran up the steps like a cat. He was sincerely glad to see his friends, and they were as genuinely delighted to see him, and crowded round him while very hearty greetings were exchanged.

I was not destined to see Vailima after all. Mr. Lloyd Osbourne, who had invited me before, had gone with Mrs. Stevenson to New Zealand, where she was taking the baths at Rotarua for rheumatism, from which she was suffering greatly. My friend, a certain Irish purser, whom Stevenson mentions in the Vailima Letters, insisted that I should stay and be introduced to him; but just then there was a good reason why the whole race of newspaper correspondents should be held in disfavour by him.

Some time before a writer for a Western paper had gone down to Samoa, and had visited Vailima, which was a sort of house of free entertainment for every tourist who happened to be passing that way. The man had been kindly received and hospitably entertained. He departed, and, with the most cruel treachery, repaid the kindness of his host by writing a scurrilous attack upon him, in which his family were included. However innocent they might be, I could not feel that other correspondents, coming after this specimen, could or would be very welcome, and I did not feel disposed to test Stevenson's forbearance; but I shall always regret that I did not at least remain on board to luncheon with him, as I was urged to do.

I had on this second visit no kind and clever Professor Koebele as guide, philosopher, and friend. I went ashore with a fretful, peevish Englishman instead, who enjoyed nothing, saw nothing, and found fault with everything. He growled at the heat, which was intense; he grumbled at the flies, which were certainly numerous and vicious; the natives worried him; and there were certainly some bad smells, which neither he nor any one else could have enjoyed. But all these were the sort of ills that the experienced traveller learns to accept as a matter of course, a part of the price one must pay for seeing the kingdoms of this world and the glory of them; and the "tuppenny ha'penny" dominion of Samoa, with its king on an allowance of $75 a month, was not an exception to the rule. The sun did pour down with intense fierceness — that I will admit; but all the ills combined were nothing to the complaints of my petulant escort. Finally I said, "It is so very warm that I think I shall go back to the ship. I have visited Apia before, and have seen it all. But don't let me interrupt your visit; I will get a boat, and the men will take me out to the ship."

I was afraid he would come trailing along, even after this palpable dismissal. He did hesitate a moment and appeared undecided, but finally concluded to remain, to my great satisfaction. I went back to the landing-stage, called a boat, and stepped into it, sitting high in the stern. My face was a blazing scarlet, and I must have presented rather a queer appearance — a solitary female sitting on my elevated perch, with the four stalwart natives at the oars.

I was undeniably in a bad temper, and they looked at me dubiously, as one inspects an animal which it is better not to disturb. Finally their overweening curiosity got the better of their doubts; they probably had never had just such a passenger, a grim, laconic, lone woman, like some sort of figure-head at the wrong end of the boat.

" You — you got no old man ? " the boldest of them finally ventured.

" No," I replied curtly.

" You never have no old man ? " he persisted.

" No," I answered again, with still sterner emphasis.

They all smiled, then broke into a good-natured laugh, no doubt mentally congratulating the non-existent "old man" on escaping a fate altogether undesirable. Mr. Stevenson had gone when I returned to the ship, and we sailed within an hour. A few months afterwards I heard of his sudden death.

While the ship was in Sydney she had been docked and her keel cleaned, and she made one of the quickest voyages from Australia to Honolulu that had ever been recorded. We entered the harbour on the morning of May 30th. It reminded me of my first visit; for, by a coincidence, it was another American

holiday — Memorial Day.   The *Philadelphia* had
arrived in my absence, one of the largest cruisers in
the American Navy, and she was beautifully decorated; and flags were floating from roofs and flag-
staffs all over the city.   The sky was cloudless, the
water reflecting all the colours of the rainbow, and
vegetation was in the fulness of its perfection.   We
docked at ten o'clock.   My friend, Mrs. W——,
was waiting for me with her carriage, and I was
driven at once to the Government building.   After
a journey of over five thousand miles, contending
with the variable forces of winds and waves, I had
reached Honolulu at ten o'clock on the very day
when the Constitutional Convention had met, and
had just an hour to spare!

The exercises of this opening session of the Convention, which did not adjourn until July, were simple, dignified, and unostentatious, after the manner
in which all the affairs of the Provisional Government
had been conducted.   It was held in one of the
larger rooms of the Government building.   The
President and the Executive Council sat upon the
platform, and there were present the diplomatic
representatives (with the exception of the American
Minister), the officers of the men-of-war then stationed at Honolulu, with the prominent citizens of
the Islands, accompanied by their wives and daughters.   All the windows were open, the bare room was
brilliant with sunshine, and the soft wind rustled in

the historic palms upon the lawn.   There was a very brief address by President Dole, which was translated by an interpreter into Hawaiian for the benefit of native delegates to the Convention whose knowledge of English was not quite perfect.   The exercises occupied but an hour.

I lunched with my friends the W——s, and we then attended the Memorial Day service at the Honolulu cemetery.   It seemed strange, indeed, to witness this solemn ceremony here in this tropical land, in the midst of surroundings far removed and widely different from the scene of that great conflict in which the dead had participated.   There is in Hawaii a Grand Army Post, and upon the 30th of May the graves of its deceased members were decorated with flowers and wreaths and American flags, as had been done throughout the United States, North and South, from the Atlantic to the Pacific, on that day.   There was a procession, with President Dole, the Executive and Advisory Councils, at its head, with the officers of the American and English ships, United States marines, and Hawaiian soldiery, infantry and artillery, with the Government and marine bands, followed by citizens in their carriages.   I had seen the observance of Memorial Day in many parts of the United States; in Chicago where in the miles of marching men were carried the flags of every European nation except Russia — the heterogeneous population putting aside their race hatred and prejudice, uniting to honour the dead who had preserved the land of their adoption, and made possible for them its liberty and its opportunities — and in many a town and village besides; but I had seen nothing that had ever impressed and thrilled me like this, where Europeans, Hawaiians, Americans, Portuguese, Chinese, and Japanese were assembled, each a part of the multitude, sharing in all that was done and listening intently to all that was said.

The bond between the United States and Hawaii seemed trebly strengthened. There they slept, those in whose memory the day was observed, and who upon other soil had suffered hardships and perils incredible, and who had shed their blood in the sacred cause of human liberty. Across the place of their repose fell the shadows of the solemn mountains, "rock-ribbed and ancient as the sun;" hither came the voice of the sea, sounding eternally upon the shore; above them bent the arch of the tropical sky, a flame of blue and gold; and gathered to do them reverence were those, like themselves, who had stood in defence of the right, and were ready to sacrifice their lives, if need be, to accomplish the overthrow of oppression.

I had never seen such flowers; for Europeans, Americans, and Hawaiians alike had remembered their dead. Some of the graves were a solid mass of sombre purple and lavender heliotrope; others were heaped with tuberoses and plumaria; upon others, outlined with *leis*, were simply branches of palm; and still others were strewn with lilies. There were palm branches again with garlands of lilies, and some were covered with gardenia and stephanotis and oleander.

There was an address and singing, after which the people dispersed. In the evening I dined with the President and Mrs. Dole, meeting Admiral Walker, who invited me to visit his flag-ship the following morning.

The Convention continued in session until July, its deliberations being marked by impartial and painstaking consideration of every question destined to affect the well-being of the new Government and of the people, irrespective of class or colour. On July 4th the Republic was formally proclaimed in Honolulu with great rejoicing. The momentous day was ushered in with a salute at sunrise, and at a very early hour the streets were thronged with people, hundreds wearing knots of red, white, and blue ribbon. Both public buildings and private residences were profusely decorated with garlands of flowers, flags, and branches of palm. At nine o'clock President Dole and his Cabinet, with General Soper in command of the Government troops, appeared upon the steps of the Executive building, and looked down upon the thousands who had assembled to participate in the exercises. The President said:

"The movement for popular government which has to-day reached such an important stage in this country began in 1839, when Kauikeaouli, swayed by the light of the new civilisation which was fast dawning upon his kingdom, surrendered his unlimited sovereign power and proclaimed to every man the rights of 'life, limb, liberty, and freedom from oppression, the earnings of his hands, and the productions of his mind.' The progress of this cause, from that day to this, has been irresistible. There have been times, indeed, when it seemed to slacken its pace, and even to turn back on its course, but obstacles only served to give it a chance to gather its strength for swifter advance. The Land Commission and the great *Mahele*, by which the lands of the kingdom were divided between the people, the chiefs, the Government, and the King; the Constitutions of 1853, 1864, 1887; and the proclamation of January 14th, 1893, are the milestones along the way. To-day, as we pass through the gate Beautiful into a new realm full of promise, we set up another milestone greater and grander than all that stand behind us. The end is not yet. The relaxing influences of peace are more demoralising to patriotism than the stern and bracing dangers of war. 'Eternal vigilance is the price of liberty.' There are still great things to be done. There are achievements in free government, as yet unattained, to be striven for — for responses to the fast-growing claim

PRESIDENT DOLE.

that the poor man, the weak man, the ignorant man, shall be recognised, in fact as well as in name, in the body politic. There are new milestones to be set up on heights which are yet to be gained. Let us see to it that our future is worthy of our past and of all the promise of this auspicious day, and that it shall grow therefrom as the tree from the sapling; that freedom shall never come to mean licence in the vocabulary of the Republic; and that the spirit of traffic shall never invade the council chamber or the halls of legislation. And now, in behalf of the men who have carried this cause along, and who have stood ready to defend it with their lives; in behalf of the women who have given it their prayers and their husbands and sons, for the benefit and protection of all the people of this country, of whatsoever race or name; and in gratitude to God whose hand has led us, —I, Sandford B. Dole, President of the Provisional Government of the Hawaiian Islands, by virtue of the charge to me given by the Executive and Advisory Councils of the Provisional Government and by Act dated July 3rd, 1894, proclaim the Republic of Hawaii as sovereign authority over and throughout the Hawaiian Islands from this time forth. And I do declare the Constitution framed and adopted by the Constitutional Convention of 1894 to be the Constitution and the Supreme Law of the Republic of Hawaii, and by the virtue of this Constitution I now assume the office and authority of President thereof. God save the Republic!"

As the last sentence was uttered the guns of the battery boomed a salute to the Hawaiian flag, which was unfurled upon the tower of the building. An old native Hawaiian bared his head to the salute, exclaiming, "There is more patriotism in a pound of that powder than in all the royalism of Hawaii."

Admiral Walker and his staff, with the diplomatic representatives, were present at the proclamation ceremonies, and Chief Justice Judd, whose father had exerted so great an influence in the civilisation of the natives, and Associate Justice Bickerton were the first to take the oath of allegiance. This was administered in the presence of five thousand people. The remainder of the day was devoted to athletic sports and yacht races and to official and private receptions, and in the evening there were brilliant illuminations.

The Constitution thus formally adopted was modelled after that of the United States, and framed specially to simplify annexation, which it anticipated. It was extremely liberal. President Dole, as I have said elsewhere, had been the devoted friend of the natives, and rights and privileges were assured them under the new Government which they had never enjoyed under the domination of their own race.

In this final triumph of liberty an effort was

made to secure equal rights and justice to the female as well as to the male citizens of the new Republic, and in favour of this the Hon. L. A. Thurston laboured strenuously, supported by the most intelligent men and women in the Islands.

There were those, however, who were timid, having yet to learn that justice is eternally an abstract principle into which questions of expediency cannot enter, and with whose administration there can be no temporising, as older governments are slowly realising.

The new Government thus auspiciously established continued to administer public affairs with the moderation and justice which the Provisional Government had manifested from the beginning.   Its pacific rule was but once disturbed, and this was in the native uprising, instigated by the Queen and the adventurers that still gathered about her, in January, 1895.   It was suppressed within little more than a fortnight, the conspirators being tried and sentenced to fine and imprisonment, most of them, however, being afterwards pardoned.   The country has now enjoyed more than three years of uninterrupted peace, during which prosperity has steadily increased.   In the financial report for 1897 the total current revenue for 1896 was $1,997,818.18, and the total expenditure for the same year $1,904,190.92.

"This shows," says Mr. Thurston, "that after paying all running expenses, interest on all loans,

19

and redeeming $16,000 worth of bonds falling due, the Treasury closed the year with a cash surplus over $71,000 greater than at the beginning," — proof that the country is, as he asserts it to be, "self-supporting, solvent, and prosperous." The sums mentioned may seem insignificant to governments whose receipts and expenditures are reckoned by millions, but it must be borne in mind that the entire population of the Islands is but 109,020, many of the natives being merely nominal tax-payers.

Mr. Thurston has thus summarised the form of the new Republic, which I quote verbatim:

"The Government of Hawaii was a monarchy until January, 1893, when Liliuokalani attempted to abrogate the Constitution and promulgate one increasing her power and disfranchising the whites.

"The people thereupon overthrew the monarchy, and established a Provisional Government, January 17th, 1893.

"Later a Constitutional Convention unanimously adopted a Constitution declaring the Republic of Hawaii on July 4th, 1894.

"*The Executive* consists of a President and four Cabinet officers. The President is Sandford Ballard Dole, fifty years of age, Hawaiian born, of American parentage, a graduate of Williams College, a lawyer by profession. He was a judge of the Supreme Court under the monarchy, which position he resigned to accept the leadership of the Revolution, which overturned the monarchy. He is respected and honoured by all classes and factions in the community.

" *The Electorate* consists of all male adult citizens who take an oath of allegiance to the Republic.

" Asiatics are not eligible to citizenship or to vote.

" *The President* has the power of veto, which may be overridden by a two-thirds vote of each House.

" *Character of Laws.* — The foundation of the legal system of the country is the Common Law of England.

" The penal law and practice are codified, and there are no penal offences except those enumerated in the code.

" The civil law, practice, and procedure are partially codified, and are in general as much like those of the several American States as the law of one State is like that of another.

" The text-books and law reports of England and the United States are cited as authority in the courts in the same manner that they are in this country.

" The members of the Supreme and Circuit Court bars are nearly all Americans, or were educated in American law schools. The attorneys in the District Courts are mostly native Hawaiians, educated in Honolulu.

"THE COURTS.

"The main judicial system consists of District and Circuit Courts and a Supreme Court.

"*District Courts.* — There are about thirty District Courts. They have jurisdiction over civil matters involving not more than $300, and over misdemeanours. They also commit, for trial by jury, persons accused of felony, exercising the functions of an American grand jury. The grand-jury system has not been adopted.

"An appeal lies from the District to the Circuit or Supreme Court.

"*Circuit Courts.* — There are four Circuit Courts, with appellate jurisdiction over appeals from the District Courts, and original jurisdiction over all civil suits involving more than $300, and over persons committed for trial for felonies; in all equity, admiralty, and probate cases, and over special proceedings, such as *habeas corpus*, etc. Each Circuit Court is presided over by one judge. All jury trials are held in the Circuit Courts.

"*Juries.* — The same class of cases are tried by jury as in the United States. Juries consist of twelve men, but nine can render a verdict in both civil and criminal cases. Jury can be waived in both civil and criminal cases, except capital cases.

"*The Supreme Court* consists of three judges, with exclusive jurisdiction to decide certain special proceedings, and the validity of elections to the Legislature; concurrent jurisdiction with the Circuit judges concerning *habeas corpus* and certain other special proceedings; and appellate jurisdiction over exceptions and appeals from District or Circuit Courts. Cases are tried promptly, and the courts are ably and honestly conducted.

"The judges are appointed by the President — District judges for two years, Circuit judges for four years, and Supreme Court judges for life.

"The required qualifications of a voter for Representatives are ability to read and write Hawaiian or English, and the payment of all taxes due; and for Senators, in addition thereto, an income of $600 per annum, or the ownership of real estate worth $1,500, or personal property worth $3,000.

"*The Legislature* consists of a Senate elected for six years, and a House of Representatives elected for two years, each consisting of fifteen members.

"*The Legislative Procedure* is practically the same as in the United States. Each measure, in order to become law, has to pass three readings before each House, and be signed by the President.

"The Committee system is the same as in American legislative bodies."

Apart from the uprising of January, 1895, the new Government, whose principles were thus defined, continued to strengthen its position and win the faith and goodwill of the people. The Hon.

Albert S. Willis, the American Minister, died suddenly in December of this year, and was succeeded by Mr. Mills, who was made Chargé d'Affaires. Upon Mr. McKinley's election Mr. Harold W. Sewell, son of the Free Silver candidate for the Vice-Presidency with Mr. Bryan, was appointed Minister. Mr. Sewell, however, was not of Mr. Bryan's political belief, having been a strong supporter of Mr. McKinley.

CHAPTER XXIII.

ANCIENT CUSTOMS.

THE ancient Hawaiians were never cannibals. It was customary among many of the Polynesians to eat portions of the bodies of enemies, the heart and the brains, as certain of the American Indians have been known to do, in the belief that they would thereby acquire the courage of an adversary which had commanded their admiration. Unlike the Samoans and Maoris, their handsome faces and figures were not disfigured by tattooing. As is inevitable among people where the authority of the chief or king was absolute, there was great oppression, great cruelty, and indifference to life. If a man of the common people stood upon an eminence where his shadow fell across the chief's path, if he climbed a tree or placed himself in any position more elevated than the chief, he was put to death. At the launching of a new canoe a man was sacrificed; and when a new hut was built, under each of the four corners was placed a portion of a human body.

I saw in the fine museum connected with the Kamehameha School for Boys a somewhat peculiar wooden tray. When I asked what it was, I was informed by the curator, Mr. W. T. Brigham, that before the advent of the missionaries shark-killing was a favourite sport with the chiefs. A man was killed, the body cut into pieces, placed in a wooden tray like that which the museum had preserved, and then left to decompose. When this was accomplished, it was taken out beyond the reef, set afloat upon the water, the odour and the ooze attracting the savage fish. The Hawaiians then darted in amongst them armed with short knives, and a furious battle followed, in which it usually happened that the natives were victorious.

Their feats with their swimming-boards were remarkable. These were made of polished *koa*, and were about eight feet in length and eighteen inches in width. With these they swam out beyond the reef, and then waited the approach of a breaker, riding in to the shore on the crest of the wave with incredible swiftness. It was a rare thing that the swimmers were ever injured, they were so skilful, being as much at home in the water as upon the land. Among games mentioned by Professor Alexander and by Jarves in their histories was one somewhat like checkers, played with black and white pebbles upon a board divided into squares. Chiefs alone were permitted to shoot mice with bows and arrows — a sport having a religious significance. Children walked on stilts and spun tops made of gourds. The men excelled in athletic sports, especially boxing, wrestling, and running; and in their boxing bouts the combatants were frequently killed. In bowling, polished stones and wooden sticks were used, and the players displayed much skill both in sending the stone between the upright sticks — not knocking them down — and in the great distance to which it could be thrown. In the museum there are also several sledges, long and narrow, with the runners highly polished and curved, and these were used in coasting down steep hillsides — another favourite amusement.

A few primitive musical instruments existed, which, with drums made of a portion of the hollow trunk of the cocoa palm and covered with shark skin, or of gourds and cocoanut shells, were used to accompany their chants, which were monotonous and prolonged. Their most important dance was the *hula-hula*, which was revived during the latter years of the monarchy, if it could be said ever to have fallen into disuse. It consisted chiefly of indecent posturing, and was formerly accompanied by lascivious songs. The dancers were women almost naked, wearing wreaths of flowers, with barbarous bracelets and anklets of dogs' teeth and pigs' teeth.

The ancient Hawaiians might almost have been called a race of poets. They excelled in improvisation, and their poems in form were like the chants of most uncivilised people, consisting of sentences and phrases repeated, without rhyme, but with a certain musical accent that was a substitute for rhythm. These compositions are divided by Professor Alexander into religious chants, prayers, and prophecies; *ihoas*, name-songs, composed at the birth of a chief in his honour, recounting the exploits of his ancestors, etc. ; *kanikaus*, dirges or lamentations for the dead; *ipos*, or love-songs. He quotes this dirge, which has been preserved, and was composed in honour of the son of the English missionary, Mr. Ellis:

> " Alas ! alas ! dead is my chief,
> Dead is my lord and my friend,
> My friend in the season of famine,
> My friend in the time of drought,
> My friend in my poverty,
> My friend in the rain and the wind,
> My friend in the heat and the sun,
> My friend in the cold from the mountain,
> My friend in the storm,
> My friend in the calm,
> My friend in the eight seas.
> Alas! alas ! gone is my friend,
> And no more will return."

Another has also been preserved, which was composed by Queen Kekupuohe, one of the widows of Kalaniopu, who reigned over the Hawaiians at the time of Captain Cook's visit in 1775. Kekupuohe was converted to Christianity, and her poem was an

invocation to the Deity. The following extracts
have been quoted by Mr. M. A. Chamberlain in a
paper on early native converts:

> " Once only hath that appeared which is glorious;
> It is wonderful, it is altogether holy;
> It is a blooming glory, its nature is unwithering.
> Rare is its stock most singular, unrivalled;
> One only True Vine !   It is the Lord, etc.
>
> God breathed into the empty space,
> And widely spread His power forth,
> The Spirit, flying, hovered o'er;
> A spirit, 't is a shadow of what is good;
> A shadow of heaven is the Holy Spirit.
> His power grasped the movable; it was fast.
>
> .   .   .   .
>
> The earth became embodied ;
> The islands also rose ; they rose to view ;
> The land was bare of verdure,
> And desolate the earth; earth also was man ;
> 'T was God that made him,
> By Him also were all things made, etc."

The ancient Hawaiian religion was essentially
gloomy, and was attended by many cruel and oppressive rites, in which the authority of the priests was
paramount.   They had an infinite number of deities,
many of whom, like the spirit that was supposed to
be embodied in the shark, the volcano, or the hurricane, were evil and malicious, to be feared and
placated.   The four chief gods were *Kane, Kanaloa,
Ku,* and *Lono,* which were also worshipped through-

out Polynesia, pointing to a common religion and a common origin. Idols were worshipped, and they were of great variety, hideous and grotesque, their purpose apparently being to augment that dread and fear through which the priesthood thrived and prospered — a motive not unknown among more civilised races and in a more enlightened age. Their idea of a future life was indefinite, and they had a superstitious dread of ghosts, avoiding battle-fields and burial-places after nightfall.

The *tabu*, which was also universal throughout Polynesia, was exceedingly oppressive: a sort of religious interdict or prohibition laid upon the people and affecting their entire life, — their habits, customs, food, worship; indeed, at some time and under certain circumstances, almost every possible act. Certain food was perpetually *tabu* to women — pork, bananas, and the better varieties of fish. There were certain solemn seasons when any sort of work was *tabu* — when absolute silence was imperative, a condition which, if violated, necessitated beginning the whole tedious business over again. Marriage was usually attended by feasting; polygamy was practised; and chiefs could divorce their wives at will. Infanticide prevailed to a frightful extent. Upon the arrival of the American missionaries in 1826, one woman confessed to Mrs. Judd, the wife of the missionary, that she had murdered nine of her children and buried them under the floor of the hut.

It was not considered a crime, and consequently was not punished in any way.

A superstitious belief prevailed concerning the hair, nails, blood, and saliva which seems general among barbarous people: all these were carefully destroyed, lest they should fall into the hands of their enemies, who were able thereby to cause illness, misfortune, or death. They had methods of embalming, and the bones of chiefs were sacred, and were hidden in caves or elsewhere with the greatest secrecy.

The people had some instinctive knowledge of engineering, as the construction of their great fish-ponds which still remain near Honolulu would indicate. They exhibited great courage in battle, fighting with spears and javelins, clubs of hard wood, and slings made of cocoa fibre and human hair, from which stones were thrown long distances with great force and unerring aim. They had no knowledge of anything that could be called the art of warfare, their battles being hand-to-hand encounters, the combatants being incited to fresh courage and deeds of daring by idols carried by the priests, who accompanied the soldiers in the field.

Their food consisted of *poi*, fish, and, after the introduction of cattle and pigs into the Islands by Europeans, of beef and pork. These were cooked in underground ovens, a custom still in vogue among those who come less frequently in contact with white people. *Kava*, which was used throughout the islands of the Pacific, was made from the *awa*, and prepared by masticating the root and pouring water over it, which was then strained. Formerly this was offered to American and European visitors; and although to drink it must have required a strong will and a still stronger stomach, to refuse it was a gross discourtesy, and therefore quite impracticable. With much to cause them sorrow and even misery, the people as a race were wonderfully light-hearted. They had a keen sense of humour, and feeling, if not profound or lasting, that was easily touched. This made them ready converts to Christianity — this added to the fact that they had discarded their idols prior to the advent of the missionaries to their shores.

CHAPTER XXIV.

PRODUCTS.

SUGAR is the leading product and the chief source of wealth in the Hawaiian Islands, the export increasing from 25,080,182 lbs., valued at $1,216,388.82, in 1875, to 294,784,819 lbs., valued at $7,975,590.41, in 1895 — totals that have more than doubled in twenty years. In the cane-growing regions of the United States a yield of three tons to the acre is considered profitable, and in many of the richer plantations of Hawaii five tons to the acre have been produced, and occasionally eight. Good crops are raised by "rattooning" — allowing the cane to produce a second crop without replanting. An effort has been made to secure Portuguese labourers for the plantations — 1,123 Portuguese having been employed in 1896. They are considered much more tractable than the Japanese, who are difficult to control and are disposed to engage in strikes; the Japanese, however, are still greatly in the majority.

There is no coffee in the world superior to the Kona coffee — the indigenous coffee of Hawaii. It combines the strength of Java with the flavour of what is sold in the American and European markets as Mocha. This industry is still comparatively undeveloped, but scores of plantations are under cultivation, and are being rapidly bought up, until it is said that lands available for coffee culture will soon be difficult to buy at any price. It requires considerable capital, and from three to five years of labour while investments remain unproductive. There are many thousands of acres planted with coffee which has not reached maturity, so that most of the crop at present is consumed by the home markets. The export in 1896 was 114,983 lbs., valued at $22,011.18. Pineapples are also profitable, the crop being easily grown and ready for market within ten months after planting. The export of bananas is also increasing, the fruit being of especially fine quality.

There are many varieties of hard wood in the Islands, which are beautifully grained and take a high polish. Of these the most important are the *koa* and *kou*, from which the natives formerly made their calabashes and other utensils. The leaf of the pandanus is still used in the market — fish, beef, and other articles being neatly wrapped up in it, the long stem serving as a handle by which to carry the parcel. Almost all the varieties of the palm — the cocoanut, which is indigenous, the traveller's palm, the royal and date palms — grow luxuriantly;

and in Hawaii the bamboo has been introduced. The algaroba, which was first planted by the French missionaries, is about the only thing that will take root in the lava; but it manages not only to live, but to flourish and multiply, and within fifty years may do much to transform the waste places into habitable regions. The tamarind, the orange, the mango, the bread-fruit, the beautiful umbrella tree, and the monkey pod add their rich and varied leafage to the general verdure.

I have written much of the flowers, but no words can convey any idea of their beauty and variety. The bougainvillea, a crimson or salmon-coloured creeper, will envelop an entire tree, its sprays, two and three yards in length, depending from the boughs like swaying garlands. The stephanotis, another trailer that we nurse tenderly in the artificial warmth of our greenhouse, there embowers an entire verandah, above and below. My friend Mrs. W—— had a plant trained on the verandah where they usually sat, but its fragrance was so oppressive that it had to be cut down; one on the walls of the stables remained, and this climbed to the highest peak of the gable. There are entire hedges of hibiscus and oleander; the splendid datura, with its trumpet-shaped flowers, attains the proportions of a miniature tree; and the nasturtium, which grows wild upon the lava around Kileauea, becomes a thing of splendour with a little cultivation. Carnations and violets

20

have also been acclimatised, with many varieties of beautiful lilies. The fern forests of Hawaii and Kauai are of unimaginable loveliness, their thick plume-like branches interlaced above the rushing streams and cascades that water their roots. The banks of the rivers in Hawaii are also matted with moon-flowers, which slowly open with the twilight. Fifty years ago the missionaries planted a hedge of night-blooming cereus along one side of the grounds of Oahu College. The hedge was five hundred feet in length, and President Hosmer has added an additional thousand feet. The blooming of one flower is an event in our cold climate, and invitations are sent by florists to the favoured few who are permitted to view the wonder. I have a photograph of this old hedge taken by a flash-light when there were three thousand perfect flowers in bloom. Imagine their suffocating sweetness, and the dazzling array of three thousand great snow-white disks coming into life and exhaling their concentrated perfume as they slowly faded!

It is a climate, however, with which the floriculturist cannot rashly experiment. What may be a valued plant elsewhere, here may become an enemy, with none of the restraint that nature has devised to keep it within bounds elsewhere. Some one introduced the lantana, and it has overrun thousands of acres of the best land, forming impenetrable thickets that can be rooted out only with plough and harrow.

HEDGE OF NIGHT-BLOOMING CEREUS, FIVE HUNDRED FEET IN LENGTH, AT OAHU COLLEGE.

At the time it was photographed there were in bloom three thousand perfect flowers.

A gentleman told me that it had cost him $1,500 in one year to clear his fields that had become overgrown with the mischievous shrub.

In Hawaii, as throughout Polynesia, there was very little animal life in the Islands until cattle and pigs were introduced; nothing, indeed, but rats and mice, dogs and cats — a fact that Professor Koebele thought was largely responsible for cannibalism in the other islands, where, through the destruction of fruit trees, food became scarce. The cattle and pigs multiplied, however, and there are still herds of wild cattle in Hawaii, especially on the lower slopes of Mauna Kea and Mauna Loa. The natives formerly captured these animals by digging pits, into which they fell, when they were destroyed with spears and knives. It occasionally happened that a man also fell into the pit, and was gored and trampled to death.

A Scotch resident described the manner in which he had seen wild pigs destroyed: the animal was driven to bay, and when it turned and charged a string was held extended firmly in both hands, against which it ran open-mouthed; the cord was then wound round and round the snout in a flash, the poor brute being finally strangled. Deer have been successfully introduced upon Molokai, with pheasants, which are also numerous in Oahu, but which take refuge in the lantana thickets, and so defy the sportsman. The mongoose, imported from Jamaica as an enemy to the rats, which were very destructive in the cane fields, has proved to be a good deal of a pest, preferring poultry to rats, and having a rapacious appetite for pheasants' eggs. Rats are ubiquitous and daring. They swarmed in the hotel, and feared neither man nor beast; they had a voracious appetite for soap, which it is supposed they applied internally. There were certain of the species with a civilised taste for fresh air and a commanding prospect, and these made their home in the cocoanut trees, which furnished both food and a nesting-place. These tree-dwellers bored into the shell, and devoured the fruit whenever prompted by hunger. I was told that the more enterprising went out upon business or to call on their friends across the street, utilising the telephone wires as thoroughfares, where they were comparatively safe from their enemies. I never saw an example of this sort of wire-walking, and cannot vouch for it.

There are no reptiles, and no venomous insects, except centipedes, spiders, and scorpions, and people are very rarely bitten. In the two visits which I made I never saw a scorpion or a centipede. The spiders, I am forced to admit, are not pleasing, except to students of entomology. They are a trifle smaller than a tea-plate, and bristle with coarse brown hair. Ants and the carpenter-bee do great mischief, boring into and destroying furniture and the woodwork of houses. The mosquito, however,

is the serpent in this paradise.   The pest was introduced at Lahina, on the island of Maui, in 1826, by
the *Wellington*, which brought them in her water-
casks from Mexico.   A friend who told me the story
had heard Dr. Judd relate his experience at the
time of their advent into Honolulu.   They came at
night in a blinding cloud, bloodthirsty and rapacious, stinging frightfully.   Half the night he sat
up fanning his wife, while she stood guard over him
the remainder of the night, and in this way they
lived until nets could be procured from China.   I
have never seen them in such numbers anywhere else.
Beds are supplied with nets, but strangely enough the
windows are not screened, as they are screened even
against flies throughout the United States.   They are
objected to because it is thought they exclude the
air, yet it is never so hot in the Islands as it is in
the United States in the months of July, August, and
September.   The mosquitos are especially vicious in
their attacks upon new-comers; they appear to prefer them to old residents, whose blood is probably
thinner.   I was always forced to go to my room and
take refuge behind the nets, and dining out was a
painful ordeal, unless one wore thick boots and
stockings, that their sharp sting could not penetrate.
They gathered around one's head in clouds as soon
as the sun set, and it was difficult to keep from in-
haling them into the mouth.   They are much worse
when the south wind blows, and *buhac*, a Chinese

drug, is then burned; it stupefies them, and they drop on the floor, and are swept up and destroyed. They breed prodigiously in the rice fields, and in the little irrigating canals which the Chinese gardeners construct through their banana groves; and no means of preventing their increase has yet been discovered.

There are no reptiles in Hawaii, this group, with all the South Sea islands, being in this respect unlike the West Indies, where the *fer de lance* and other deadly species abound. Another stupid meddler very nearly brought about a calamity, which fortunately was averted. He returned from India with a boxful of what he supposed to be harmless house-snakes, intended to destroy rats, which, when they had been out at sea several days, displayed the unmistakable marks of pythons. When their identity was fully established they were tossed overboard, and no experiment of the kind has since been attempted. There are very few birds except on the islands of Kauai and Hawaii, where the *oo* (*Acrulocercus nobilis*) and the *mamo* (*Drepanis pacifica*) are found — the honey-suckers which yield the precious yellow feathers from which the royal mantles were made.

The ubiquitous English sparrow has made himself at home in Honolulu, with the pigeon, the German dove, and the mynah, which has been brought from India. The latter is fearless and impudent, riding about the fields upon the backs of pigs and cattle, and stealing whatever it can find and carry off. The superintendent of a mill told me that there was, in the building over which he had supervision, a room which had been closed for several months. When they finally opened it, they found a great heap of rubbish in the centre of the floor, for which no one could account until a hole in the roof was discovered, through which it was realised immediately that the mynahs had entered, bringing frequent additions to their hoarded stealings. Rags, string, paper, handkerchiefs, bits of lace and ribbon, were found in the heap, which had been growing steadily during the entire time that the room had been closed.

CHAPTER XXV.

THE PASSING OF THE NATIVE.

HAWAII is a veritable land of the lotus-eater. After a few days one is content to drift along indifferent to the realities of life, and to what in the exacting temperate zone we call "duty." The climate explains a great deal in native character that has defied the Christianising of half a century, and yet finds solace in certain rites and ceremonies, surreptitiously performed, which are a very marked contrast with the belief in abstract virtue, as it is embodied in orthodoxy. Flowers, music, ease, enough to eat — these seem to be the essentials of life among the Hawaiians. As a people they are physically attractive. Many of them are tall, vigorous, well proportioned, with a freedom and grace which are the result of loose and simple clothing and of life spent almost wholly in the open air. They have dark skin, silken, jet-black hair, flashing black eyes, with long lashes, rather thick lips, and teeth of dazzling whiteness. They are a most amiable and light-hearted people, the embodiment of generosity, cheerfulness, and hospitality. The latter trait I have already noted; what is theirs is yours, freely and without reservation. If a native is hungry, he does not even ask food of his neighbour, but enters his house, and the calabash of *poi* is at his service — the common supply of all who come. Clothing is borrowed in the same manner, and it would be despicable meanness so much as to hint that a return, even though delayed, is expected.

I had a very touching example of their affection. I had accompanied Mrs. H——, the ex-Queen's chief lady-in-waiting, to an entertainment given at the Kawaiahao Church. We occupied one of the elevated pews in the rear which had been set apart for the ladies of the Court. Near us were seated many of the Hawaiian friends of Mrs. H——. At the conclusion of the programme she introduced me to several of them, explaining that I was Admiral Brown's sister.

"Not sister," I corrected, "but cousin."

"We have no word ' cousin ' in the Hawaiian language" (she had been speaking in Hawaiian to her friends, many of whom could not speak English); "our only terms are ' mother ' and ' sister; ' we do not recognise the relationship of cousin."

It requires very little to support life here. There is no winter that demands outlay for fuel, heavy clothing, and meat, which are so expensive and so necessary in colder climates; cotton trousers and

shirt and a straw hat constitute the ordinary attire
of working men, while the women consider themselves sufficiently well clad with a chemise, a single
petticoat, and a *holoku.*

It is said that the vices that have decimated the
Hawaiian race so fearfully have been those with
which our own vaunted civilisation is not unfamiliar
—gin and licentiousness. The Islands were at one
time so densely populated that artificial ponds for
fish-raising had to be constructed; and out upon the
mountain sides, enclosed in low stone walls, are
yet to be seen the small tracts allotted to families,
upon which they were forced to raise additional supplies of food.

Alcohol in any form, it is well known, is fatal
in hot climates; and the natives of Hawaii, although
enjoying a more moderate temperature than might
be expected in this latitude, have not greater physical resistance against its ravages than is met with
nearer the Equator. The census of 1896 fixed the
total population at 109,020, of which there are but
31,019 native Hawaiians. The native population in
1890 was 34,436, of which 18,364 were males and
16,072 were females. The loss since 1884 had been
5,578, a decrease which the census of 1896 shows
has continued. On the other hand, there has been
a gain of 1,968 half-caste — a gain that has been,
perhaps, proportionally maintained.

The natives, like all aborigines, are peculiarly

susceptible to contagion, all contagious diseases being amongst them extremely fatal. In 1848 the measles, which were introduced from California, spread through the Islands, and it is estimated that one-tenth of the people died from the disease.

In 1853 smallpox was introduced, also from California. Every precaution was taken to prevent its spread, but again there was terrible mortality, although vaccination was resorted to as a preventive measure. The total number of deaths was between two thousand five hundred and three thousand.

With their decay in numbers their skill in the beautiful arts which they once employed is becoming obsolete — that, especially, of building what are called "native houses." I was taken out to the plantation of Mr. S. M. Damon to see two which Mr. Damon had had constructed as examples of the work of old Hawaiians. A grass hut, as such a house is commonly called, conveys an idea of a rude habitation, roughly constructed, with little idea of comfort or beauty. These houses have both the latter qualities in high degree. The framework consisted of upright timbers of native wood, those at either end of the house lengthening towards the centre timber, which was the highest. There was no ridge-pole, but across the top slanting lengths of bamboo had been placed at close intervals, and tied to the timbers at either end with fine cord made of cocoa fibre. The grass attached to this beautiful frame was, in reality, a sort of woven mat, intricately braided in a handsome pattern nearly six inches in thickness. It not only excluded the rain, but the heat of the sun.   There were an aperture for a window and a doorway so low that the tall Hawaiian was forced to stoop as he entered. Along one end of the single apartment was the bed composed of fine mats, piled one upon another, with a single round bolster, also of woven matting. The floor was covered with a mat; and the bed, which was occupied by an entire family and any chance visitor who might be enjoying their hospitality, was amply provided with coverings of *tapa* — a sort of paper made from the bark of the mulberry, macerated and beaten with heavy billets into sheets, one being joined to the other by beating the edges smoothly together. The pieces of cloth were then tastefully decorated in stripes or simple geometrical figures with a wooden tool, or tinted with bright vegetable dye pink, brown, or purple. The clothing of the natives, which before the advent of the missionaries consisted of flowing mantles, was made of the same material. Some of the *tapa* was as thin as fine muslin, and other qualities were as thick as heavy cloth. After the arrival of the missionaries the women not only donned the *holoku*, which was made of calico or muslin, but learned also to make patchwork quilts, in which they became very expert, using rich materials and the brilliant colours in

GRASS HOUSE AT WAINAHU PLANTATION.

which they delight. Professor Alexander states
that the house of a chief was sometimes from forty
to seventy feet in length by twenty in width, the
principal furniture being polished calabashes for
holding fire and water. The houses which Mr.
Damon was fortunate enough to have had constructed were built by a native then nearly eighty
years of age. He was no longer able to work, and
when he dies the art will probably die with him.
There was one other native house occupied by a
native family at Waikiki, which had one dark room
in the rear, with a roofed space in front of it, the
earthen floor being covered with a coarse mat, upon
which a company of women sat huddled together.
There were a half-dozen children, several lean cats,
and the inevitable yellow dog, without which no
Hawaiian *ménage* seems to be complete. Not one
of the family could speak a word of English, but I
was greeted with friendly smiles and gestures and
the kindly "*Aloha.*"

Anglicising is slowly doing its work, apart from
the gin and the restraining clothing which are held
partially responsible for the decay of the race.
They are losing their joyousness by slow degrees.
Most of the customs are passing away which gave
a picturesqueness to Hawaiian life. It grieved me
inexpressibly to see, in evidence of this, a native
woman of the finest type wearing a trained *holokn*
which had a fashionable skirt edged with plaiting

sweeping the sidewalk, her graceful carriage seriously hampered by the French-heeled slippers into which she had squeezed her well-developed feet. The custom of wearing *leis* is also falling into disuse. The lower classes still adorn themselves with garlands of flowers — marigold, plumaria, and tuberoses; but the better classes, those who, you are immediately told, were educated abroad, scorn this decoration, which they consider distinctly barbarous.

There has been a great deal of sentimentality in the cry of theorists, "Hawaii for Hawaiians." The conditions which exist are largely of their own creating, and the only alternatives that remain, as I have said many times, are to leave the Islands in that state of nature when the most cruel rites of paganism prevailed, or to accept the civilisation ordained and perpetuated by the so-called missionary element. The charge made against the latter is succinctly this: They found here a simple people in possession of the country, who received them with unquestioning generosity, accepted the religion which they taught, discarded their idols, and discontinued human sacrifices. The Anglo-Saxon proved to be the stronger race, and multiplied steadily where the natives visibly decreased, and the possessions of former powerful chiefs and chiefesses became the estates of their teachers and of their descendants. It is certain, however, that violence has not been resorted to. Gifts of land were voluntary, or the land was purchased, and, coming into the possession of provident and industrious whites, has been held by them up to the present time. Putting aside all prejudice, it must be frankly admitted that the Hawaiian is inherently averse to work. He is improvident, and has a passion for gambling — a passion, however, that seems to be one of the characteristics of human depravity all the world over. He is apparently devoid of forethought, and deficient in judgment to an astonishing degree. It has been these two last traits, with his improvidence, that have made him unfit to exercise authority or to administer public affairs with any of the ability requisite in leadership.

Some of the proceedings of native legislatures are an indication of what might be called the childishness of the people as a race. One was, to give an example, that there should be an Act promulgating the statement that leprosy did not exist, and another was to repeal the Act which provides for the necessary segregation of the lepers on Molokai. Among those who are wealthy and educated a lavish extravagance in living seems to be the rule. They reside in beautiful, luxuriously furnished houses, surrounded by extensive gardens; they entertain like princes; their children are sent to Europe to be educated. With their dark Oriental beauty and native languor they have acquired a Parisian polish, which is in striking contrast to American nervousness and angularity. It is said by those whose word cannot be doubted that many of even the intelligent retain under the surface the ancient faith of their ancestors. They consult their *kuhunas*, their native physicians, in preference to English or American medical men. I heard of a case of this sort which had occurred only recently. A child had been sent to the Hospital with a dislocated hip, which had been encased in a plaster cast. She was progressing favourably, when the parents became dissatisfied, and finally, notwithstanding the protests of the Hospital authorities, insisted on removing her and placing her under the care of a native doctor. The cast was taken off, and the child will be lame for life. What has been done for Hawaiians by Hawaiians is traceable, always, to foreign influence in the Government. There are now throughout the islands millions of dollars worth of highly improved property, a perfected system of public instruction, and a civilisation almost ideal in its character. It has been charged that it is puritanical, hard, and narrow — an easy accusation, always upon the tongue of the demagogue, and of those who confound liberty with licence. The only real question involved, when all the charges of clamouring factions are sifted and their demands are analysed, is: Shall what now exists — society, wealth, comfort, in which even the poorest shares — be dissipated by hands incapable

of administering law and order; or shall it be trans-
ferred to those who created it, and who, in saving
their own, must save with it that which yet remains
to the natives?

This is the sum and the substance of the whole
situation; and if America is not ready and willing
to assume the responsibility, England may be induced to accept it, and, before her, Japan, who has
already upon Hawaiian soil a representation of over
twenty-five thousand souls. No matter what the
outcome may be, the Hawaiian is a fading race, with
remnants of heathen customs still hampering it,
confronted by the stronger and the newer, trained
in government and refined, or at any rate strengthened, by civilisation. It is one of those crises
which come to individuals and nations alike, when
destiny leaves little choice to the actor in the
drama, and events move on irresistibly through that
transition which evolves, at last, higher and better
conditions. It is the apparent triumph of the strong
over the weak; it is, in reality, the natural dissolution of that which has served its time. It seems a
hard and pitiless doctrine, but it is the unvarying
law of nature and of history.

INDEX.

Adams, the U. S. S., 214, 265.
Adler, German war-ship, 268.
Ah Fong, the merchant, 185.
Aholo, L., 4.
Ahulas, 128, 129.
Aki, the Chinaman, 4, 7.
Alameda, the s. s., 264, 265.
Alexander, Prof. W. D., his account of the crisis of 1887, 3, 10; criticism of King Kalaukaua, 11; official report to the Senate, 151; his history, 296, 298.
Algaroba, the, 305.
Alliance, the U. S. S., 74, 150.
American flag, hoisted at Honolulu, 56; notification to President Dole that it would be lowered, 153; lowering of the, 159–162.
American naval officers, 114, 162, 163, 262.
American protectorate, close of the, 163.
Annexation, favourably viewed by President Harrison, 22; opposed by President Cleveland, 22; growth of the desire for, 28, 33, 85, 144, 157.
Annexation Club, the, 151, 152; Mr. Blount's reply to, 152.
Ants, 308.
Apia, 266, 278.
Armstrong, Mr. W. N., Commissioner of Immigration, 8.
Ashford, Mr. C. W., 6.
Australia, a visit to, 277.
Australia, the s. s., 43, 145; the surgeon of, 70.

BAMBOO, growth of the, 304.
Bananas, giant, 240.
Beetle, a destructive, 228.
Bickerton, Justice, 19, 288.
Birds, 240, 310, 311.
Bishop, Mrs. Bernice Pauahi, 9.
Bishop, Mrs. Isabella Bird, 73, 243; the old home of, 114; visit to Mr. Sinclair's estate, 132, 133, 134; description of the Leper Settlement, 201; account of Hilo and Hawaii, 225; of King Lunalilo's reception, 226; Manual Training School founded by, 253.
Black, of San Francisco, Mrs., 202.
Blount, Mr. J. H., mission of, 3, 22, 145, 164; credentials of, 146, 147; treatment of the Provisional Government, 148, 150, 151, 156, 160; "Southern" proclivities, 149; reply to the Annexation Club, 152; first official order, 163; close of his administration, 209–214; succeeds Mr. Stevens as American Minister, 210; succeeded by Mr. Albert S. Willis, 210, 211; investigation into the sources of his report, 213.
Boston, the U. S. S., 18, 24, 74, 117; ordered to Hilo, 153; a ball on, 262, 263.
Bo'sun bird, the, 71.
Brigham, Mr. W. T., 296.
Brown, Mr. C. A., 109, 187.
Brown, Admiral George, 10; takes back King Kalaukaua's body to Honolulu, 11, 37; a member of

President Cleveland's Commission, 139; affection of Queen Kapiolani for, 192; affection of Queen Liliuokalani for, 205–207.

Brown, Mr. Godfrey, 5.

Brown Cabinet, the, 6.

Buhac, use of the drug, 310.

Bush, Mr. John, 140, 164.

Call newspaper, the correspondent of the San Francisco, 78.

Calliope, H. M. S., 268.

Camp Boston, a visit to, 114, 158; the American marines at, 114; the routine of, 115.

Candle nut, the, 240.

Cane fields, 237.

Carpenter bee, the, 308.

Carter, Charles L., death of, 27.

Casey, Dr., 275.

Catholic nuns at Molokai, 200.

Chamberlain, Mr. M. A., 299.

Charleston, the U. S. S., 10, 11.

Chicago, a visit to the World's Fair at, 210.

Chinese fire brigade, a, 185; fruit-vendors, 169; merchants, 184, 185; mothers, respect shown to, 184; New Year, the, 96; peasant woman, a, 183; servants, 94, 95; schools, 180–184; temples and worshippers, 179, 180.

Circuit Courts, 292.

Civilisation, effects of, 317.

Cleghorn, Mr., 101; a visit to his grounds, 101–105.

Cleveland, Mrs., receives Princess Kaiulani, 176.

Cleveland, President, 3; opposes annexation, 22; dispatches Commissioner J. H. Blount to Hawaii, 22; favours Queen Liliuokalani's restoration, 22; unpopularity of his policy in the States, 24; his attitude towards the Republic, 25, 26; takes the oath of office, 131; recommends the withdrawal of the Hawaiian treaty, 138; his hostility to the Provisional Government, 139; his letter to President Dole, 146; his connection with the "Blount Mission," 209–211.

Climate, 250.

Coffee plantations, 238, 239, 303, 304.

Committee of Public Safety, the, 20.

Constitution, amendments of the, 6; establishment of a new, 17, 18, 19; drafts for a new, 27, 214; formal adoption of the new, 285–288; summary of the, 290–294.

Constitutional conflict, a, 15–19.

Constitutional Convention, a, 24; meeting of the, 282.

Contract labour system, the, 87, 88.

Convicts, 240.

Cooley, Judge, 139.

Corwin, the U. S. S., 23.

Courts of Justice, 292, 293.

Crisis of 1887, the, 2, 3; of 1893, 16, 17.

Croton, fine specimens of the, 107.

Cumming, Miss Gordon, 226, 243.

Customs, 255–261; ancient, 295–302.

DAMIEN, Father, 200.

Damon, Mr. S. M., 14, 160, 178–183, 315, 317.

Dancing, 297.

David, Prince, 141.

Davies, Mr. Theophilus, 172, 175.

Diamond Head, 73; secret meetings at, 26; a drive to, 81.

District Courts, 292.

Dole, Judge Sandford B., appointed Head of the Provisional Government, 21; his integrity and courage, 21, 28; chosen President of the Republic, 25; attitude towards President Cleveland's Commission, 143, 156; action as to the lowering of the American flag, 160; opposed to the claims of Princess Kaiulani, 174; a dinner with, 203, 285; presents me with my passport, 264;

his address to the Constitutional Convention, 283, 286–288.
Dominis, a portrait of Mr. John, 124.
Draper, Lieutenant, 160, 162.

EDUCATION, 253.
Electorate, the, 291.
Ellis, Mr., 298.
Emma, Queen, 9; her education and training, 12; a photograph of, 123.
Emory, Mrs., 184.
Engineering, knowledge of, 301.
Ethnology, a study in, 170.
Executive, the, 291.
Expenditure, 290.

FARALLONES, the, 71.
Ferns, beautiful, 238, 239, 306.
Filial piety, the god of, 180.
Finnegan, the dog, 119, 120.
Fire brigade, a Chinese, 185.
Food, native, 301.
Franklin, Lady, 243.
Funerals, costly, 10.

GAMES, 296.
Garnet, H. M. S., 74; a ball to the officers of, 260.
Gay, Mr. Francis, 132, 133, 134; political views of, 134–137.
Gibson Cabinet, the, 4; dismissal of, 5.
Gibson, Mr. W. M., 4, 5, 80, 272.
Gods, the chief, 299.
Golden Gates, the, 71.
Green, Mr. W. L., 6.
Gresham, Mr. Walter Q., 24, 138, 139, 176.

HAILSTORM, a heavy, 244.
Harrison, President, favourable views of annexation, 22; enmity between, and the Secretary of State, 163.
Hawaii and the United States, bond between, 284, 285.
Hawaii, Kamehameha III.'s cession of, 30; relations of, with the U. S.,

1–31; political affairs of, 35, 37; my departure for, 63, 64; first impressions of, 75–77; staple diet of, 97; the approach to, 215; my first ride in, 220–225; commercial and social status of, 250; ancient customs of, 295–302; poetry of, 298; religion of, 299; population of, 314.
Hawaii Ponoi, the, 261.
Hawaiian whalers, 74; natives, 81; society, 85; race problem, 91; women, 97; honesty, 100; firemen, 109, 110; patriotism, 130; mutton and wool, 136, 137; horsewomen, 142, 143; League, the, 145, 150; Commissioners, the, 157; flag, the hoisting of the, 162; Board of Health, 196; Boys, Royal School for, 206; meals, 255; hospitality, 256.
Hawaiians, affection of the, 196, 313; light-heartedness of, 198; character of, 312–315; vices of, 314; susceptibility of, to disease, 315.
High-binders, 69.
Hilo, the whaling trade in, 74; a visit to, 218; roads in, 220; lava above, 221; Japanese houses and Portuguese farmers in, 224; life in, 226–234; Chinese quarter in, 237.
Holoku (garment), the, 76, 98, 188, 190, 193, 238.
Honolulu, the Brighton of, 73; the whaling trade in, 74; my arrival in, 84; Japanese Consulate at, 88; cleanliness of, 89; Chinese and Portuguese quarters in, 89, 96, 179; churches in, 90; vehicles in, 90; drivers in, 91, 92; seasons, rainfall, and temperature of, 92; houses in, 93; population of, 93; the paradise of the Chinese, 94, 178; servants in, 94, 95; streets of, 96; society in, 99; Chinese population of, 178–186; social life in, 250–263; changes in, 252.
Hookupu, ceremonial, the, 11.

Hooper, Major, 67.
Hosmer, Harriet, 211.
Hosmer, President, 306.
Hui Kalaiaina, the royalist society of, 18.
Hula-hula dance, the, 297.
Hurricane of 1889, the, 268, 269.

Ide, Miss, 278.
Idol worship, 300.
Ié-ié vine, the, 240.
Ihoas, 298.
Iowa, the prairies of, 66.
Ipos, 298.

Japanese superstition, 63; immigration, 88, 89; labourers, 86, 87, 237; frugality of, 88; officers, 99.
Jarves, 296.
Judd, Chief Justice, 19, 288; letter of introduction to, 38.
Judd, Colonel C. H., 8.
Judd, Mrs., 300.
Judicial system, the, 292, 293.
Juries, 292.

Kaae, Junius, 4.
Kahili, the, 104, 124, 125, 126, 189, 204.
Kahoolawe, 72.
Kaiulani, Princess, named heir-apparent, 15; house of, 101, 102, 103, 104, 105; portrait of, 106; her life in England, 172; education of, 172; her appeal to Congress, 173-175; departure from England, 174; her reception by Mrs. Cleveland, 176; her return to England, 176; her relations with Liliuokalani, 191.
Kalaukaua, King, descent of, 1, 9; turbulence of his reign, 1; jealousy of foreigners, 2; Cabinet, 4; asks the European Powers to form a protectorate, 4, 5; struggle to regain power, 6, 7; debts, 7; tour round the world, 8; rejoicings on his return, 8; coronation ceremony, 9; extravagance, 9, 10; summons a revolutionary convention, 10; dies at San Francisco, 11; election, 13; names Liliuokalani as heir-apparent, 13; scheme for a national lottery, 16; a presentation to, 80; personal effects, 122; a photograph of, 123; the library of, 124; portraits of, 189, 190; his attachment to Admiral Brown, 192.
Kalaukaua's Palace, a visit to, 122; funeral, a survival of, 128; sword, 129; Singing Boys, 142, 260; crown jewels, theft of, 166-168.
Kamehameha, King, offers the island of Niihau to the Sinclairs, 133.
Kamehameha III., his cession of Hawaii, 29.
Kamehamehas, the old, 1; photographs of, 123.
Kamehameha School for Boys, 296.
Kanaloa, the god, 299.
Kane, the god, 299.
Kanikuais, 298.
Kapiolani, Queen, at the Golden Jubilee of Queen Victoria, 14; the crown of, 167; her estates, 187; reception by, 187-194; villa, 188; manner, 190; strained relations with Liliuokalani, 191; popularity, 191; gratitude to Admiral Brown, 192.
Kauai, 72, 132; fern forests of, 306.
Kava, the manufacture of, 274, 275, 302.
Kawaiahao School for Girls, 206, 253.
Keelikolani, Ruth, 9.
Kekupuohe, dirge composed by Queen, 298, 299.
Kemoa, P. P., 4.
Kileauea, volcano of, 216, 235-249; the hotel at, 241; the crater of, 242-249; visitors to, 243; activity of, 247.
Knapp, Miss Adeline, 78, 81.
Koa wood, 241, 296, 304; a cylinder of, 192.

Koebele, Professor Albert, 232, 233, 234, 266, 275, 307.
Kona coffee, 70.
Kou wood, 304.
Ku, the god, 299.
Kuhunas, the, 320.
Kukui, the, 240, 241.

LABOUR system, the, 87, 88, 89.
Lady-bird, a useful, 232, 233.
Lahina, 309.
Laird, Lieutenant, 115, 122, 127, 131, 158.
Lanais, 72, 79, 93, 141.
Laws, character of the, 291.
Legislative procedure, 293.
Legislatures, native, 319.
Leis, garlands of, 75, 97, 141, 142, 190, 204, 318.
Leper receiving station, the, 196.
Leper Settlement, the, 195-202; improvements at, 201.
Lepers, the, 72; tax for, 198; cheerfulness of, 199, 202; the plan of isolating, 200.
Leprosy, first signs of, 197.
Like-Like, portrait of the Princess, 106.
Liliuokalani, Queen, accession of, 12; named heir-apparent by King Kalaukaua, 13; misrule, 15, 16; schemes for a new Constitution, 17, 18, 19; throne declared vacant, 20; restoration favoured by President Cleveland, 22; freedom allowed her, 25; plots *v.* the Republic, 26; sentenced to imprisonment, 27; formally abdicates, 28; regret at her dethronement, 77; the adherents of, 85; the home of her girlhood, 114; a photograph of, 123; relations with Queen Kapiolani and Princess Kaiulani, 191; an audience with, 203-208; her town house, 203; simplicity of her life, 208.
Lono, the god, 299.
Lottery, national, 16, 17.
Louis Philippe, a portrait of, 123.

Luau, a, 230, 231, 232.
Ludlow, Captain, 104.
Lunalilo, King, 1; death of, without heirs, 12; a reception given by, 226.

McGREW, Dr. J. S., 152.
McKinley, President, effects of his election, 28; his message to Congress, 29.
Mahan, Captain, his views of the situation, 29.
Mahukona, 217.
Malietoa, King, residence of, 271, 272, 273; bed-chamber of, 273.
Mamo bird, the, 311.
Mamos, the sacred, 125, 126.
Manchester products, 267.
Manners and customs, 255-261.
Mariposa, the s. s., 170, 265, 277.
Marsden, Mr., 140.
Maui, 72, 216, 229, 309.
Mauna Kea peak, 216, 218, 229, 236, 238; wild cattle on, 307.
Mauna Loa peak, 216, 221, 229, 236, 238; wild cattle on, 307.
Memorial Day, 282, 283.
Mills, Mr., 204, 294.
Missionaries, the, 85.
Mohican, the U. S. S., 74, 150; the captain of, 104; a reception on board, 203.
Molokai, 72, 195-202, 216; division of, into sanitary districts, 196; Catholic nuns at, 200; formation of, 201.
Monarchy, President Cleveland's schemes for the restoration of the, 22, 23; abolition of the, 24, 25, 91.
Monowai, the s. s., 71.
Mongoose, importation of the, 307, 308.
Mormon, the Book of, 272.
Mosquitos, 117, 308, 309, 310.
Mouse-shooting, 296.
Musical instrument, native, 260, 297.

Naniwa, the Japanese ironclad, 74, 86, 144; crew of, 98, 99.
Nasturtium, luxuriant growth of, 244, 305.
Neumann, Mr., 140, 141, 176, 204.
Nevada, crossing the, 66.
New Zealand, a visit to, 264-277; the climate and people, 277.
Niihau, 72; offered to the Sinclairs by King Kamehameha, 133.

OAHU, 72, 216, 228.
Oahu College, 100; flowers at, 306.
Oakland, 67.
Ohalo shrub, the, 244.
Olona, or native hemp, 127.
Omaha, 66.
Oo bird, the, 126, 127, 190, 311.
Opium, sale of, 16, 17.
Osbourne, Mr. Lloyd, 276, 279.
Ostrich farm, a visit to an, 109 *et seq.*

PACIFIC, the, 71.
Palm, varieties of the, 304.
Pandanus leaf, the, 304.
Patriotic League, the, 164.
Pearl Harbour, cession of, 13.
Pelé, the deity, 244, 249.
Philadelphia, the U. S. S., withdrawal of, from Honolulu Harbour, ordered by President Cleveland, 26; return to Honolulu, 282.
Pigs, the killing of wild, 307.
Pine-apple plantations, 239.
Plantations, the multiplication of, 254.
Poetry, 298.
Poi, the staple diet, 97, 98; vessels for holding, 125.
Police, a visit from the ex-Chief of, 165.
Porter, Mr. Robert, 160.
Portsmouth, the U. S. S., 13.
Portuguese, the, 73, 98.
President, the powers of the, 291.
Products, 303-310.

Provisional Government, the, 21, 152, 290; organises a Republic, 24, 25; the friends of, 157.
Public Safety, Committee of, 20.
Punchbowl crater, the, 78.

RAGSDALE, William, 201.
Rainbow Falls, the, 220.
Reciprocity treaty, the, 250; the effect of, 254.
Reform party, the, 6.
Religion, 299.
Reptiles, absence of, 308.
Republic, establishment of a, 24, 25; the first President of, 25; attitude of President Cleveland towards, 25; ex-Queen's plots v., 26; attempt to overthrow, 28; prosperity under the, 28; formal proclamation of, 285.
Restoration of the monarchy, President Cleveland's scheme for, 22, 23.
Revenue, 290.
Revolution in Hawaii, announcement of, 56.
Revolutionary convention, a, 10.
Riding, the method of, 142, 143, 244, 245, 257, 258.
Robertson, Colonel J. W., 122, 123, 129, 130, 167, 203.
Rooke, Dr., the adopted daughter of, 12.
Rosa Antone, 4.
Roses, wholesale destruction of, 228.
Rotarua, the baths at, 279.
Round Top peak, the, 73.
Royal Hawaiian Hotel, the, 78, 79; the servants and officials of, 81.
Royal mantle, the cost of a, 127.
Royal School for Hawaiian Boys, 206, 252.
Royal succession, Hawaiian law of, 12.
Rush, the U. S. cruiser, 144.

SACRAMENTO Valley, 67.
Samoa, 266, 267; natives of, 267; a

rebellion in, 271, 276; prisoners in, 271; native R. C. Church in, 274.

Samoan dancers, 170; headdress, 269; customs and language, 270; houses, 270; chief, a, 274; nuns, 274; love of cigarettes, 275.

San Francisco, 67; death of King Kalaukaua at, 10, 11; a visit to China-town, 68; the Mid-Winter Fair at, 211.

"Scale-blight" parasite, the, 233.

Schofield, General, 140.

Scientific farming, 254.

Scott, Mr. John A., 254.

Screw palm, the, 240.

Seal Rocks, the, 68.

Servants, 250.

Severance, Mr. Henry M., 148.

Severance, Mr. Luther, entertains the officers of the *Boston*, 154; the home of, 225; culture of, 226.

Sewell, Mr. Harold, 204; appointed American minister, 294.

Sierra Nevada mountains, the, 66, 67.

Shakespeare class, a ladies', 229.

Shark-killing, 296.

Sinclairs, the, 132, 133.

Singing Boys, King Kalaukaua's, 142, 260.

Skerrett, Admiral, 150.

Smith, Mr. W. O., 160, 174.

Society, 85, 99, 250–263.

Soil, productiveness of the, 254.

Soper, General, 160, 161, 162, 285.

Sparrow, the English, 311.

Spiders, 308.

Squid, 98.

Stevens, Mr., U. S. Minister, succeeded by Mr. Albert S. Willis, 22; letter of introduction to, 38; his part in political affairs, 86; his resemblance to Mr. Lincoln, 153; a guest of the U. S. S. *Boston*, 154; death of, 156; a call upon, 203.

Stevens, Miss, visit of, to Hamakua, 154; death of, 155.

Stevenson, Mrs., 279.

Stevenson, Robert Louis, his views on the Leper Settlement, 202; a meeting with, 266, 278; death, 281.

Strong, Mrs., 276.

Sugar manufacturers, 254, 303.

Sulphur banks, 244.

Superstitions, 301.

Supreme Court, the, 293.

Swimming, 257–261.

Swimming-boards, feats with, 296.

Swinburne, Captain, 86, 114, 117, 118, 120, 121, 158.

Sydney, 281.

Tabu, the, 300.

Tantalus peak, the, 73.

Tapa, 266, 316.

Taro (*Colocasia antiquorum*), 97, 98.

Tenedos, H. M. S., 13.

Thurston, L. A., 6; on Japanese immigration, 88; on the streets of Honolulu, 93; message of President Cleveland to, 138; his handbook, 253; efforts on behalf of Hawaiian liberty, 289.

Ti leaf, use of the, 192.

Trade winds, 92.

Trenton, scene of the wreck of the U. S. S., 268.

Tropical forest, a, 238.

Tropical showers, 72.

Tuscarora, the U. S. S., 13.

Twain, Mark, 243; his experiences, 251.

UNITED STATES troops requested to maintain order, 20.

VAILIMA, 276, 279.

Vandalia, scene of the wreck of the U. S. S., 268.

Vedalia cardinalis, the, 232.

Victor Emmanuel, a bust of, 80.

Volunteer troops, 131.

WAIKIKI, 73, 81; a ball at, 260.

Walker, Admiral, 26, 285, 288.

Washington's birthday, celebration of, 74.
Washington Place, 203.
Wellington, the s. s., 309.
Whalers, Hawaiian, 74.
Wilder, Honourable W. C., 139, 140.
Willis, Mr. Albert S., instructed to restore Queen Liliuokalani, 22; his negotiations with her, 23; absents himself from the Constitutional Convention, 25; succeeds Mr. Blount as American minister, 210; death of, 294.

Wilson, Mr. C. B., 15.
Wiltse, Captain G. C., 18.
Women, the daring and resolution of, 38.
Women of Hawaii, the, 97; professions open to, 229.
Wood, varieties of hard, 304.
Wool-growing, 132, 133-137.
World's Fair, the, 192; a visit to, 210.

ZIEGLER, Captain, 161.